# BETWEEN
# *Floors*

## VALKYRIE BROTHERS - BOOK 2

BY

# BETHANY MAINES

 Blue Zephyr Press
2661 N. Pearl, #360
Tacoma WA 98407

Cover art by **LILT**.

ISBN-13: 979-8-9867745-8-9

# Contents

BETHANY MAINES

# BETWEEN Floors

# 1

*Forest*

## THE ELEVATOR

The elevator bell chimed at the same time as Forest Valkyrie's phone, and he hesitated—torn between answering and getting inside. Forest picked up the phone—already expecting an emergency—and stood with one foot in the hall, one in the elevator, blocking the door, knowing that the cell reception would cut out once the elevator doors closed.

"Yeah, Jim. What's up?"

Forest had a stack of emails filling up his phone, and he'd only been out of the office for three hours. The afternoon had been a waste of his time. None of the nanny candidates had been worth a damn. They all had degrees, experience, and first-aid training, but none of them seemed to grasp the seriousness of the job. Well, except for the weird one.

He couldn't have a purple-haired nanny—no matter how pretty she was. He needed someone educated, regimented, and in control. Someone who would take Oliver's care seriously. The doctors had no idea if or when the autoimmune disorder that had killed Oliver's mother would kick in with Oliver, and Forest needed a nanny who could adequately assess for signs of illness. But the entire afternoon hadn't met Forest's goals and had put him further behind at work.

"Hey," said Jim. "The project managers are freaking out. Detroit just emailed that they can't make the full I-beam delivery. They say they can do a partial, or we can wait six weeks."

"Take the partial and start calling around to fill the rest of the order. Even if Detroit makes it with the rest of the shipment, we can use it on the Sound Transit Project."

"And if they don't, then we'll need it," said Jim. "Got it. And speaking of the Sound Transit project..."

"Yeah?" The ink on the Light Rail contract was barely dry. Forest wasn't sure how there could be problems already.

"Our surveyors just got back to the office. They've been in the Emergency Room all day. Apparently, half the initial build site is a homeless encampment, and while they were being chased off the site, one of our guys put his hand down on a used needle."

"Oh, God. Tell me he's OK." Forest ran his hands through his hair and then tugged nervously at his beard.

"They bagged the needle, and it tested clean, so he's just going to be on a series of antibiotics for the next six weeks."

"Don't let the insurance give him crap on this. Make sure everything is covered."

"I'll make sure. But this is going to be a problem."

"Get legal involved. At a minimum, it's a failure to disclose from the City. I'm not endangering our guys, and I'm sure as hell not clearing a homeless encampment for them."

"On it," said Jim.

Seattle was in the middle of a building boom, which was great for him since he was trying to get his construction and engineering firm up over the half-billion dollar mark for gross revenue, but it was also pushing him and Seattle close to the breaking point. The building boom was nothing compared to the peak in income disparity and accompanying spike in drug use that was forcing Seattle to grow in unprecedented ways.

"You coming back to the office?"

Instinctively, Forest looked at his watch, even though he knew the answer was no. It was nearly five. Seattle traffic was a disaster at rush hour.

"No, I'm out. I've got to pick up Olly, and then we're heading home, but I'll be on email after he goes down."

"OK, got it. Talk to you tomorrow."

Forest stepped fully into the elevator, pushed the button for the parking garage, and looked at his watch again, trying to estimate how long it would take to get to his brother's office. Rowan was one of the few people he trusted to watch Oliver. Rowan was six years older than Forest and had spent most of their childhood as "the man" of their house. At thirty-six, Forest knew it was ridiculous to still think of Rowan as their grown-up, but that didn't make it less true. Rowan was retired Marine Force Recon and ran his own security firm. If Rowan couldn't protect Oliver, then no one could. But on the other hand, Forest hated being late or looking incompetent in front of Rowan. Rowan always seemed to have his shit together—Forest always felt like he was one step ahead of disaster.

Forest looked up just as a graceful arm waved between the doors, and the auto-sensor froze them in place. Forest nearly groaned out loud when they trundled back open to reveal the least qualified of the nanny candidates—purple-haired Chloe Jordan.

She looked him up and down, and he half-expected her to declare that she would wait for the next car, but instead, she gave a little shrug and walked in. He wasn't sure he would have the balls to do that.

Forest moved to the opposite side from the panel and watched as she pushed the Lobby button. That meant they would have to endure the entire ride together, both of them knowing that he'd ended the interview early with what he hoped was a polite enough *I don't think we're a match.*

He surreptitiously took another look at her as she turned to face the front of the car. Purple hair, nose ring, no sign of a tattoo, but he guessed there was a tramp stamp under the green linen dress. Once upon a time, that would have had him saying hello and asking where she wanted to eat breakfast. Free spirits had once been his preferred type. But then, once upon a time, he'd been a bit of a wandering soul himself. Not anymore. These days, he took zero unnecessary risks.

He looked down at her feet. Doc Martens. She was wearing Doc Martens. He hadn't noticed those earlier. He'd been too busy trying not to stare at her dreamy blue eyes. Who showed up to a job interview in punk boots and a dress? Was she trying for the Most Seattle-ite of the Year Award?

He looked up as the LED panel above the door counted down the floors. Sixteen, fifteen, fourteen, twelve—clunk.

The car bounced and then stopped. The counter hovered between fourteen and twelve.

"Floor thirteen," muttered Forest.

"Twelve," said Chloe, looking up at the counter. "Or maybe fourteen?"

"They skipped thirteen out of superstition. They can say fourteen all they want, but it's thirteen."

"Hm," she said.

"The doors should be opening," said Forest.

The lights went out.

Forest's heart seemed to stop and only restarted when the emergency lights flickered on. It gave Chloe's purple hair an ethereal, glowing, blue cast.

"OK," he said, stepping in front of Chloe to rip open the emergency phone panel and hit the call button. Nothing happened. Forest reached up and loosened his tie. It felt like it was trying to strangle him. He tapped the call button again, and this time, there was a burst of static that immediately went to silence. He fumbled for his phone. He dialed Rowan, but the call dropped before ringing through.

"I can't do this. I have to get Oliver," he muttered. He pulled at his tie again. He felt like the walls were getting closer.

"Are you OK?" asked Chloe.

"What? No, I'm not OK. I'm stuck in a damn elevator, and I need to pick up my son. I need..." He looked around the elevator again. He was sweating, and he felt like there wasn't enough air. "Do you think it's getting hotter?"

"No," said Chloe. "The temperature is fine. Are you claustrophobic?"

"I need to get out. I need to get Olly. I can't be late. I need..."

"You need to breathe," she said and put her hand on his chest. He looked down. Her fingernails were clipped short. She had a ring on her thumb and a set of Buddhist prayer beads looped around her wrist. He couldn't remember the last time someone had touched him on his chest.

"Inhale," she said, and he obeyed. "Exhale." He looked into her face and stared into her impossibly glowing eyes with little flecks of silver blue. It was the emergency lighting. She couldn't really have the universe in her eyes. He let the air in his lungs out.

"I need to get my son. I can't be late."

"Where is Oliver now?" she asked.

"With Rowan. My brother."

"Inhale. That's good. Does Olly like spending time with Uncle Rowan?"

Forest let out a snort. "Rowan is his favorite. Uncle Rowan gives him tanks and lets him eat Cheerios off the floor."

Her eyes crinkled in laughter. "Yes, of course, delicious floor food. Always a winner. Exhale."

Her hand was warm on his chest as he exhaled. He felt like it was radiating soothing heat to the rest of him.

"What else does Uncle Rowan do?"

Forest shook his head. "The same shit he did for us. Cartoons and sugar and how to get your shoes on the right feet and..." He shrugged. What didn't Rowan do?

"So Uncle Rowan loves Oliver?"

"Of course!"

"So we can recognize that whether you arrive early, on time, or late, Uncle Rowan will take care of Oliver?"

Forest felt like his brain was trying to fight itself. Of course Rowan would take care of Oliver. It was so obvious when she said it, but the urgency of needing to get out of the elevator and get to Olly still felt real.

"Yes, but..."

"Inhale and hold it for ten seconds. Here we go."

He watched her inhale through her nose and copied her. The air went into his lungs, and he kept inhaling until her lips puckered and she let her breath out. Her lips were lusciously pouty.

"I don't do well with enclosed spaces since I got locked in a coolant tank in Qatar," he blurted out. He hadn't meant to tell her that. He just hadn't wanted to say the thing about her lips.

"That sounds really frightening," she said, nodding. "But this is an elevator, and it isn't enclosed."

"It is enclosed," he snapped, regaining some of his composure through sheer annoyance.

"There are two exits," she said, pointing to the emergency hatch in the ceiling and the doors. "We can and will get out."

His first instinct was to argue with her and then he realized that was stupid. Her head cocked to one side, and her eyes twinkled as if she knew what he was thinking.

"Why did you even apply to be a nanny?" he demanded in irritation. "You have no experience working with children."

"No paid experience, it's true, but I do have some experience working with childish individuals," she said, a smile quirking up one corner of her mouth.

He glared at her.

"I also have a degree in Nutrition, two years experience in children's game development, and I'm certified by the Certification Council for Professional Dog Trainers."

"You think being a certified dog trainer qualifies you to work with children?" he demanded in outrage.

She nodded. "Yes."

He stared at her in disbelief.

"I also find that my time as a Buddhist nun is helpful for dealing with both humans and dogs."

"I cannot... Why are you weird?"

"I'm not weird," she said. "I'm confident and comfortable with who I am. I believe that many parents would like to have that trait shared with their children."

"Parents don't want that."

"They don't? That's interesting. What do they want?"

"They want successful children."

"What does success look like to you?"

"Good schools and jobs and a retirement account. Do you even know what a 401k is?"

"No. I mean, I'm aware of their existence, but I don't really know what they do."

"You see? How can you care for children?"

"Do children need to know what a 401k is?" Chloe looked surprised.

"No, they need to be shown how to be successful. You can't just leave them to flounder around and hope they turn out all right. Do you know where we would be if we hadn't had Rowan?"

"No," she said, shaking her head. "Where?"

"Not here," he snapped. "We got lucky. And I'm not letting Oliver floor food his way through life. We do *not* eat scraps."

"Ah," she said nodding. "I see. You're right. That is important."

"Yes! Wait, what?"

"It's important to you that Oliver knows he deserves food that is made for him. Proper meals, yes? At a table?"

"Yes!" Forest felt confused. How had he ended up in this argument? Was it an argument if she was agreeing with him?

"So, you make Oliver dinner? That's really wonderful. Do you make sure he gets all the food groups?"

"I try. He doesn't like vegetables and keeps demanding those horrible chicken nuggets shaped like dinosaurs."

She laughed. "Have you tried cutting his food into funny shapes?"

"I... No?"

"Funny shapes are way more fun for children. Also, you have to consider that children's taste buds are vastly different from adults."

"They are?"

"Yes, children have more taste buds than we do, which makes eating a very intense experience for them. Also, their taste buds are more concentrated in recognizing sweet and salty things, so they'll inherently reject sour and bitter flavors."

"Oh. I didn't know that."

"It makes vegetables a hard sell, but there are some options. Toss a teaspoon of brown sugar over something that's a little bitter. Change vegetable choices periodically. You could try snap peas or yams. Green beans can be delicious when pan-fried. Fresh tomatoes can be fun to squish, which would be a food he's allowed to play with."

Those were all good ideas. Ideas that Forest would never have come up with on his own.

"OK," she said, looking up at the ceiling. "Nothing appears to be happening, so we should probably attempt to escape on our own. Why don't I boost you up through the roof hatch?"

"No," he said, shaking his head. "You're smaller. I will boost you up, and then I'll climb up."

"That sounds like it makes more sense, but I'm not wearing underwear, so no."

He'd heard the phrase *struck dumb* before but never thought it was an actual thing that could happen until he realized that his lips were moving and no words were coming out. Finally, he cleared his throat.

"You can't be a nanny and not wear underwear!"

"I'm not nannying right now," she objected.

"It's a job interview! How do you not wear underwear to a job interview?"

"Well, I wasn't planning on showing you my underwear, for starters, and for seconds, all five of my panties are still drying. It's laundry day."

"How do you only own five pairs of underwear? No, don't answer that."

"I don't believe in owning a lot of things. I do want to get two more pairs, though. So I'll have one for each day of the week. Why? How many pairs of underwear do you own?"

"A lot more."

"Like ten?"

"At least twenty."

"Really?" Her eyes were big as if he'd announced that he owned eighty-two BMWs.

"I cannot believe I'm having this conversation. OK, we're leaving the elevator now. I will boost you up, and I will not look up your skirt. And, really, no underwear, and you chose to wear a dress?"

"It goes below my knees, and it's comfortable."

He made an inarticulate noise of disbelief and frustration, then squatted down and cupped his hands.

"Hurry up before you say something else that will scar my psyche."

"OK," she said with a shrug, putting her boot in his hand.

He pushed upward and kept his eyes closed. "Not looking," he muttered to himself.

"I'm not sure that saying it makes me feel reassured that you're not doing it," she said. "Almost there. One second." There was a sharp click, and then he felt some of her weight shift. "Sorry, can you get me a little higher?"

He pushed upward, and then her foot pulled free of his hand. He had expected some fumbling, but once her foot was gone, it was like she had floated away. He heard the flex of metal as she gained the elevator roof.

"Is it safe yet?" he asked, lifting his face up but not opening his eyes.

"Yes," she said, a giggle filling out her voice.

He opened his eyes and stared up at her face in the hole in the ceiling. Her purple hair was falling all around her. It was disorienting and beautiful all at once.

"How do we do this?" she asked, looking around.

"You move so I can grab the edge," he said.

"Uh, OK." She moved back, and he launched himself upward to grab the edge. Then he pulled himself up onto the top of the elevator.

"Right," Forest said, dusting off his hands and looking around. The elevator shaft was grimy and filthy like every other one he'd ever been in. The thick, greased cable rose up the shaft, and over the edge of the car, he could see that the second elevator was at the ground floor and not moving. He took a bigger breath. Everything felt much better now that he wasn't stuck in a box. He turned to look at Chloe and was surprised to see that she looked nervous.

"Don't worry. This is the easy part."

# 2

## *Chloe*

# THE STAIRS

The easy part.

The man had just gone from almost having a panic attack to not only hoisting her above his head but doing a massive pull-up to get himself onto the elevator roof, and now he was looking over the edge like it was nothing.

Forest Valkyrie was a type-A, arrogant, rich jerk. Or at least that was how he'd come off in the interview. He'd barely let her get two words out before sending her packing. She'd had to take a few minutes in the bathroom to do some meditative breathing before she'd been ready to face the world again. And a little crying. There had been a lot of meditation and crying of late. Ever since she'd returned to Seattle, Chole had felt slapped around by the realities of modern life. Rent was one of the realities that seemed particularly aggressive.

She was living in a postage stamp-sized crap-hole, and it was still more than she could afford. She didn't have a lot of needs, but she did need to be able to sleep *somewhere*. Unfortunately, living in a Buddhist monastery for two years, while valuable life experience, wasn't exactly a selling point on a resume. The temp agency had taken to throwing her at anything and everything, and a live-in nanny position would have solved so many of her problems. She'd actually had hopes for the job. Maybe that's why it had hurt so much to be so summarily rejected.

Chole took another look at Forest. He was six feet of handsome with hazel, gold-flecked eyes and a crisply trimmed beard that gave him an aura of barely tamed ruggedness. He also clearly thought she was insane. If Chloe was honest with herself, she would have to admit that part of the reason she'd barely been able to string together a sentence in the interview was because she had been staring at him. Four years of celibacy had collided with her libido like a sports car into a brick wall. Having him dismissively tell her they weren't a match had been an excellent way to stop that little daydream, though.

"OK, let's see… this is a Thyssenkrupp."

Forest continued to mumble to himself as he examined the mechanism below the door to floor fourteen. He wiggled something, looked up at the doors, and made a pleased noise.

"OK, you come over here and hold this bit up. I'll climb up that ladder and open the door, and then once I've got them open, you'll climb up."

She had several questions—starting with how he knew that would work? But as she stepped toward him, the entire elevator swayed slightly, and she froze.

"It's going to do that, but all the brakes are in place," he said calmly.

"You know how you have coolant tank-induced anxiety? I kind of have a slight fear of heights since that one time in Hoi An."

"Did you fall off a building?" he asked, raising an amused eyebrow.

"No, I jumped."

And then the brake on her wire hadn't kicked in until she could see the lines in the pavement. Overall, Chloe was fine with dying but thought she would prefer not to know about it until after it was over.

He laughed, clearly assuming she was making a joke. Chloe decided she didn't want to bother to correct him. What was the point?

"Well, the elevator is probably stuck because of an electrical malfunction. It's not going anywhere. So don't jump off, and everything will be fine."

Surprisingly, his eyes stayed locked on hers, and his expression was reassuring and kind. Chloe controlled her breathing and took another step.

"How do you know all of that?"

"My business is construction and engineering," he said. "I've been putting all the Legos together to make buildings since I was Olly's age. I just happen to be a lot more comfortable with elevators when I'm not in them."

"I usually take the stairs," admitted Chloe. "But sometimes speed and convenience seem like nice things."

"Serves us right," he said. "Should have gotten our leg work-out in."

She made it to the edge of the elevator, and he smiled at her. It was a genuine smile, and once again, she found herself a little short of breath, but this time, it had nothing to do with the elevator.

"OK," he said, taking her hand and moving it to a bit of machinery right at her eye level. His hands were warm and gentle on hers—for some reason that surprised her. "You lift this part up when I say so. Got it?" He showed her how the part moved up and down.

"Got it," she said, nodding to show she understood. Sometimes, body language meant more than words.

"All right. Hang tight."

He pushed his messenger bag more fully to his back, swung up onto the ladder beside the doors, and climbed swiftly up the door above them.

"OK, now."

Chloe dutifully lifted the part, and he dangled from the ladder and wedged his fingers into the crack between the heavy metal slabs. With creaking slowness, the doors parted. He stepped off the ladder onto the fourteenth floor, braced the door open, and turned back to her.

"Your turn," he said, beckoning to her.

Cautiously, she stepped onto the ladder and climbed up. Forest waited for her, holding out his hands when she reached his level. He wrapped his arms around her, lifting her off the ladder as if she were made of porcelain. She couldn't remember the last time anyone had treated her with such delicacy, and she was overwhelmed by the scent of bergamot and sandalwood and the feeling of safety.

"Solid ground," he said as he placed her feet on the floor. Then he stepped back and smiled at her.

She nodded back, not trusting herself to say anything.

"Stairs are this way," he said, pointing down the hall.

"I guess we still get our shot at leg day," she said.

They walked down the stairs, but Chloe found that without an immediate problem to solve, her conversation had dried up.

"Not going down to the parking garage?" he asked in surprise as she reached the door for the lobby.

"No, I took the bus."

She opened the door, and they both could see the sheeting downpour outside the glass-fronted lobby.

"And besides, someone should tell the front desk that the elevator is stuck."

"Right," he said, nodding. "Well, good luck in your job search."

"Good luck finding your nanny match," she said, walking quickly through the doorway before he could reply.

The front desk had only seemed mildly concerned about the stuck elevator. She was willing to bet they would have reacted with much more excitement if Forest had told them about it. She pulled her poncho out of her bag and trudged to the bus stop down the block. She was pretty sure that she now had a thirty-minute wait before the next bus. The October wind gusted up her skirt. Maybe Forest was right—she should buy an interview outfit. But it seemed silly to have an additional set of clothes that she only wore for interviews. On the other hand, her legs were freezing, and she couldn't wear yoga pants to an interview.

A black Mercedes pulled up in front of the bus stop, and the window rolled down. There were a lot of European vehicles in Asia that ran the gamut of beater to luxury. The Mercedes logo didn't mean as much there, but even she could tell that this car was top of the line, and she looked into the car in confusion. If she got propositioned again, she was going to be spitting on someone.

"Where do you live?" Forest demanded, leaning across the center console.

"Capitol Hill," she said, bending down to look at him through the window.

"Get in. I'll drive you home."

"You don't have to."

"You're getting rain on my leather seats. Get in."

Chloe tried to remove her poncho so it wouldn't get more water on his upholstery and then shoved it and her bag down with her feet on the floor. By the time she got situated and seat belted, he was giving her a look.

"What?"

"Is that a WWII poncho?"

"Vietnam-era," she said. "In fact, I got it in Vietnam."

"When you tell me ridiculous things, it makes my head hurt," he said, pulling back into traffic.

"That is not ridiculous," said Chloe. "It's a perfectly reasonable piece of rain equipment in a rainy city."

"It's weird. Normal people do not wear ponchos with dresses and boots. You look like a Studio Ghibli character."

Chloe laughed. She didn't mind the comparison—Studio Ghibli movies were unique and creative.

"Well, maybe you should consider that normal isn't all it's cracked up to be."

"Being normal makes things easier."

"Does it, though?" she asked.

"Fewer problems."

"Hm," she said. "I guess it depends on what problems you're

worried about. Turn left up here."

He wound his way through the traffic, rain splashing the windows, and Chloe directed him toward her rundown apartment building. She was renting a three-hundred square foot studio that had once been a two-bedroom that had been split up. It only had a mini fridge and no stove or oven, and they were still charging an arm and a leg.

Forest Valkyrie drove with assurance and more than a hint of non-Seattle-like aggression, bullying his way into lanes with a flair she associated with driving in Asia.

"Did you live in the Middle East long?" she asked. He looked at her in surprise. His hazel eyes looked gold in the glow of the car dash. "You said you'd gotten stuck in a coolant tank in Qatar."

"Oh. Yeah. I started out in Dubai when I was eighteen. Bounced around the Middle East and Asia with various projects and companies. I came back home to start my firm about six years ago."

"Was it hard to adjust to living here again?" asked Chloe, wondering if the trouble she'd been having was typical.

"Yeah. I mean, construction crews are construction crews, but the political infrastructure is different. Much less open to bribery. And that does make me proud of us as a country, but it can be inconvenient."

Chloe laughed, and he looked over at her in surprise.

"Construction crews are indeed the same everywhere," said Chloe, thinking of her family. "But those are work things. I was asking if it was hard for you as a person."

He looked as if he had no idea what those words meant.

"Uh... It is what it is. No point in complaining."

Chloe frowned. The answer implied that there was something to complain about but that he didn't want to think about it. Chloe disapproved of not thinking about emotions. She couldn't appropriately judge her actions and decisions without investigating her feelings.

"Up ahead on the left," she said, pointing.

"Really? Here?" he demanded as they pulled up.

"It's not the best," she agreed. "But it's better than the place I lived in Malaysia."

"I had a six-month contract in Kuala Lumpur. If this is better, I'm willing to bet you were living in a cardboard box over there."

"Not quite, but I don't need a lot. Thanks for the ride."

She got out of the car before he could say anything else. Forest Valkyrie was devastatingly handsome, but he was right—they were not a match.

3

*Forest*

## THE DECISION

Forest stood with his forehead pressed against Olly's door. Inside his room, Olly was sobbing; it was all Forest could do not to walk back in and pick him up. The day had been an unmitigated disaster from top to bottom. The only part of the day that he hadn't been fighting with Olly was dinner time. And that was because Forest had cut the sandwich into a star shape and given Oliver cherry tomatoes to squish and eat.

Just like Chloe had suggested.

Forest wearily walked down the stairs to the living room, ignoring the discarded piles of toys and books even though the clutter bothered him. He paid for a cleaning service and could make it twenty-four hours until they tidied.

Forest stood staring out at the darkened lawn. He could see the toys in the reflection in the window and realized that by the time he got home the next day, Olly would have put the clutter back. Forest would never experience the brief moment of clean—he would always exist in this moment of perpetual disarray. A moment where everything was disorganized, and he still had work to do. There was at least another hour of responding to email before he could be done. Forest ran his hand over his face. All he wanted was to grab a bottle of Jack off the bar and go cry and drink in the shower.

He needed help. He couldn't keep going like this. But the agency hadn't come up with a new panel of nanny applicants yet. The thought of nannies made him inevitably picture Chloe. Her vibrant purple hair and universe eyes had filled out all the dark corners of his thoughts for the last three days. He couldn't understand it. They were incompatible. But he kept thinking about her.

Outside, the wind tossed the tree branches in a temper tantrum of October rain, and drops hit the window with sharp little smacks. Which just reminded him of the way Chloe had looked in her ridiculous poncho.

Forest's phone dinged. The slight noise bounced off the wall of glass windows and came back, sounding louder than it should.

He'd bought one of the largest houses he'd looked at. From the eight-foot-tall double front doors to the massive central island that stood like a battlement of marble between the kitchen and the expansive family room with the two stories of windows—it screamed expensive. Which was why he'd bought it. But he hadn't counted on the echo. It made the house feel empty. He'd hired a designer who had provided top-of-the-line modern furniture and shelving, but he found that without Olly around, he tended to hide away in one of the smaller rooms—like his office or the gym. Although, the shower—with or without the bottle of Jack—currently sounded way more appealing than either.

Another alert forced him to look at the phone. They had six major projects running, two of which were nearing their handover dates, and the Sound Transit rail line job was threatening to become a political hot potato since they would need to clear out the homeless encampment to move the project forward. They also had a slate of what he considered minor projects that were below the twenty million budgetary mark. Those were great for keeping everyone employed, but it also meant that marketing was up his ass wanting quotes for press releases and opinions on proposals as they went after new work. He loved the head of his marketing department—she was pure genius at her job—but he was starting to hate the sight of her name on any email. It always came with attendant to-do items.

He kept telling himself that if he could just get the company to that next rung financially, he could afford to ease back and spend more time with Olly. Every time he was at work, he felt like a failure for not being with Olly, but every minute he spent with Olly came with a soundtrack of dings as work stacked up in his inbox. Forest had promised Vera that Olly would have the best. But right now, Olly was getting a half-assed father and an endless round of background-checked babysitters while the company was getting a distracted CEO who was so tired he couldn't remember the day of the week without checking his phone.

Every day was starting to feel like he was stuck in an elevator.

*Inhale for ten seconds.*

Chloe hadn't seemed to judge him or why he was claustrophobic.

Forest inhaled as Chloe had done in the elevator, held it for the count of ten, and then exhaled. Then he did it again. By the time he reached the third one, he'd started to feel better. On paper, Chloe was the worst decision of all time. Chaotic job history. Clearly alternative lifestyle. But in person, she had been... calm. Even when she'd gotten scared of the elevator's movement, she hadn't panicked. She had been able to ride out the chaos of the moment, and she had listened to him. To tell the truth, he couldn't remember the last time he'd actually felt that heard.

He looked at the digital picture frame sitting on the mantle. It showed a rotating slideshow of Olly's mother. Her red hair and dimpled smile flashed by again. Forest had tried to only put healthy-looking photos of her in the frame. Olly loved looking at it. Vera had been the last of Forest's chaotic decisions. He'd met her on a work trip to Germany. She was an Australian working in Germany as a data analyst. He hadn't known it at the time, but she'd been on the run from a life sentence. Vera had Lupus, but decided she'd had enough of living in fear of flare ups. She'd packed a bag, told her over-bearing parents to go to hell, and gone off to live in the land of the free, which for her had been Germany.

But a year after they'd met, Vera had shown up on his doorstep with an infant and one request—that he take care of Olly. Vera's health had been impacted by the pregnancy, and she was determined not to let her autocratic parents raise Oliver. Olly had been almost one when Vera passed away. Forest was never sure if he'd been in love with Vera, but it didn't matter. He loved what she had given him. Oliver was the most beautiful little being Forest had ever met, but Forest knew he was failing as a father. He was failing both Vera and Olly.

An idea formed in his mind, and he turned it over, feeling guilty.

He knew where Chloe lived. What if he just went over there and asked her to come home with him?

Chloe had wanted the job before. So what if she was weird? She was also smart. And soothing. And pretty. No, that didn't matter. Smart was what mattered. Her tips had worked. They were the only damn thing that *had* worked. It didn't have to be forever. It just had to be until he got a proper nanny. Someone who wasn't a dog trainer and whose life goals didn't include purchasing two more pairs of underwear. He could still get Olly the best super nanny ever, but Chloe would be light years ahead of the nothing he currently had.

He pulled out his phone and looked at his contact list. He couldn't call Rowan. He couldn't let his hyper-competent older brother know how badly his life was going. That just left Ash. Reluctantly, he dialed his younger brother's number.

"Hey," said Asher, sounding cheerful. "Where's my Olly pic of the day?"

He knew Ash didn't mean it to, but the question hit him like a sucker punch. He couldn't even meet the minimum requirement for being a good father and take a damn picture of his kid.

"It hasn't exactly been a cute day," said Forest.

"Oh. Is it a Monster Olly day? What'd that lady on the TV call it? Being a threenager?"

"Sounds right," said Forest, tiredly. "Honestly, I don't remember you being this hard to deal with."

Ash gave a startled guffaw of laughter. "That is because I was an angel baby."

"Uh..." said Forest, distinctly remembering several incidents from their childhood. "No."

"Well, you were what—six or seven when I was Olly's age? You may not be remembering accurately."

"Yeah, or maybe Rowan was better at all this stuff."

"No," said Ash firmly. "Rowan would have been eleven when I was Ollie's age. You can't tell me he was a better parent at eleven than you are now."

"Maybe?" Forest offered weakly, and Ash snorted.

"Still no nanny?"

"No," said Forest. "Actually, maybe. At least a temporary one. But I have to go get her. I don't suppose you could come over and be in the house while I do that? Olly's already in bed."

"Um, I'm kind of in the middle of something."

Forest's heart sank.

"It's fine. I'll call Rowan."

"No, um... Let me just... I'll pack up my computer and come over."

"Thanks, Ash. I really appreciate it."

Forest hung up and rubbed the back of his neck. Was he really doing this?

Could he afford not to do it?

# 4
## *Chloe*

# THE WAY FORWARD

Chloe was about to start dinner preparation when her intercom buzzed. She stared at it in surprise and then answered cautiously. No one came to her apartment on purpose.

"Hello?"

"Chloe?"

"Yes?"

"It's Forest Valkyrie." There was silence, and Chloe tried to decide what she was supposed to do with that information. "Can I come up?"

"Um... Yes?" She hit the buzzer for the lobby door, and the intercom static dropped.

She wasn't sure what to do now. Was she supposed to meet him at the door? She looked back at her wok sitting on her single electric burner on the floor. The oil was at the right temperature now. She didn't want to lose her moment. She returned to her spot on the floor and whisked her rice flour mixture again. She was about to pour it in when there was a knock on the door.

"It's open," she called.

Forest came in and paused on the threshold as she poured the batter into the wok. It made a perfect sizzling noise.

"Do you always leave your door unlocked?" he demanded.

"Yes."

"That's not safe. You can't—are you making *Bánh Xèo?*"

"Yes," she confirmed.

"Like real *Bánh Xèo?*" he demanded suspiciously.

"I guess? I'm not sure how we're defining the reality of food."

"With the sprouts and shrimp and the *nuoc cham?*"

"Yes. Would you like some?"

The answer was yes. It was written all over his face.

"No, I'm fine. I ate dinner." He stepped into her apartment but stopped before she could say anything and took off his shoes, placing them neatly on the shoe rack next to the door. "These are all the shoes you own, aren't they?" He asked, looking at her four pairs of shoes—Doc Martens, green ballet flats, Teva sandals, and sneakers for running and her sporadic dog walking jobs. She had tried to cut back, but she'd found each useful for their own distinct purposes.

"Yes."

"Uh-huh. OK." He looked around the rest of her room, took out his phone, and pushed several things as he walked over to her. Finally, he sat cross-legged on the floor and looked directly at her. She looked back. He wasn't wearing a jacket or a tie, but he still looked like he'd just come from work. Too bad for her that he was someone who looked dreamy in work clothes. He also didn't look bothered to be sitting on the floor. That was interesting.

"Did you find a job?" he asked.

"No," said Chloe.

"Great. Then you can come work for me."

"Hm," said Chloe, using her chopsticks to flip her crepe. "I thought we weren't a match."

"We aren't. You are not qualified to raise a house chicken. But I need help, and I need it now."

"So you thought you would lower your standards all the way to me, and I should accept that?"

He froze. He clearly hadn't considered his house chicken comment an insult before saying it out loud.

"You have no degree in child-rearing. You have no medical

experience! Those are must-haves."

She considered that. He was asking for proof of specific skills. It was a pretty linear way of thinking, but that also meant he perceived a particular need and thought those were the only answer. They weren't arbitrary requests.

"Why medical experience?" Chloe asked, sliding the crepe out onto the plate. The turmeric colored it a beautiful golden yellow.

Forest hesitated. "Oliver's mom died of Lupus. The doctors don't know if Oliver is going to get it too. Everyone has to have medical knowledge in case... Just in case."

Chloe nodded as the truth became clear to her. Forest Valkyrie was scared shitless that his son was going to die. He was trying to control the uncontrollable and doing a terrible job at it.

"But you're smart," said Forest, leaning forward, his voice urgent and desperate. "All your stuff worked. So if you stayed with us for a little bit, we would probably be OK until I found someone permanent."

"My stuff?" She looked up, puzzled.

"Your food stuff. He liked cherry tomatoes and star-shaped sandwiches."

"Hm." She dumped her pork into the wok. It was also interesting that he'd tried any of her ideas.

"God, that smells good." He shook his head as if refusing to be distracted by the wafting smell of cooking pork. "Look, I don't know how this works. But I know I need help now—not next week or next month or whenever the agency finds someone suitable. I will pay you double whatever it said in the ad— just stay with us for a month."

Chloe thought about that. Double what he'd had in the ad was a lot. And since he was hiring her directly, she wouldn't pay the agency fee. It was the kind of money that could get her a plane ticket back to Asia.

"I'm not sure that being a nanny is what I should be doing. I came home because I thought it was time I reconciled with my past," she said thoughtfully, "and because I thought I should make some decisions about my future."

"You should definitely make some decisions about your future," he said. "You should decide to not fucking live here. Don't you have any family? My brothers would shit a brick before either of them let me live here."

Chloe added the shrimp to the pan.

"I do have family. I haven't told them I'm back in Seattle. They don't approve of my lifestyle."

"I don't approve of your lifestyle. The neighborhood is dangerous and unsafe. This apartment is not up to code, and you don't own enough underwear."

Her family would theoretically care about those things. But mostly, they would care about what she looked like. Safety was secondary to appearances. The fact that they would probably approve of nannying was one of the things that made her ambivalent about the job. But she was trying to free herself of the idea that she had to push against whatever they wanted in order to be right.

Chloe added the mung beans, carrot, and mushrooms and watched his eyes follow the food longingly.

"You wanted the job earlier. Why are you stonewalling me now?" Forest demanded, tearing his eyes away from the wok.

"I'm not stonewalling. I'm taking my time to think. Go grab the bowl out of the dish drainer, please," she said.

He did as he was asked, but huffily.

"The extra chopsticks, too."

She tossed the mixture in the wok, lifting it off the burner and letting the ingredients turn in the air. After a few turns, she added everything to the center of the crepe and tucked them neatly inside. Then she cut the crepe in half and scooped it into the bowl he was holding out to her. He made a confused noise.

"Sit," she ordered. "Eat."

"That's your dinner."

"And I am sharing my food with you as a guest in my home."

He stared at her and then sat down in his previous spot. He set the bowl down in front of him and started to roll up his sleeves, revealing dark trailing ink on both forearms. Apparently, he wasn't quite the clean-cut businessman he looked like from the outside. She put the *nuoc cham* in a small bowl in front of him. Once done with his sleeves, he peeled off a chunk and dipped it in the sauce, negotiating it to his mouth without dripping it everywhere. She approved of his technique.

"Mmmmm." The groan he made was practically sexual, and he melted in on himself, his spine curving as he chewed. As far as complimenting her cooking, that was about as good as it could get. "God, the sauce is so good. Where did you get it? I can't find any that's right."

"I make my own fish sauce," she said. "You can't get it right with store-bought fish sauce."

He paused, his next bite hovering above the dip, clearly torn. "You can't make fish sauce in the house."

"Garage?" she offered. He had an expensive car, so she assumed he had a garage.

"Perfect," he said, looking relieved.

They ate in silence for a few moments. The pleasure he got from eating made her think Forest Valkyrie hadn't properly enjoyed a meal in years. She watched as he licked his fingers after the last bite.

"You'll come live with me," he announced, setting his chopsticks on the edge of his bowl. "You'll take care of Oliver. You will buy at least two more pairs of underwear."

"The underwear really bothers you?"

"They are a necessity of life!"

"Meh," she said with a shrug. "Only one week out of the month."

He made a groaning noise and covered his face with his hand.

"Why are you weird?"

"I'm not weird," she said. "I am the way I like to be."

"You like to be poor?" he demanded.

"Money is helpful," she said. "But it's not the goal of my life. I would like more money so I could live the way I like, but I don't need a lot of stuff."

"How do you like to live?"

"I like to travel. I like to talk to people. I like to learn new things. And I like to cook."

His phone dinged, and he checked it.

"Those are nice things, but they're nicer with money."

"Money is only tangentially related to any of those things."

"We can argue about this in the car after I pack your things," he said.

"What?"

"I DoorDashed a large bin. It's downstairs."

"When did you do that?" she asked with a frown.

"When I walked in. I'm going to put all of your things into it, and then I'm going to take you home."

"But I hadn't agreed when you walked in," she said.

"Yeah, but I generally get my way, so I figured you would have agreed by the time it arrived. And I was right. Be right back."

He left, and Chloe continued to eat her dinner. Forest Valkyrie was a puzzle. She wondered if she ought to be offended by his presumption that he could get his way. He had a lot of money, so she supposed he did get his way most of the time. That was probably why he was freaking out so much about Oliver's potential for illness. He couldn't control it. But as much as he was horrified by her lifestyle, Forest also thought she was smart. He had tried her suggestions and didn't seem to think she didn't know what she wanted or couldn't make her own choices. He obviously had no idea *why* she was making her choices but didn't think she was incapable. Did she want to go be his nanny? She had to admit that her attempts to reintegrate into Seattle life had not been very successful. Her intention to talk to her parents hadn't materialized. She was living on the fringes of this life because she was afraid to let go of her old one and was scared of her past. Forest challenged her, but he didn't frighten her. Perhaps this was her way forward.

"OK," he said, coming back in with a large plastic tub. "I'm assuming anything not nailed down is yours?"

"Yes, but you can leave the food. We'll put it in the box down in the lobby."

"No, I'm taking the fish sauce."

"Well, obviously, we're taking the fish sauce, but I'll put that in a plastic bag."

She rinsed her bowl, and by the time she had separated the food items she was leaving, he was dithering over how to place her sketchbooks into the crammed bin.

"No," he muttered to himself, taking the sketchbooks back out, and setting them aside on the floor, "we'll carry those." He glanced up. "Too important," he said and Chloe realized that she must look surprised. "I learned early on never to mess with anyone's sketches. Architect's lose their shit."

"I'm not an architect," said Chloe.

"Doesn't matter. You made those with your brain and a pencil. They can't be replaced."

Chloe sat with a feeling of surprise and gratitude as Forest wedged the lid down on the large bin. No one had ever taken her designs seriously before. They were just doodles of designs that *could* be. Maybe. In the future. If she could figure out her present. Forest didn't know about her idea of making custom artisan tiles as a business, and he would probably have opinions about it if he did, but he still valued her sketches.

"Got it all in," he said, looking pleased. "Knew it would fit." He looked up at her, and she knew she was making a face but couldn't stop. "What?"

"I can't believe I own so many things," she said. "That's just a lot."

"It literally all fits in one box."

"But you had to really push the lid down. I've become lazy since coming back here. I shouldn't have bought that extra pillow."

He was staring at her. "I cannot respond to that in any coherent way."

"Does it need a response?"

"It needs something. Come on. I promised Ash that it would only take me an hour."

Chloe turned and looked at her now barren studio apartment.

"Thank you for sheltering me," she said and bowed to it.

"Trust me, it doesn't deserve that much thanks," said Forest. "Are you going to need to contact the landlord or something about canceling your lease?"

"I didn't pay rent last month, so... I'm sure it's fine." Forest gaped at her, and she patted his arm. "Come on. Let's go."

## 5

# *Forest*

# THE ADVENTURE BEGINS

That morning, Forest carried a sleepy Oliver out to the kitchen where Chloe was waiting. Forest thought she looked nervous.

The previous night, Chloe had seemed to think the nanny suite was huge. It was admittedly bigger than his first apartment, but he didn't think it was *that* impressive. She had made little excited noises about the big bathtub, though, so that was a winner. Now, if only she could win with Olly.

Olly eyed her with suspicion and didn't want to talk to her, even after breakfast. When it came time to leave, Forest's stomach was in knots. By the time he got through his commute and into the office, he was convinced he'd made the wrong decision.

Forest answered the bare minimum of questions and ran into his office to get to his computer. He felt guilty about not mentioning the nanny cams to Chloe, but not enough to *not* check them. The camera started recording once he alarmed the security system and filed a chunk of video once an hour. He clicked on the first clip of the day right after he had left and held his breath as the footage flickered into movement.

Chloe and Oliver were in the kitchen, having obviously just watched him leave.

Oliver looked up at her. Forest could tell that he felt uncertain. Then Chloe sat on the floor, meeting the toddler at eye level.

"I know your dad said my name, but sometimes adults talk fast.

I'm Chloe." She pointed at herself. "And you're Oliver?"

He nodded.

"Who is this guy?" she asked, pointing at his stuffie. "What's their name?"

"Bear," he said. There was the heavy implication that she'd asked a stupid question.

"Oh. Dog?"

"No. Bear."

She mimed puzzlement, scratching her head and screwing up her face.

"Mm. Bird?"

"Bear!" he exclaimed in exasperation.

"Oh, I know. Cat!"

"Bear!"

"Ohhhh. Bear. Got it." He laughed. "I was being silly, wasn't I?"

"Silly," he agreed.

Forest felt himself unclench his jaw muscles. This was OK. She'd made him laugh. That was a positive start.

"Usually, in the morning, I like to stretch. What do you like to do?"

"Legos," said Olly promptly.

"Oh, cool! You know, when your dad was your age, he liked to play with Legos, too."

Forest felt surprised to hear her mention that detail. Olly cocked his head as if interested.

"Can you show me where the Legos are?"

Forest fast-forwarded through the next few minutes. Olly took her to the playroom and showed her the Lego bins. They played together for a little bit, or at least Chloe tried. Olly snatched all the Legos away from her. Sharing was not in his skill set. After a few moments of uneven playing, Olly started to look upset, and Forest slowed the playback to regular speed to see how she handled her first Olly meltdown.

Then the video ended. Forest blinked as he realized that he'd run out of recording. Panicked, he tapped over to the live stream.

Chloe had started some music and was stretching in the open area of the playroom. At first, Olly seemed triumphant—smashing the Legos together loudly—but the longer Chloe ignored him, the more he watched her. Forest watched Olly come to stand uncertainly at the edge of the rug.

"Do you want to stretch with me?" Chloe asked, smiling at him. "I like having friends stretch with me."

Olly stepped onto the carpet, but he still looked tentative to Forest.

"Stretching is fun. First, we reach all the way up to the sun, and we say good morning, Mrs. Sun!"

Chloe reached her arms all the way up, and Olly hesitantly copied her, reaching above his head and wiggling his fingers.

"Oh, that's wonderful. Good job. Now we reach down to the ground, and we pat the ground because he is our friend. And we say *Hello, Mr. Earth!*"

"Hello!" bellowed Olly, and Forest waited for Chloe to tell him to be quiet.

"That's right! We must be loud because Mr. Earth is much bigger than us. Hello, Earth!" she yelled at the ground as she bent over from the waist. Her ass was conveniently pointed toward the camera, and Forest had to take a deep breath and think about cold showers for a moment. It had seriously been too long since he'd seen a woman naked.

"Hello! Hello!" Olly yelled. He loved any excuse to be loud.

Chloe continued to stretch and lead Oliver through various movements, alternately whispering, yelling, dancing, and spinning. Her yoga poses seemed odd, but she was probably modifying them to something more active for Olly. At each new attempt, Chloe told Oliver that he was wonderful, and Forest watched as Olly lost his shyness and tried each new thing with less and less hesitancy.

Forest felt his stomach unclench, and he closed out the nanny cam as Jim came through the door, tapping on his tablet and a sheaf of paperwork pinched under one arm.

Jim was nearly sixty and had joined Forest's team a few years ago. He'd been a project manager for Boeing for twenty years before being unceremoniously laid off. Jim usually wore his hair shaved down tight but was tentatively growing it out. Forest still wasn't used to the small afro—it looked very 1972 to him—but he would have died before breathing a word because he knew that thanks to Boeing's old-school attitudes, Jim felt self-conscious rocking natural hair in an office environment. Forest had made one awkward comment of encouragement. He wanted Jim to know that his hair was as welcome as the rest of him. But didn't really know how to approach a conversation with another man, let alone an older Black man, about their hair. Jim managed the other Project Managers so that none of the balls in the air got dropped. Jim wasn't intimately familiar with construction, but his skill with timelines and calm demeanor made him the best first mate on a ship that Forest was privately always convinced was moments away from sinking.

Forest reviewed Jim's list, putting out as many fires as possible. He needed about three more Jim's before he felt comfortable cutting back on hours.

It wasn't until lunch that Forest had a chance to check the nanny cams again. He logged in and went directly to the live stream as he shoved half a sandwich in his mouth.

"Shit," Forest said, sitting bolt upright and nearly choking. Olly and Chloe were in the kitchen, and instead of having him strapped down in his booster seat, she had him standing on the step stool. What the hell was she doing? There were knives and ingredients out. Olly could be into anything in an instant. Didn't she know how dangerous this was?

"OK," said Chloe, "you have selected your bread. I think the brioche buns are a wonderful choice. Now, what do you want *on* the sandwich?"

Olly surveyed the jars and piles in front of him as Forest's hand covered his phone, preparing to call Chloe but not also not wanting to distract her at the wrong moment. Olly pointed to one stack that Forest couldn't see.

"Cheese. Good one. Sliced or shredded." More emphatic toddler pointing. "Shredded. Interesting. What shall we pair it with? Oh, the Nutella. Your taste is fascinating. All right, here is your cheese to sprinkle, and I will spread the Nutella."

Forest couldn't believe that she was letting Olly have whatever he wanted. That was not nutritious!

"Now, we put it on your plate, and you get to carry it to the table." She waited until Olly was on the ground before handing the plate to him. Forest watched as Olly proudly, if precariously, transported the plate to the table and then willingly climbed into his booster seat. Olly never wanted to be in the seat—it was always a battle.

"And here," said Chloe, bringing a sippy cup to the table, "is your kale, yogurt, banana, berry smoothie. Isn't it fun to make new things?"

Olly was never going to eat any of that.

"Yum!" crowed Olly, taking a giant swig of the drink.

"Yum!" agreed Chloe, raising her own glass in cheers.

Forest watched in disbelief as his son munched happily on his Nutella and cheese sandwich and powered through a kale-based smoothie.

"Hey," said Jim, leaning through the open office door. "Uh, you look like someone already told you that Harborview retracted their sign-off," said Jim, scrutinizing him.

Forest groaned. "Seriously?"

"Yeah, but they don't want to pay for the changes."

"Oh, but they're going to anyway," said Forest. "That's what sign-off means."

"They're dangling that new building as leverage," said Jim.

"They can dangle all they want, but the funding is through the city. That means they have to go out to bid. So unless they've got an end run around that, they've got nothing."

Jim looked thoughtful. "I'll look into it." He turned to go but then stopped. "If that wasn't what had you looking shell-shocked, what was it? Everything OK?"

"I was checking the nanny cam," said Forest, feeling embarrassed. "It's Olly's first day with the new person."

"Oh, great! You found someone! How's it going?"

"She fed him a kale smoothie."

Jim grimaced. "Temper tantrum for the ages?"

"He said *yum.*"

"So you hired a witch doctor," said Jim, nodding. "I'm not sure I approve of messing with satanic forces, but it's clearly effective."

Forest laughed and glanced at the live feed again. Olly was grinning and trying to clink glasses with Chloe.

"Yeah, I guess it is," he agreed.

They were waiting for him when he got home. Chloe had bundled Oliver in his rain suit even though it wasn't raining. It covered Olly head to foot, making the toddler look like a traffic cone. They were running around the front yard waving sticks. When Forest pulled into the drive, they cheered like he'd won a race.

"Daddy!" crowed Oliver as they came into the garage after him.

"Hey bud!" Forest exclaimed, opening the car door.

"We're prats!"

"Uh..." Forest looked to Chloe for an explanation. She was also carrying a stick and laughing.

"We're pirates. These are our swords," Chloe said. Her purple hair was damp and sticking to her face, but her cheeks were flushed pink. She looked wild enough to be a pirate.

"Oh," said Forest. "Pirates. Got it. OK, but we have to leave the swords outside."

Olly glared at him and then looked to Chloe.

"He's right," said Chloe, nodding. "That is good sword manners. We leave our swords outside unless we're attacking."

"Attack!" yelled Olly, lifting his sword high, which made Chloe throw her head back in laughter. Olly grinned at her response.

"No," she said, ruffling his hair. "That's enough attacking for one day. It's time to feast and tell tales of our adventures!"

"He won't know what those words mean," said Forest.

"This is how he learns what those words mean," said Chloe, picking Olly up. "Feast means to eat all the good foods. And we learned what adventure means today, didn't we?"

"Best day ever!"

"That's right!"

Forest watched in disbelief as Olly handed over his sword, and Chloe carefully placed the sticks next to the door to the house.

"We can play more swords tomorrow," she said. "They will be right here."

"OK," said Olly.

"Satanic forces, indeed," muttered Forest, following them.

Inside, Chloe started to take off Oliver's rain suit, and Forest hurried to help.

"It went OK today, though?" he asked, worried that while Olly appeared to be in a good mood, Chloe had found it too hard and might ditch out on him.

"Best day ever," said Chloe, tweaking Olly's nose before peeling off his sweater.

"It's an adventure," said Olly, his baby voice muffled as the sweater went over his head.

"An adventure," repeated Forest, and Chloe laughed.

"Don't look so shocked," said Chloe. "He may not be a house chicken, but we still survived the day."

Forest blushed. "I shouldn't have said that. I'm sorry."

Chloe looked up at him as if measuring his words. "I forgive you."

She said it with all seriousness, and Forest felt a pop as if something in his chest had fallen back into place. He didn't think anyone had ever said that to him before. Then her head cocked, and her eyes twinkled.

"Although, I'm afraid I may have promised Olly that when you came home, you would make the TV work because that actually *is* outside of my skills. You have three remote controls, and none of them say on or off."

"Oh," said Forest. "You went an entire day without screen time? That's..." That was one of his primary methods of bribery. If she hadn't had screen time, how the hell had she gotten through the day? "That really was an adventure, then."

"Best day ever!" chirped Olly, coming out of his sweater, and Forest smiled at him. Without hesitating, Olly ran in for a hug, and Forest wrapped his arms around his son's tiny body and picked him up. It felt like the first time in weeks that they hadn't been mad at each other. He breathed out a sigh of relief and hugged Olly tighter.

"Best day ever," agreed Forest.

# 6
## *Chloe*

## BEDTIME RITUALS

Chloe could hear Forest talking in Olly's bedroom. After tooth-brushing, Olly came out to say goodnight to his mother in the digital picture frame, and then he and Forest read books in Olly's bed.

Chloe's mother had always been too busy to read to any of the children, and her father didn't do women's work. Chloe remembered asking one of her brothers to read to her, and he'd thrown her book across the room. She tip-toed to the bedroom and looked in.

Forest made growly bear voices to go with the story as Olly was snuggled into his side, eyes closed. Chloe could feel everything in her soul melting at the sight of them. Forest read to the end and gently closed the book.

"OK, bud," he said softly, easing himself away from Olly. "You sleep tight."

Olly's eyes sprang open. "Chloe!" he barked, and at the door, Chloe jumped. "Didn't say night." Olly's eyes fluttered closed as he yawned.

"It's fine," said Forest, tucking Olly in. "You can see her in the morning."

"Want Chloe."

Forest looked up in exasperation, and Chloe edged into the doorway, hoping Forest wouldn't be mad. Instead, he looked relieved and beckoned to her.

"See? Here's Chloe. Say goodnight, and then it's bedtime." Olly held out his arms, and Chloe hurried forward to get a hug.

"Goodnight, Olly," she whispered and kissed his head.

"Night-night," he murmured sleepily.

As always, Forest held the door for her and gently closed it behind them. They walked down the stairs together, reminding Chloe of the first day they'd met. He'd seemed so dismissive then. Chloe wanted to grab his hand and make him look at her, but kept his eyes straight ahead. She consciously went into the kitchen as they reached the ground floor—attempting to give Forest some space—but he followed her.

"Ugh," Forest said, rolling his head around on his neck as they reached the ground floor. "What a day."

"Bad day at work?" she asked.

"Yeah. But this evening went great!" A smile lit up his face, and Chloe couldn't help smiling back. "Olly ate all of his dinner!"

"Well, yes?" Chloe didn't know what else he was supposed to do. He was an active little boy.

Forest laughed and shook his head. "You don't even know. He and I have been locked in a death match over dinner. I don't know how you did it."

"I made you do it," said Chloe.

"What?"

"I put food on your plate and told you to try it, and then he watched you. He did what you did."

He had copied Forest move for move; it had been the most adorable thing ever. Forest stared at her, mouth swinging wide.

"I need a drink," he said at last.

Chloe shrugged. It wasn't magic. Olly worshipped his father and was at the stage where he wanted to do everything himself, just like Forest.

"Do you want one?" asked Forest, going to the bar cart in the family room.

"No, thanks."

"You don't have to cook us dinner, you know. I *do* cook. I've just been ordering out because it's your first week, and I didn't want to think. I have one of those meal kits that comes to the house."

"Yes, I used part of it," said Chloe. "But I saw a new recipe on PBS today and wanted to try it."

He'd seemed very stressed when she'd started to make dinner. He'd also seemed upset when the lawn care guy had fixed the loose back gate hinge with a few quick twists of a screwdriver. She suspected that Forest put people in boxes and didn't like it when they wandered out—even in positive ways.

Forest sank onto the couch and held his tumbler to his forehead. Chloe watched him, eyeing all the parts of him, trying to decide how they all came together to make such a beautiful shape.

"Are you sure you don't want a drink?" he asked with a sigh.

She wanted to draw a finger down the arch of his nose. Such an odd thing to want. Noses weren't known for their eroticism, but the idea of being able to trace his outline in such an intimate way gave her a little flutter in her belly.

"Thanks," she said, trying to pull her mind away from his body. "But I decided when I got out of the monastery to only drink if I was going to really enjoy it. Right now, I feel like it would just be a thing to do."

"Is it weird if I drink?" he asked, opening his eyes, and Chloe tried to make sure her face wasn't doing something stupid.

"It is not weird for me, but I have been told that my not drinking makes others feel judged. So my question back is… will it be weird for *you* if I don't?"

He looked puzzled. "I have no idea."

"That's such an honest answer. Thank you."

"But it doesn't answer the question."

"But now we can find out the answer together!"

He snorted and closed his eyes again. Chloe tried not to sigh. Forest thought she was insane, and, for once, she wished she could conform a little more. She wasn't usually attracted to people who were so tied to normal. Before her self-imposed dating hiatus, she had been interested in individuals who walked on the wild side of life.

"I think I will make tea," she said. Tea was a beverage of stability—he couldn't say that was weird. "It's so nice that you have proper tea," she said, selecting an herbal blend and scooping the leaves and flowers into the strainer.

"I always mean to make it, but I never seem to have the time. Or if I do have the time, I always forget about it and then end up burning the leaves and throwing it out. And then I get mad that I wasted tea."

She nodded. Wasting tea was a sacrilege, but considering how much money he spent on other things, she wouldn't have thought he cared. She set the water to heating and tidied up while she waited.

"Mrs. Vlatsk will get it in the morning," he said. "You really don't have to clean."

"I like to respect my home, and part of that is putting things away."

He was silent, and Chloe wondered if he'd taken her statement as a judgement.

"Chloe?"

"Yes?"

"Why did you join a monastery?"

Chloe paused. This was the first time he'd asked her anything that wasn't Olly-related.

"It's none of my business," he said quickly. A flush of pink was rising above his dark beard. "Don't answer if you don't want to."

"No, it's fine. You're just the first person to ask since I've been back in Seattle. I don't have a problem discussing it. Or any part of my life, really. I feel like most of the things people don't want to discuss are centered around shame, and I have given that up."

Forest laughed. "You gave up shame? Just boom—no more shame for you?"

"I accept the good and bad decisions of my past, and if I am true to myself and my philosophies in the present, then I will have nothing to be ashamed of in the future."

"So you have no three a.m. cringe?"

"I don't know what cringe is," said Chloe. "I keep hearing people describe things as *cringe,* but I don't understand it. I don't think I've been paying attention to slang recently. Or possibly ever. My childhood was pretty sheltered."

"Cringe is when you do something so lame that I'm embarrassed for you, but also the emotional bleck you feel about your own past actions."

"Oh."

Forest laughed. "You don't have it, do you? Like at all?"

"No, I don't think I do."

"OK, then, I'm jealous. Do all Buddhist nuns get this superpower?"

Chloe laughed. "I have no idea. Everyone is on their own journey. To answer your question, I joined because I wanted to learn more about myself. Which I did. And one of the things I learned was that I shouldn't stay there."

"So it was a mistake?" Forest looked horrified.

"No! It was an amazing success! Once I was separated from the world, I was able to think clearly for perhaps the first time in my life. I was able to examine the patterns of my life and my ways of thinking."

"Like what?" he asked.

"I'm the youngest of nine children. My parents are very religious. It was expected that I would get married by no later than twenty, and college was unnecessary. I got around that by doing the Running Start program in high school to get college credits and then picking nutrition as my degree. That would be useful in child-rearing, and since I could be done by the time I was twenty, there wasn't any reason not to let me go."

"Jesus. Sorry. But for fuck's sake. There are people who still think like that?"

He abruptly stood up and began to gather Olly's toys.

"More than you would suspect," said Chloe. "But after a while I realized I wasn't one of them."

Forest dumped the toys into their decorative basket, then stood back and breathed out one long exhale as if releasing some sort of stress.

"That can't have been easy. What did you do?" he asked, returning to the couch. Chloe was surprised again. She had thought his chore had derailed his listening.

"After some blowouts," Chloe remembered her father angrily waving his hammer as she dove into her friend's Honda Accord. The memory was still bitter, but mostly now, it made her sad. "I moved out, and they said not to come back, so I didn't. My time in the monastery allowed me to reflect on some of the patterns in my life. One of which was a matter of balance. I wasn't living in an intentional way. I pushed against my parent's life by going in the opposite direction and doing everything they hated."

"Sex, drugs, and rock and roll?" suggested Forest with a grin, and Chloe laughed.

The kettle reached a boil, and she picked up the pot and poured the water over the tea leaves.

"Yes. And I enjoyed that for a while, but then I realized it wasn't fulfilling or meaningful to me. So then I went back to my parent's pattern of looking to religion. Admittedly, I went Buddhist, but I was still looking to a greater source for answers."

"Nothing wrong with that," said Forest.

"No. And now I can comfortably say that," said Chloe, taking her mug and a dish for the strainer over to the family room to sit on the opposite end of the couch from Forest. There was plenty of room for them both, but Forest still moved his feet to the ottoman to make space for her.

"So is that why you came back to the States? You'd absorbed all the wisdom of the ages?" His eyes twinkled. He was enjoying all the Buddhist clichés.

"Well, I've reached the point where I need to make some decisions with my life. Partly I want to know if I fit in here anymore—if this is the place I want to start building something. But also…" Chloe sighed for her past self who had been so angry and hurt. "I made a bunch of declarations back when I was twenty and giving the world the finger. I was never going back to the States. I was never getting married. I was never having kids. I was never talking to my parents again. That was a whole lot of Nevers. And I realized that I should probably reevaluate those statements if my goal is to live with intention rather than simply rebelling."

"Mm," he said, taking a drink. "I feel that. Moving toward something is so much better than moving away."

"Yes," she said, happy that he understood. He had adjusted his feet again, and one was closer to her. Instinctively, she stretched out a toe and tickled the bottom of his foot. He yelped out a bark of laughter and pulled his foot away.

"Did you just play footsies with me?"

"Oh. Uh… sorry? Olly and I do that while we're stretching. It makes him laugh. But I should have asked before touching you." She sat with that for a moment, feeling a little embarrassed. "Oh! Cringe?"

"Not even close," he said, shaking his head, then stretched out his leg and poked her foot with his.

Chloe chuckled and held her foot steady as he tried to wiggle his appendages at her, but they only ended up with toes touching each other. Chloe tried not to think that their big toes were kissing, but they kind of were. There was pleasure in feeling even that tiny bit of skin against hers, and Chloe flushed at the realization.

"I think you have more control over your toes," said Forest, clearing his throat and withdrawing his foot. He looked down at his glass as if just remembering he was holding it and took a sip.

Chloe stared into her tea and blurted out the first thing that came to mind.

"You said moving toward was better than moving away. Did you have a moment of realization in your life?"

He looked up, seeming surprised.

"I spent a good chunk of my life looking for ways to stand out," he said. "Everyone just listens to Rowan automatically and everyone adores Ash because he's like a damn shiny firefly. I guess I always felt lost between my brothers. It took me a while to realize that I needed to dig into my strengths, not copy someone else. But once I started pursuing goals and not reacting, stuff started to click for me."

Chloe nodded and wished he would put his feet back.

"So, have you come to any decisions on all your declarations?" Forest asked. His mouth twisted in a smile around the rim of his glass as he took a sip. She could tell that he found her funny, but there was sympathy in it this time.

"Some. I do think I should talk to my parents at least once more. I haven't done it yet, though. It's my own fear that's holding me back. I know it, but going to see them or calling is easy to avoid."

"Meh. I mean, sure. Call them if you want, but take it from someone who's been there—they will *not* give you what you want. My father's been AWOL since I was eight, and I don't want to see that abusive asshole again. And my Mom is... always looking for something that isn't me. Or Rowan or Ash. I've tried having genuine conversations with her, and it goes nowhere. She'll just trot out some sort of inane platitude, say how proud she is of us, and then manage somehow to make our childhood sound like our fault. I've given up. Whatever closure or recognition I could hope for will not come from her."

"It's frustrating not to have your pain recognized," said Chloe.

"She sounds really damaged."

Forest sighed. "Yes. But it gets tiring being the strong one in a relationship. And that means that I have limited contact with her because I can't help her, help myself, run a business, and be a parent. When it comes to her, I've run out of fucks to give."

"And that's completely reasonable. With my parents, I think it's more for me. The last things I said to them were childish and hurtful. I think I will feel better if I attempt to leave in the spirit of kindness."

"Well, I wish you luck, but I advise you to guard your heart against high expectations."

"Thank you," said Chloe. His unexpectedly honest sentiments touched her. She felt like her old college friends had taken sides about it being the best or worst idea ever. Neither side had felt accurate. Forest's pragmatic advice felt genuine.

"What about the other Nevers?"

"I'm not sure about living here," said Chloe. "I really haven't come to any conclusions. But one of the reasons I wanted to be a nanny was to help make up my mind about kids."

"So kids are out, is what you're saying? Sorry. I swear it's worth it most days."

"Oh, no. Olly has convinced me that I absolutely want kids. I want two more just like him." Chloe stopped as she realized how possessive of Olly she sounded.

"You're kidding," said Forest, in shock.

"He's marvelous. I find being with him to be very joyful. It's very unexpected. When I was caring for my nieces and nephews, I felt resentful. Probably because I was forced to, and I didn't have the tools I needed. But with Olly, it's different. For one thing, I now have data-based child-raising knowledge, and, of course, not being twelve helps. But I feel honored that I can help shape him as a human."

"I think most days I'm just trying to keep him alive."

Chloe chuckled. "Well, yes, I had that moment today when he tried to dive off the slide. But in general, I love it and him. Of course, I suppose this means I really will have to find someone to have sex with."

Forest had been in the middle of a swallow of bourbon and promptly spit it back into his glass.

"Sorry, what?"

"Well, I've been celibate since I joined the monastery. And when I got out, I made the same decision on sex that I did on drinking. But it's been four years, and I'm starting to worry that I've forgotten how to do it."

"Can you stop saying that shit when I'm trying to take a drink?" demanded Forest, wiping bourbon off his chin.

"It's just sex," said Chloe. He seemed very upset. She suspected this was going to be another underwear issue. She shrugged as she took the tea strainer out of her mug and set it aside.

"If that's what you think, then you've been doing it wrong. Sex is a vital and significant part of life."

"Yes, but it's not satisfying to me if I'm not invested in the person I'm doing it with," she said, taking a cautious sip. The temperature was still a little too hot, but she could taste the chamomile with a delicious vibrancy. "Which means that I need to meet someone and spend time with them. And that's been difficult since I've been here. The friends I've reconnected with say to try the apps but to be honest, the idea of swiping left or right or whatever it is on someone is abhorrent to me."

"OK, yes, for you, the apps would not be right."

"It's one reason I've considered returning to Vietnam. I had a community, and there were several people who I thought were worth my time."

"I am sure there were," said Forest, and Chloe thought his tone was oddly frigid.

Forest's phone beeped, and he looked at it with a deep sigh.

"Who sends you emails at this hour?" asked Chloe.

"Well, this one is from my guy in Dubai, so it's probably a normal time for him. The others are just emails I haven't gotten to today."

"I think you should hire an assistant to respond to your email. I had a friend in Singapore who did that as a job."

Forest paused his glass halfway to his mouth. "How would that even work?"

"She would read all the emails, compile a list of questions, and then ask the boss the questions and then respond to the emails. He never read any emails."

"That is either the height of luxury or a sign of the apocalypse."

Chloe chuckled. "It might be both."

Reluctantly, Forest picked up his phone and stood up. "Might as well get it over with," he said. "I don't have an email assistant."

"Thank you for spending time with me," said Chloe. "I enjoyed talking to you."

He blinked down at her. "I enjoyed it too," he said, smiling, and Chloe felt herself flush again. "I don't remember the last time I talked about something that wasn't work with another adult."

"Same time tomorrow?" she asked, holding out her tea mug. He tapped it with his bourbon.

"It's a date."

Then he looked at her tea mug.

"I didn't feel judged for having a drink. I think anyone who tells you that is saying more about themselves than you. You always make me feel accepted as I am."

Chloe was so touched that she had no idea what to say.

"See you at breakfast. Wish me luck in the email mines."

"Good luck," whispered Chloe as he left.

Five days. And every day brought Chloe a fresh way that Forest Valkyrie was not at all what she had thought. She had assumed that seeing him day in and day out would ruin her crush, but five days had only made it worse.

# 7

*Forest*

# THE TRUCK

It was Saturday. They had made it all the way to Saturday. Usually, Saturday was Forest's day to try and catch up—with Olly, working out, sleep, the house, and probably email too. But all week had been filled with cheerful Olly and playing after work. Forest had slept through multiple nights without interruption and had even gotten a decent approximation of the workouts he was supposed to be doing. Having Chloe living with them didn't seem like it should take that much pressure off, but it was like she made everything magically better. For once, Forest felt like he had the head space and energy to attempt something more than the bare minimum. But he didn't know what that would or should be—he'd forgotten what else he used to do.

"OK," said Chloe, coming back into the kitchen. "You're home, and you don't need me? So I could go out for a bit?"

Forest looked up at Chloe and realized that she was wearing her Doc Martens and a jacket, and his answer was noooooooooooo. Olly was in such a good mood; everything was calm and perfect, and Chloe was the one who made that possible. But, of course, she wanted to have a life of her own.

"Um, yeah, of course," said Forest, sucking up his own feelings.

"OK, I'm going to try out the car."

"What?" He'd told her she could use the SUV he usually used as the Olly-mobile, but she hadn't driven anywhere all week. He had been meaning to ask, but it hadn't come up.

"Well, it's been about ten years since I've driven in the U.S., and I haven't ever driven anything like that."

"It's got the top safety rating," said Forest automatically.

"I'm sure it does, but it's a lot of vehicle, and I don't feel comfortable taking Olly out in it without doing some practice drives. I'm going to find an empty parking lot to drive around for a bit."

"Oh," said Forest. Rowan and Asher seemed to think he was too safety conscious and needed to relax. But Chloe was planning on doing extra work on the weekend so she could properly protect Olly. Forest wanted to hug her so much that he took a step forward. Chloe probably wouldn't mind. She seemed like a hugger, but that wasn't an appropriate boss thing to do.

"I didn't realize… Thank you so much for being careful. Um… what if we all go?"

"No," said Chloe, laughing. "That's the whole point! I don't want Olly in the car while I'm driving for the first time."

"No, I can drive us to a park. Olly and I can play on the swings, and you can drive around the parking lot. And that way, I'm there if you have questions."

"Oh, OK!" Chloe's smile was huge. "That would be great!"

Getting Olly ready was usually a challenge. He never wanted to put on his shoes and coat. But the idea of going somewhere with Chloe *and* Daddy was tantalizing to the three-year-old, and he willingly shoved his arms into his jacket.

"OK," said Forest, unlocking the SUV and preparing to break down its finer points.

"Wait, there's more garage?" Chloe went around the SUV and opened the door into what had initially been for RV or boat storage. Then she made a little squeal.

"You have a truck?"

"Uh, well, yes."

"Truck!" bellowed Olly, breaking free of Forest's grip and

running for the truck. Which was why it was parked in the separate section of the garage to begin with.

"I know!" exclaimed Chloe, bending down to grin at Olly. "It's a truck!"

Olly was shocked. Usually, he got pulled away from the truck, kicking and screaming.

"Look, Olly," she said, scooping him up to look into the extended cab. "It's a four-door Ford F-150. That's a lot of F's. Can you say F-150?"

"Fffffone-fity!"

"That's right! Why am I driving that beast?" she demanded, waving dismissively at the SUV. "I want to drive the truck."

"Uh... Well, Olly..."

"Olly wants to ride in the truck, too, don't you? Do you want to ride in the truck, Olly?"

"Yes!"

"OK," she said, beaming, "we'll need a couple of minutes to put your car seat in there, but then we'll ride in the truck."

"OK!" Olly glanced at Forest like he couldn't believe he was getting away with this. Then he looked at Chloe, his eyes wide to see if she could pull off a miracle.

"But..." began Forest. "It's not a kid-friendly vehicle."

"Are you kidding? Trucks are the best. Here." She hefted Olly up and plopped him into the truck bed. "See? Now he's contained while we put the car seat in. And the tailgate makes a great changing table. Olly's out of that zone, but I used to use the tailgate on my brother's truck all the time. Plus, its high wheelbase makes it super safe in traffic. And we'll put the car seat in the middle, which is the safest position. So it's completely safe, and I can totally drive a truck."

Forest didn't know if he was horrified, pissed off, or really sad. Olly began to do laps around the truck bed. Chloe smiled at Olly and then turned to look at Forest. Her smile faltered when she saw his face.

"What's the matter?"

"I stopped driving it when I got Olly because I thought I couldn't do that."

Chloe put her hand on his arm and stared at him earnestly. As usual, whenever she touched him, he felt warm all over. It didn't seem fair that she could make him sweat just by bumping into him and footsies the other night had been the first time he'd ever felt short of breath just from feet.

"That was very noble of you to sacrifice your truck for your son, but parents are still allowed to have a vehicle they like."

"It's just a truck," said Forest, feeling his cheeks heat up. "I'll get the car seat."

Twenty minutes of sweating and swearing later, Forest was feeling anything but noble, but he was feeling triumphant that he had bested the car seat.

"That was a testament to perseverance," said Chloe.

"If that means I am stubborn as fuck," said Forest, "then you are correct." Then he grimaced and glanced at Olly. Olly was bouncing up and down and yelling *truck* repeatedly. He didn't appear to have noticed Forest's swearing.

"OK, who wants to ride in a truck?" asked Chloe, holding out her arms for Olly.

"Me! Me!"

"What? You do? No way!"

"Yes way!" Olly dove into her arms over the side of the truck, and Forest took a panicked step forward, intending to catch his son. Instead, Forest ended up with his arms around both Chloe and Olly.

"Oh!" exclaimed Chloe in surprise as Olly lunged over her shoulder to hug Forest, throwing her off balance and locking her against Forest's chest. Forest held on tighter, feeling how every curve of her body fit against him. She was leaner than he'd thought, but just the right height for her ass to press against his—

"Daddy!" said Olly, grabbing Forest's face with both hands.

"Truck!"

"Yup," said Forest, disentangling himself from Chloe and trying to free his face from Olly's grip. "We're going in the truck!"

On autopilot, he opened the door for Chloe, then stopped, unsure how she would lift Olly into the car seat that was too far away for her to reach easily.

"OK," Chloe said, putting Olly on the bench seat. Her tone was cheerful. Apparently, he was the only one who found getting smashed together by a toddler erotic AF. He needed to get a grip on himself.

"Go get in your car seat, and I'll buckle you in."

"No," Forest began, "he's not going to..."

Olly walked over, plunked himself into the seat, and fumbled with the straps.

"Uh..." Forest was dumbstruck. Chloe climbed in next.

"Oh, you are so close," she said, fixing one of the straps. "What a good try. We'll keep working at it. I'll bet you get it next time." She snapped him in, and climbed back out and held out her hands for the keys.

Forest watched as Chloe backed out of the driveway and followed the circular drive down the street. He didn't like being driven by someone else, but she'd spent a few minutes adjusting everything and seemed so incredibly happy that he hadn't been able to say anything.

"I love trucks!" she yelled as they pulled onto the street. Forest jumped in his seat, but Olly laughed.

"Trucks!" Olly yelled back.

"Sorry," she said, looking over at him. "I learned to drive in a Ram 1500. When I started driving in Asia, I never really felt safe. Everything was so tiny! Even that tour bus I drove for a while felt underpowered. I hate to say it, but Americans just do trucks better."

"You drove a tour bus? I don't think that was on your resume."

"Oh, sure. I left out lots of jobs. I drove a tour bus for a summer, and I was a brick-layer for a bit. Sadly, they were very sexist. Same as here. Then, I did some waitressing. I am *not* good at that. And I was a stunt double in some action movies. Let's see what else..."

"You were a what?"

"A stunt double. Not many white actresses know kung fu, so they'd use me. That's when I started dying my hair. The wigs kept flying off!"

"You were seriously in movies?"

"Well, not good ones. And you don't see my face. But they're out there somewhere. But the director that liked me got arrested, so I had to move on."

"Arrested for what?" demanded Forest in horror.

"Illegal animal sales? I think he was smuggling pangolins."

"You are making this up," said Forest.

"No, pangolins are real. They have these fun scales and long tails. I'll show you a picture."

"I know what pangolins are! That wasn't the unbelievable part."

"Oh. What was the unbelievable part?"

She pulled up to a stop light and turned to face him.

"The bricklaying," he said because he wasn't going to dignify her ridiculousness with a real answer.

"Oh. Yeah, not a lot of women bricklayers out there. But I'd always wanted to do it. It was my dream. My uncle is a bricklayer, and I watched him do our patio when I was eight, and I thought I could grow up to do that. I didn't realize then that there was no way my family would allow that."

"What's wrong with bricklaying?"

"It's for men."

"That is dumb. The foreman on my outdoor kitchen was a woman. Forewoman. Foreperson?"

"I love your outdoor kitchen! The joints are so tight! And the curved corners had my jaw on the floor. So impressive."

"I know, right? I pointed it out to my brothers, and they just gave me a look."

"People don't appreciate the skill," said Chloe as the line of traffic in front of them moved. "Anyway, I enjoyed bricklaying, and I learned tons. I loved building."

Forest felt surprised to hear his own passion echoed in Chloe's words.

"Yeah," said Forest. "It's addictive to see something come together out of nothing."

"Exactly! And I discovered a passion for making bricks, but I want to do something custom and personal." Chloe made a dismissive noise, as if trying to quell her own excitement. "In the future. I'm not ready. Anyway, there were some issues with safety on that job, and getting a visa for bricklaying was problematical."

Forest grunted in understanding. Visas were always a problem. People heard words like *bricklayer* and categorized it as unskilled manual labor, which couldn't have been further from the truth.

"Ooh! There's the Goodwill! Should we get you a Halloween costume, Olly?" She called over her shoulder.

"We don't buy used clothing," said Forest. "Olly gets his own clothes."

"Buying used clothes is environmentally friendly."

"Olly deserves clothes that are his. Hell, all kids deserve that. And do you know how many times my brothers and I started the winter without coats because there weren't any at the Goodwill? I'm not buying something another kid could use when I can afford to go somewhere else."

Forest expected an argument, and he braced for impact.

"That's a really valid point," said Chloe nodding. "It's hard to balance social justice and environmental concerns. But I want to get Olly a pirate costume with a sword."

"I want a sword," muttered Olly from the backseat.

"And I have a hard time buying something new that he'll only wear once," continued Chloe.

"We will go to the Spirit Halloween three blocks up further and make sure we donate the costume afterward."

"Well..." Chloe looked like this was severely trying her *buy-nothing* ethos. "Maybe one time it would be OK. It *is* for Olly."

Forest felt like he'd just discovered the key to winning any argument with Chloe. It just had to be for Olly, and she'd cave.

At the Halloween store, Forest quickly found a miniature Captain Hook costume, but when he turned around he saw Chloe wistfully eyeing an adult size Tinkerbell costume. The idea of Chloe in a green mini-dress made him short of breath.

"I always wanted to be a fairy," she said regretfully. "My parents said Halloween was from the devil."

"Wings!" bellowed Olly, pulling wings of a low rack and shoving them at Chloe. Forest hadn't realized that Olly could be the best wing-man ever.

"Should we get Chloe wings?" Forest asked Olly.

"Yes!" Olly waved his sword above his head with a triumphant, wiggling dance.

"Done," said Forest taking the Tinkerbell costume and wings out of Chloe's hands.

"Oh, I don't know," said Chloe, trailing after him.

"It's for Olly," said Forest, heading for the register. Chloe made a distressed noise, but didn't actually argue.

They were walking out of the store, each with a hand holding onto Olly, who wanted them to be his swing every three steps, and Chloe was still dithering about the purchase.

"I just don't know," said Chloe for the fourth time. Forest said nothing and tried not to look too smug.

"Chloe?"

Forest paused to look at the woman approaching them. She probably was only a few years older than Chloe but looked eons more... Forest tried to put his finger on it. It wasn't more mature or older, exactly. She had a toddler on her hip and two more children in tow as they approached the store. He was still trying to pin down what it was when Chloe stopped in her tracks. Boring? Polished? The kids were all blonde, tidy, and wearing khakis. They gave him *Children of the Corn* Vibes.

Fake.

From her impeccably curled hair to the perfectly pressed children—the woman didn't look authentic. Forest glanced at Chloe and realized that even if he thought she was insane in a poncho, she always looked uniquely herself.

"Uh..." said Chloe. "Regina?" He watched Chloe look at the children as if counting them.

"Kids," said Regina, hoisting the youngest a little higher. "This is your Aunt Chloe."

"Dad says you're going to hell," said the oldest boy, and Forest felt shocked.

"Your father doesn't get to decide that," said Regina, smiling tightly. "Chloe, it's really good to see you. We're going to buy Halloween costumes."

"Oh. Will is OK with that?" Chloe looked like she had difficulty believing the answer was *yes.*

"No, but since we got a divorce, he doesn't get to decide that either."

"Oh!" exclaimed Chloe, looking strangely relieved. "I didn't know that."

"Yeah, I figured you wouldn't. It was finalized last year. I changed churches."

"That's a tough adjustment, Regina," said Chloe. "Are you OK?"

"Yes. Happier anyway. And I can see that I will be fine even if I'm not there yet. God will rebuild." Chloe smiled and nodded silently. "Thanks for not asking *what happened* like you're surprised."

Chloe gave an unhappy shrug. "I understand."

Forest wasn't sure he did.

"Yeah, I know," said Regina. One of the kids tugged at her shirt hem. "Anyway, I'd better go get everyone costumes."

"I'mma be a pirate," announced Olly. Regina smiled at him.

"Have fun trick-or-treating," Regina said kindly, and Forest retracted some of his mean thoughts.

Regina and the kids headed inside, and Chloe took a deep breath.

"Well," she said, looking at them, "that was... unexpected. I
didn't think she and my brother were a good match, but I didn't want
to be right. I will definitely have to meditate on this."

Forest didn't know what to say. The more he heard about Chloe's
family, the more he thought some of them needed to be punched in
the face. Who told kids that their aunt was going to hell?

"Snack?" asked Olly, and Chloe laughed.

"Yes, possibly over a snack."

## 8

## *Chloe*

# FAMILY VALUES

It hadn't occurred to Chloe that she would accrue additional nieces and nephews while she was out of the country. Somehow, they had stayed in her head exactly as they had been—immobilized in the amber of her memory.

However, seeing Regina and Will's three children—that she had never previously met—brought it forcefully into her awareness that time had moved on. And Regina's casual handling of their meeting also made Chloe realize how far removed she had become. Regina hadn't offered a hug because they weren't, and never had been, close. Regina hadn't told her the children's names because they weren't part of each other's lives and never would be. At best, they were casual acquaintances who had once been related. Regina had given Chloe the information she felt was necessary and moved on. Chloe found that surprisingly sad.

After her first year overseas, there had been no more emails or text messages. No phone calls, birthday messages, or letters. And Chloe had reciprocated with equal silence. It was freeing in many ways. Horrifically lonely in others.

It had taken some meditation for Chloe to identify that her sadness was grief for a family that would never be. She would never be what her family wanted, and they would never be the welcoming, warm family she longed for. But accepting that meant letting go of the hope that it ever would be. Chloe knew she needed to call her parents and close the door to her past once and for all. She needed to say goodbye in a way that wasn't reactionary or childish. It would free her to move forward.

And that was frightening.

Sometimes high ideals and logic ran straight into the scary soup of emotion.

Olly was playing with Legos. Forest was at work. The cleaning staff that randomly popped in and scared her for the first week had finished for the day and disappeared again. If she was going to do this, there wouldn't be a better time. Sitting at the kitchen island, Chloe took out her ancient, clunky phone that Forest kept making fun of and dialed the number that, despite her best efforts to forget, she knew by heart. On the third ring, Chloe didn't know if she was hoping to go to the answering machine or not.

"Hello, Jordan house," said her mother's unmistakably sweet voice.

"Hi, Mom," said Chloe, pleased she didn't sound nervous. "It's Chloe."

"Yes, it says that on the caller ID. I didn't believe it."

"Well, the technology is correct," said Chloe.

"Yes," said her mother. "Was there something you wanted?"

"Well, I... I know we didn't say goodbye very well. So, I wanted to say thank you, that I appreciated you, and tell you that I loved you."

"And?"

"That was it, Mom. Just that."

Chloe found herself unexpectedly on the point of tears. Forest had been right about her heart.

"Oh."

Chloe exhaled sadness.

"OK," said Chloe. "Thank you for picking up the phone. I'll go now."

"Chloe," said her mother, sounding suddenly more urgent.

"Yeah, Mom?"

"Where are you living?"

"I'm actually in Seattle. At least for the next few months." They were almost through Forest's one-month emergency, and she'd seen zero movement on finding a replacement for her. She also knew damn well that she would never leave either Forest or Olly high and dry, so she was probably in for the next little bit.

"But you do have someplace to live, right?"

"Oh. Yes. I'm fine. I'm... Um... I'm working as a nanny for right now and I live with the family."

"Oh! That's... that's a good job."

Chloe tried not to sigh. Her mom was making an effort. Chloe should meet that energy, not tell her mother why she was wrong.

"Yeah, it's been fun. I really like them."

"I'll have to tell your father you called," said her mom abruptly.

"Um... Yeah, of course," said Chloe. The unspoken message was that her mother would not hide any of Chloe's screw-ups from her father. Whatever happened was on Chloe's head. "I would have called when you were both home, but I'm usually doing stuff for dinner then." And she didn't want to listen to her father yell or threaten her.

"Oh. OK."

"Anyway," said Chloe, deciding that she had reached the end of her energy reserves for protecting herself, "that's my number. You've got it on the caller ID. You can call or text me if you want to talk to me." Then she wondered why she'd said that. The point had been to close the door for good—not leave it open a crack.

"I don't text," said her mother. "I don't have a cell phone."

"Oh. OK."

"I'll pray for you," said her mother.

"Um... If that makes you feel good, then you should do that. You are always in my heart."

"OK. Goodbye."

"Bye, Mom."

Chloe knew two things, and she tried to sit with them simultaneously. The first was that her mother's offer of prayer for her was a massive concession. The second was that the suggestion made Chloe's hands shake in rage. She was still sitting at the kitchen island, her hands resting on the cold granite and trying to remember that she was in control of her body, when she felt a tiny hand on her knee.

"Chloe?"

Olly held up his Lego construction. It was in two pieces, and he looked frustrated.

"It broke."

"Oh," said Chloe. "Do you want me to help?"

"Yes, please."

"Of course," said Chloe, taking the chunks of blocks. "Thank you for saying please. I really like it."

Olly beamed at her as she fit the pieces back together and handed them back.

"I want to show Daddy."

Or at least that's what she thought he said. Sometimes, toddler speech was a little garbled.

She remembered her own childhood and how she would go days without seeing her father. Jobs could run hot or cold, and when he was the foreman, he often returned after bedtime and was gone before she got up. One of the things she admired about Forest was his focus on being there in the evenings for Olly.

Olly went back to playing, and Chloe glanced at the binder on the counter with all the numbers and emergency plans that Forest could think of. She flipped it open and looked until she found the number for the Assistant. But that number was crossed out, and Jim, the PM Manager—whatever that meant—had been written in along with the note UNTIL NEW ASSISTANT IS HIRED. Jim's last name was not Manager. It was Neal. Chloe locked that fact away in her memory so that she could stop thinking of Jim as his job and then dialed the number.

She doodled a random design while waiting for the call to pick up. It had a nice symmetry, and she thought she might try it again in her sketchbook later.

"Hello," said Jim, sounding nervous.

"Hi, Jim? This is Chloe Jordan. Forest's new nanny. I would have called Forest's assistant, but the book of who to call hasn't been updated, and it just has your number."

"Is everything OK? God, please, tell me everything is OK."

"Everything is fine," said Chloe in surprise.

"None of the other nannies called!"

"Well, um, we just want to bring Forest lunch."

"What?"

"Olly and I. I thought it might be nice. Olly wants to show him some Legos, and I thought they could eat lunch together. Sorry. I just thought you would know if there was a new assistant for me to call so I could check if Forest had any free time. I don't know. Maybe he'll hate that."

"He will love it so much," said Jim. "Um... Just a sec. Let me open his calendar. The new assistant's name is Amir, by the way, but we hired him a month ago, and I think if you call him without warning, he will freak out."

Chloe tried not to ask if he would freak out more than Jim was freaking out.

"I told Forest he should hire an assistant to read his email, but he seemed to think that if he didn't do it himself, it was some kind of sin," said Chloe, and Jim laughed.

"He does seem to think he has to do everything himself. OK... Let's see what the calendar says."

"It doesn't have to be today. I know he's busy."

"No! No, we had a lunch meeting, but it got canceled. So if you came today, it would be great."

"Oh! OK. Awesome. Olly loves making lunch." She heard the slight gurk in Jim's breathing. "Don't worry. I will make sure Forest doesn't get three-year-old lunch."

Jim laughed. "He'd eat it anyway. He loves that kid."

"I know! They are so cute!"

"I know!" Jim laughed, and Chloe felt relieved that other people in Forest's life found him as adorable as she did. "This will be great," continued Jim. "It's been kind of a grind today, and I know this will cheer him up."

"Oh," said Chloe, suddenly feeling like she was hoarding all the fun Olly time. "Well, we can do it any time. So if he ever ends up with a free lunch, you or Amir or whoever can text me, and I can bring Olly over."

"Really?"

"Yeah? Olly's three. He doesn't have a lot of appointments. We can be pretty spontaneous as long as we maintain a sleep schedule and get enough play time and snacks."

"I'm not sure spontaneous is something I associate with Forest's schedule."

Chloe snorted. "Yes, I'm not sure Forest knows the meaning of the word, but spontaneous and I are old friends, so if there's a spot to wedge us in, just let me know."

"I... might actually do that," said Jim, surprised.

"Cool. OK, Olly and I are going to go work on lunch. Noon?"

"Yeah," said Jim. "Noon will be perfect. I'll text you some info on parking and where to come in."

"Thanks!"

Chloe hung up the phone and looked at Olly. "We're going to go see Daddy," she said, and Olly looked up instantly with a smile. Packing the lunch kept her from thinking about her own family and she managed to stay in that space right up until she was pulling into the Valkyrie Development parking lot and she saw a Jordan and Son's truck pulling out.

Chloe found that her hands had gone clammy. She didn't recognize the driver and she managed to not sink down behind the wheel to hide. Forest's company was big. She should have realized that his company would have crossed paths with her family. She took a deep breath and reminded herself that she and her mother had been civil, and there hadn't been any hint of anger between either of them. But Chloe also knew that talking to her mother was different than talking to her father or brothers. It didn't matter what women did—sometimes men were just angry.

# 9

## *Forest*

# LUNCHTIME

Forest walked briskly down the hall, letting his feet guide the way while he checked email on his phone. The day had been filled with his least favorite people, but at least things were getting checked off the list.

"Hey," said Jim, popping out of the breakroom and matching his stride. "Your two o'clock canceled, so I had Amir put in that meeting with the project managers."

"Oh, good. Because we wouldn't want me to have free time or anything. Chloe's right—I need an email assistant." Forest stopped walking dejectedly.

Jim looked around, surprised not to find Forest keeping up with him.

"That's not a bad idea," said Jim.

Forest shook his head. "It was a joke." He took a few quick strides, heading toward his office, and Jim joined him again.

"I don't joke about time management," said Jim. "Meanwhile, I also booked you a lunch meeting."

"Amir said I had lunch free," protested Forest. He'd been thinking about trying to sneak in a workout. Or a pizza.

"Yeah, but it's a VIP client, so you'll have to take it."

"Wait, who is it?"

But Jim was already opening the door to Forest's office.

"Daddy!" shouted Olly, and Forest had just enough time to tuck his phone away before Olly slammed into him. He scooped up Olly and tossed him in the air, which made Olly yell in happiness. He heard Chloe chuckle and looked around to see her sitting on his prim and proper guest couch with a picnic basket.

"What are you guys doing here?" asked Forest.

"Lunch!" yelled Olly.

"We made you lunch," said Chloe.

"I saw a bulldozer!" said Olly. Only it came out as *bulldother*. "Anna ex-ka-vaytor. Anna dump truck."

"All those?" asked Forest.

"Anna..." Olly looked at Chloe.

"Backhoe," said Chloe.

"Is he making you memorize all the construction equipment?" asked Forest. "Sorry."

Chloe laughed. "No, I have them all memorized from child-hood. It did take me a minute to remember the difference between an excavator and a backhoe. But then I remembered the backhoe has wheels."

"Yeah, it does," said Forest, feeling surprised and impressed. "Hey," he said, hefting Olly up to get closer to eye-to-eye, "do you want to sit on the backhoe after lunch?"

Olly's legs kicked in unsuppressed excitement. "Chloe!" he gasped. "Backhoe."

"Yeah, baby! I heard!"

Olly squealed in excitement and kicked until Forest was forced to release him. He sometimes swore his child was part alligator with all the rolling and twisting.

"We really did bring you lunch," said Chloe, hefting the picnic basket.

"I made it," said Olly as Forest reached for the basket.

Forest froze and met Chloe's eye. "I supervised," she said with a grin.

"Then I'm sure I will enjoy it," said Forest.

Lunch turned out to be a hand-packed bento box with a treasure trove of goodies. Olly had a peanut butter and jelly. Then he shared Chloe's hummus, and they experimented with dipping things into it to discover what might be good. Peanut butter and jelly was declared *not good,* but carrots were crunchy and Forest shook his head. It still seemed like a miracle to him. Chloe and Olly were done much sooner than he was, but watching them play with the set of toy trucks he kept on display made the best lunch entertainment he could imagine. He heard and ignored the email alerts pinging periodically on his phone, but he couldn't ignore it when it started ringing. He leaned over to check the caller.

"Hey," said Forest, seeing his older brother's face on the phone and picking up after the first ring.

"Hey," said Rowan. "You sound like you're in a good mood."

Forest looked over to where Chloe and Oliver sat in the sunshine patch on his office rug and back down at his lunch.

"Yeah, it's a pretty good day. What's up with you?"

"I am... also in a good mood."

"That was the most awkward statement of well-being I've ever heard," said Forest, feeling suspicious.

"It really was. Sorry. Uh. I'm calling about Thanksgiving."

"Yeah, I'm looking forward to it! Chloe can come, right?" His brother's plan to divvy up the holidays among the Valkyrie siblings had initially put Forest into a panic. But then he realized it meant that he had no responsibility for Thanksgiving and, since his designated holiday was Christmas, he had *months* to plan.

"Chloe?"

"Uh... my nanny. I hired a nanny. Temporary nanny. To fill in while I look for someone with all the certifications."

"Oh, sure. Actually, another girl would be great."

Alarm bells sounded in the back of Forest's brain.

"Another girl? Is there a first girl?"

"Uh... so... You remember Vivian? You met her when you came

to pick up Olly a few weeks ago?"

Forest tried to recall the day. He'd been frazzled and late from getting stuck in the elevator with Chloe. And then there had been a girl in Rowan's office. A late twenties brunette with a great rack. She worked for the law firm downstairs from Rowan. Rowan had said she was his tenant rep. Now that Forest was thinking about it, Rowan had seemed oddly casual with her. Usually, when talking to a business acquaintance, Rowan was Mr. Marine, but Rowan had stayed on the floor playing with Olly.

"Yes," said Forest, "Vivian very kindly put me back in touch with Grant Ichikawa at Hoskins, Kato, and Branch. I have a will now. And a trust because, apparently, that's better for Olly and my taxes."

"Oh. Great. You seemed worried about that."

"Well, I don't want to die and have you guys have to sort everything out. I did put you down as getting Olly. There's a paper for you to sign."

"No problem. Just email it or whatever. But, uh, so, Vivian."

Suddenly, Forest realized what his brother was very awkwardly leading up to and laughed. "You dog. You are dating your building rep."

Rowan's sigh was audible even over the phone. "Yes."

"Your *twenty-something* building rep."

"Please don't say anything about our ages when you see her," said Forest. "She gets mad."

Forest laughed again. "Good for you. That's great. And she's coming to Thanksgiving? That's serious. Is her family OK with you stealing her away at the holidays?"

"It's really just her. Her dad passed, and her Mom lives down in Texas."

"OK, is it horrible that I literally just thought, *that's convenient?* That's probably bad. But I feel like we've always gotten the short end of the holiday stick. I don't want to share what little family time we have with someone else's weirdo family."

Rowan chuckled. "Yeah, I hear you. But uh… I'm not sure where Vivian and I are going, but she is coming to Thanksgiving, so if you could at least share the holiday with her, I'd appreciate it."

"Yeah, of course. That is the literal point of Thanksgiving, after all. I'm an American. I understand the assignment." Forest tensed but then gathered his courage to press for more. "I guess you really like her, though?" Forest wasn't privy to the innermost workings of Rowan's life, but lately, it had felt like Rowan had wanted more connection, too. And while Thanksgiving was an inclusive holiday, Rowan had never brought anyone besides Marine buddies.

"Yeah, she…" Rowan's voice softened in a way Forest hadn't ever heard before. "Vivian's kind of amazing. And, more relevant to you, she says that Olly is about the cutest thing ever every time she sees his picture."

"Oh, well, I already like her better than Ash's ex. She yelled at Olly for spilling something on the carpet, and he cried."

"Yeah, hopefully, that breakup sticks," said Rowan drily. "I didn't like her."

"Me either, but she had that old money aesthetic that Ash likes, and I know he likes…"

"He likes looking established and confident and not like we just rolled into money last week and have no fucking clue what we're doing."

"Ha! Yes! Even though that's exactly what we did."

Rowan chuckled. "I buy so many bullshit things just because I can. And it's entirely possible Olly will be getting too many toys for Christmas."

"I may have ordered a fully operational mini-excavator," whispered Forest, and Rowan gave a booming laugh that made Forest grin just to hear his brother so happy.

"Awesome. Although, hey, tell Chloe—is that what you said her name was?—that our building is doing a trick-or-treat thing. She can bring Olly down. If you're fine with that. It's indoors and safe, and the businesses seem kind of pumped about it. There's kind of a kid carnival in the lobby."

"Oh, that sounds fantastic. He's really excited about his costume, but I have not been excited about the weather. That might be the perfect Halloween activity."

"Yeah, I'll send you an email. Or tell me Chloe's, and I'll email her? Is that better? What's the least stressful for you?"

"Oh, send it to me. I haven't gotten her set up on email yet because she won't take a real phone."

He said that last part loudly in Chloe's direction.

"If it makes phone calls, it's a real phone!" she called back. "I don't need to be online to experience life."

"She doesn't need to be online to experience life," repeated Rowan. "Well, that is..."

"Somewhat incomprehensible?" asked Forest. "Yes. I don't even know how she got a plane ticket back into the country without an email address."

"I walked up to the counter and bought one," said Chloe.

"I didn't know you could still do that," said Forest. "Anyway," he returned to the call with his brother, "just email me. Maybe we can all go. That will be fun."

Chloe looked puzzled.

"Rowan's building is doing a kid's Halloween thing."

"Oh, fun!"

Forest laughed as Chloe's face lit up. "Yeah, we're in."

"Great," said Rowan. "Looking forward to it."

Rowan hung up, and Forest looked at Chloe. "I really do need to get you a new phone. It's ridiculous that you use a computer to get email."

"It gets texts," said Chloe. "Anyone who really wants me just calls or texts."

"It's literally an old person phone."

"I like the big buttons."

"Why are you weird?"

"I don't think you hang out with enough people if you think I'm weird."

"Mmm..." said Forest, "gonna have to disagree." He finished the last orange wedge and grinned at Chloe and Olly. "Who is ready to sit on a backhoe?"

Chloe laughed as Olly jumped in the air.

They were walking down to the yard with Olly between them when Forest realized he was grinning as big as Olly was.

"Thanks so much for coming," he said, looking at Chloe. "This was great."

She smiled at him, and his chest felt oddly tight. "I thought..." She shrugged. "I thought it would be nice to see you. For Olly to see you."

Forest nodded, but he felt warm as they stepped out into the cold Fall air. Somehow, the day seemed better than it had an hour ago.

## 10

*Forest*

# FIRST DATES

Forest lay on the couch and missed Chloe. Her friends had called during dinner and invited her out. She seemed excited about it, but he and Olly missed her at bedtime. Which was ridiculous. She'd barely been here a month. There couldn't be a routine to disrupt after only a month. They couldn't miss someone after that short of a time, could they? He also realized he had never bothered to call the agency back about their new nanny candidates. He probably ought to do that. He looked guiltily at his phone. If he opened his email, there would be more emails. Was he really going to do that?

No.

He was going to lay here, drink, and wait for Chloe to come home.

That sounded depressing as fuck.

Reluctantly, he got up and went to the home gym that was just off the laundry room. It had a yoga mat in it now. And one of Olly's stuffies. Forest had gotten in a few sets and was amusing himself by trying some of Chloe's stretches when he heard the garage door go up. Moments later, the door from the house to the garage slammed.

He stepped out into the hall.

"Chloe?"

She turned to him, and he felt a wave of panic. She looked like she was about to cry.

"Are you all right? What's the matter?" He hurried toward her, forgetting he wasn't wearing a shirt.

"I..." She seemed to be having trouble getting words out. "I am very upset!" She wasn't yelling, but her voice was as intense as if she had.

Forest didn't have a response for that. What was he supposed to do for upset feelings? He wanted to hug her. She looked rigid and tense. Maybe not hugging?

"I will make you tea," he blurted out.

Chloe's shoulders dropped about two inches, and she took a deep breath.

"Thank you. I would appreciate that. I will go change. I don't like these clothes on my body anymore."

He looked down at her shirt and jeans. He thought she'd looked cute. It showed off her fantastic figure.

"OK."

"OK."

By the time he got the water boiled, Chloe had returned to the living room in her yoga gear. Forest let the tea steep the appropriate time, pulled the strainer, and brought it to her. He set down the tea and tried to ignore her perfect ass that was lifted in the air in downward dog. Having her around would either make him a monk or drive him to drink.

He put on some music. She seemed to play classic rock and mellow stuff with Olly and instrumental music while stretching. He wasn't sure what she listened to when she was alone, so he put on some classic Portishead, figuring it was close enough to her stretching music to be acceptable. She moved through some other poses, and he valiantly focused on doom-scrolling through his phone and ignored the bends and twists of her body. Finally, she came to a stop, kneeling on the rug, and picked up her cup. She definitely looked more relaxed as she sipped the tea. He wondered if it was OK to ask what had upset her.

"My friends set me up on a date without telling me," she said as if reading his thoughts.

"Blech," he said, and then realized that might not have been the upsetting part. "I mean... I would find that upsetting, but I'm assuming nothing else happened?"

"He was an asshole," she said derisively. "I honestly don't know what they were thinking. I told them I wanted to date, but could they maybe have checked that I wanted to date *him?*"

"Was that it?" he asked cautiously. "You seemed pretty upset when you came home."

"I was surprised," she said reflectively. "I felt ambushed, and that upset me, but it was more than that, and I can't tell what about the sensory experience was triggering."

"What do you mean?"

"I wasn't really prepared for dating the first time around. It took me some time to realize I didn't have to get along with everyone."

"Well, you're a go-with-the-flow kind of person," said Forest. He was uncomfortable with the idea that someone could have taken advantage of Chloe and didn't want it to be true.

"There is a big difference between accepting what the universe has brought to you and accepting the shit pile that someone tries to hand you," said Chloe drily.

Forest laughed at the unexpected analogy, and Chloe smiled.

"I think," she said, taking a sip of tea, "probably because of my upbringing, I didn't know how to set boundaries. It took me some time to realize that I don't have to accept unacceptable treatment. And while I told my friends that I want to start dating, being shoved into an unpremeditated date in a crowded bar with a douchebag... The experience felt too much like my past, and I didn't like it."

"Mm," said Forest. He wanted to say that she needed to ditch her so-called friends. They sounded like a bunch of immature bar-hopping idiots.

"I don't know... Maybe I'm not ready to start dating again."

"Maybe you need a parking lot," said Forest.

"What?"

"You were going to take the car to a parking lot to get comfortable driving again. Maybe you need the parking lot of dates. Something you can control, with minimal risk that allows you to sort of get the feel of how to do it again."

Even as he said the words, Forest wanted to take them back because he realized he didn't want her dating at all.

"That's a great idea." She picked up her tea and got up. He watched her in confusion as she plunked herself down next to him on the couch, placing her tea carefully on a coaster on the ottoman. "OK, go on a date with me."

"What?"

"We'll do a fake first date right here, and then I can figure out what triggered me."

"Right now?"

"Are you doing something better?"

He looked down at the meaningless video on his phone. "No?"

Was it better to be her practice date and be close enough to kiss her or to send her out with some other guy where he'd be thinking about *that* guy kissing her?

"OK, we have walked into the bar-slash-restaurant and figured out we are who we're looking for. Now, do we shake?"

She held out her hand.

"No, it's a first date, but we've already talked online, so we awkwardly hug."

"See? You're way better at this than me. OK, awkward hug." She leaned in, and Forest found himself matching her to give the patented first date only-shoulders-touching hug. "Ooh. You smell good. What is that? Cinnamon?" She turned her face into his neck and huffed him. At the feeling of her breath on his neck, his skin prickled all the way down his side.

"Well, you've successfully made it awkward," he said, and she chuckled as she pulled back. He reached up and touched his neck.

"I put cinnamon on Olly's applesauce. Yeah, pretty sure that's cinnamon and Aquaphor that I put on his knee scrape."

"Eau de Parent. Sexy," she said, giving an over-the-top leer and wink.

He laughed and rubbed his neck again. "Yeah, OK, but being awkward is my job. Let's see..." He looked around. "Ah. Here, woman! I have bought you this beverage, and now you are financially obligated to me." He moved her tea closer, and she laughed.

"Mmm, delicious trade-value-for-my-body beverage," she said, taking a dramatic sip. "OK, what else do douchebags do?"

"Um... Oh." He put one hand on her knee and stretched his arm along the back of her section of the couch so he could lean into her personal space. "Hi. I'm going to touch you in an attempt to build connection, but I won't actually listen to anything you say."

"Yes! Yes, he did do that!" Her eyes went wide as he nailed the douchebag maneuver. "But..." She looked down at his hand with a frown. Then she grabbed it and moved it to her other knee. Then, her waist. And then pushed it back down toward the knee so that it slid across her soft, supple thigh.

"Uh..." he said, trying to keep from blushing. This was not helping him at all.

"You're not doing it right," she complained. "It's not icky when you do it."

"Well, *not icky* is kind of the minimum I generally shoot for. But I think it never will be when you do it like that."

"What do you mean?" She looked confused.

"You're moving my hand. You're in control. I think it's probably the lack of consent that triggered you."

"Consent and intention," Chloe said, blowing out a frustrated breath that ruffled her violet bangs. "They really are everything. OK, let's try that again." She closed her eyes. "OK, go."

"Go, where?" All he could think was that he should kiss her.

"Touch me somewhere, so I'm surprised."

"I... no."

This was such a bad plan. All the places Forest wanted to touch, he certainly, absolutely was *not* going to.

"Oh, come on. I'm looking for what physical sensations trigger me."

He needed something intimate but not grope-able.

"Mm... OK." He curled his fingers around the back of her neck and ran his thumb along the ridge of muscle there, kneading ever so slightly.

"Ohhhhh," she groaned, arching toward him, her eyes still closed.

"You're not supposed to like it," he muttered.

"But it feels so good," she whispered back.

Her face was inches away from his. The faint whisper of her rose petal lotion teased his nose. Her lips would be so soft.

"We should end this date," he said, mostly to himself. Before he did something incredibly idiotic.

"OK," she agreed. Her eyes blinked dreamily open and then closed again. Then she leaned in and kissed him.

Forest knew he ought to pull back, but he didn't want to. Her soft lips invited him to linger, but he was unprepared for how much he wanted to stay.

Luxury.

That was the word that came to mind. Silk, velvet, anything expensive and heavenly. That was what kissing Chloe was like. It was everything he'd wanted in life—he just hadn't known it was a person.

## 11
## *Chloe*

# FIRST KISSES

Chloe firmly believed in the interconnectedness of energy throughout the universe, but never in her life had she felt as electrically connected to anyone or anything as she did to Forest Valkyrie.

He pulled back, and Chloe stared at him in shock. She felt like every nerve ending in her body was tingling. He made a noise. Possibly, it sounded confused.

"Do people not kiss at the ends of dates anymore?" she asked breathlessly.

There was a half a beat where he seemed to consider that.

"Yes, absolutely, they do," he said and pulled her into his lap.

Chloe liked that and wiggled around until she had her legs wrapped around him. This was clearly the best position to make out with anyone. Why hadn't she thought of this before? It felt more intimate than merely kissing. It felt like an exchange of breath.

With an exhilarating feeling of exploration, she slid one hand under his shirt. She had been upset when she'd come home, but she hadn't been blind—ink-covered, shirtless Forest was worth seeing again. He reciprocated, and Chloe leaned in, relishing the heat of his hands across the small of her back.

Forest nuzzled into the crook of her neck, and Chloe moaned at the prickling sensation of his scruff and the delightful feeling of his lips. His fingers moved up her back – half massage, half delicious petting – and Chloe breathed out. Having his hands on her body was better. The taste of him was better. *Everything* was better with Forest.

She could feel some part of her trying to send up a signal that possibly making out with her boss was not the best idea, but she ruthlessly squashed it. She wanted Forest. She didn't want second thoughts and pausing to consider.

A flat *E* tone followed by a sharp *C* echoed through Chloe's brain, and she struggled to attach meaning to the hollow ding-dong. It wasn't a gong sound. She wasn't at temple.

"What the hell?" demanded Forest, pulling back and staring in disbelief toward the front door. He grabbed his phone and pulled up the front door cam. Chloe could see a man on the front porch. His hand raised, finger outstretched, heading for the doorbell again.

"Touch the bell again, and not only will I break your finger you will be the one getting my toddler back to sleep," said Forest, speaking into his phone.

The man on the video feed looked startled. "Uh... Sorry," said the man, leaning toward the bell and speaking loudly. "I have a package for Forest Valkyrie that needs to be signed for."

Forest tossed his phone down angrily and moved Chloe a square over on the couch. He stood and stomped toward the door. Chloe stared at the image on his phone. Something was wrong. The guy on the porch did have a package, but it was flat like an envelope, and he wasn't wearing a uniform.

"It looks like papers," said Chloe, following him through the kitchen and into the front hall. "Ask for ID." In her experience, papers were never good news and always worse than any package.

Forest yanked open the door. "Who the hell are you?" he demanded, glaring at the man who looked about fifty and was wearing jeans and a tidy button-up.

The man held out a clipboard and the envelope. Forest signed it impatiently and grabbed the fat manila envelope.

"I'm a process server," said the man. "Sorry to bother you."

Then he turned around and walked quickly toward a car idling in the drive.

"A process server?" repeated Forest, sounding confused. Chloe looked over his shoulder as the car pulled out onto the street.

"That is it. I'm getting a gate installed. I swore I didn't want to be one of *those* people, but I'm not having people randomly pull up to my house."

Forest shook his head and then glared at the envelope in his hand.

"And why not give it to me at work or call our lawyer?"

Chloe knew why not. Papers that were about business went to lawyers. Only when a lawsuit was personal did it go to an individual. She had learned that from her very short stint in the children's game development company. Disney had not taken kindly to having their intellectual property ripped off by a tech start-up in Taiwan and sued the company and all the employees individually. Fortunately, disappearing into Cambodia for a year had been enough to make them forget about her. But she didn't know how to communicate this to Forest without having him bring up house chickens again and revoke her Olly privileges.

Forest closed the door and tore open the envelope as he walked back toward her. He pulled out a thick sheaf of papers and frowned at it. His steps faltered until he stopped, and his face went pale.

"They can't do this," he whispered. "They can't. They can't." He looked around wildly. "Where's my phone? I won't let them do this."

"Forest?" Chloe walked toward him. He put his hand up to his face, and she saw it shaking. He shoved the papers at her and swiftly returned to his phone in the living room. Chloe looked at the letter on top of the pages. It took her a while to decipher what it meant.

In the living room, she could hear Forest trying to talk to Rowan.

"They can't do this. I will drive to Canada. I will put him in the car right now. We will go to fucking Canada."

He paused briefly to listen to his brother, but she could tell he wasn't hearing what was being said.

"I can't," he said. "I can't let them do this. I will... I will do something."

He hung up the phone and turned to her, his eyes wide.

"I can't breathe," Forest said, gasping for air. "I think I'm having a heart attack."

His phone lit up with a quick succession of texts.

"You're not having a heart attack," said Chloe.

"I can't feel my fingers."

Chloe put the papers on the kitchen island and went over to him. "It's going to be OK."

Forest looked at his phone again.

"Rowan says not to go to Canada."

"He's right. We should not go to Canada. You need to breathe."

"I can't breathe! It feels like there is an elephant on my chest."

His phone pinged again. Chloe tried to take it out of his hand, but Forest pulled it further away.

"Rowan says to text Grant Ichikawa. I should do that, but I can't feel my fingers. I think I'm dying."

"You're not dying. You're having a panic attack. I don't know who Grant Ichikawa is."

"He's the lawyer that did Olly's citizenship and my will a couple of weeks ago."

"Well, then, he is the appropriate person to contact. Give me your phone. I will text him."

Forest finally relinquished the phone, and Chloe shoved him onto the couch.

"You need to stimulate your Vagus nerve. Sit there and take deep breaths."

Forest was freaking out, and unlike the elevator, she wasn't sure how to get his brain to stop firing all of the emergency signals.

Chloe searched for Grant's name in his contacts and sent a quick message.

Olly's grandparents just served me with custody papers. What do I do?

## 12
## *Forest*

# CUSTODY AGREEMENTS

Chloe had told him to breathe, but he couldn't. Every time he tried to inhale, his lungs wouldn't cooperate. It felt like there was an anvil on his chest.

"OK," said Chloe, setting down his phone and sitting down next to him. "We're going to try butterfly tapping."

Chloe was insane. He knew this was a fact because she had just used the phrase *butterfly tapping* as if those words meant something.

He grabbed his phone and texted Rowan again, fingers fumbling to communicate what the hell was happening. Chloe took the phone out of his hand and set it down again.

"Please look at me," she said, forcefully crossing his arms over his chest as if he were an Egyptian mummy. "I want you to tap your shoulders. First, one hand, then the other. It helps regulate the nervous system and reduce anxiety."

He stared at her and tapped a few times because he didn't know what else to do. He felt like an idiot.

"This isn't working," he gasped, standing up. "I need to… I'll…"

His phone dinged.

Listen to Chloe.

"Forest," said Chloe, standing up too. "There is literally nothing you can do."

"There has to be something. I can't let them take him away from me."

"Your body wants to fight something."

"Yes, damn it!"

"But currently, the only threat is that piece of paper."

Forest looked at the sheaf of papers on the counter. He wanted to rip them up.

"Tell me what you're feeling," she said.

"I'm so angry," gasped Forest. "They never listened to Vera. Never. They didn't want Olly. They still don't want him. They just don't want me to have him because it's what Vera wanted. How dare they? How dare they try and take my son?"

"But they won't," said Chloe. "Olly will stay here with you where he belongs."

She said it with such confidence that he was startled into taking a deep breath.

"Tell me what your fear is. Name the fear. Say it out loud."

She was waiting for him to say it. Why was this so hard? He knew why. Saying it made it real. Saying it made it more likely to happen. But those papers said it for him. The fear was now right there in front of him.

"I'm scared of losing him," whispered Forest.

Chloe nodded as if she already knew.

"I never knew I wanted him until he was here. I didn't know I could love anybody as much I love him, and I'm scared."

Chloe nodded again.

"OK. Now tell me, how much money do you have?"

Forest blinked at her, trying to calculate his net and what he had in investments.

"Lots?" he suggested, shaking his head.

"Millions? A billion?"

"Not in savings. The company is worth that much. But… if I liquidated, I could maybe raise a couple hundred million without too many problems."

"But you have a lot. And your brothers have a lot. And you have an army of staff, and you have me, and I live here to take care of Olly at all times."

"Yes. I don't understand…"

"By all ways of measuring, Olly is cared for to the very best standard of care that money can buy."

"I try," said Forest, looking around the messy living room. "I could hire more people. But I feel like that just puts more people between me and Olly."

"Exactly. You *personally* take care of him. Objectively speaking, no one is going to take a child away from his wealthy father, who has been there all of the child's life and takes care of him like you do. They just won't. And you have the money to afford lawyers who will make sure of that."

Forest took another breath. "Yeah." The tingling in his fingers was dying down. "I do."

"And if something insane happens, we will take Olly and go to Cambodia."

"Dubai," said Forest. "I have friends there."

"OK, that works too. My point is that the only place there is an army is between Olly and your fear. And if we do get down to your fear, there is a contingency plan."

Forest looked at Chloe. She had said that the three of them would go to Cambodia.

"I've never been to Cambodia."

"It's beautiful."

"I've always wanted to see Angkor Wat."

"We should go. Olly would love it. You would love it. They make good fish sauce."

They had been kissing before this happened. Should he say something about that? It seemed like he should, but what was he supposed to say?

"Listen to me," said Chloe, putting her hand on his shoulder. "This feels terrifying, but it's going to be OK. You aren't alone. You have family and help."

His phone dinged again, and he saw Grant Ichikawa's name.

I'LL LOOK AT THE PAPERS ON MONDAY, BUT THE SHORT ANSWER IS: DON'T DO ANYTHING. DON'T RESPOND IN ANY WAY UNTIL I CAN TAKE A LOOK. THEY CAN FILE WHATEVER THEY WANT, BUT YOU HAVE SOLE LEGAL CUSTODY. THEY DID NOT CONTEST THE CUSTODY AT THE TIME OF VERA'S PASSING, AND THERE HAS BEEN NO CHANGE IN CIR-CUMSTANCE. THERE IS NO VALID REASON FOR CHALLENGING YOUR CUSTODY. OLLY'S NOT GOING ANYWHERE.

He handed the phone to Chloe.

"Yes," said Chloe, nodding at the text. "Yes. See? Olly is staying right here."

Forest realized that, logically, Chloe, Rowan, and Grant were all correct, but he still felt like he was waiting for a fight to start. And Chloe wanted him to tap himself. The only way that was going to work was if he punched himself in the face. Maybe that's what he was doing—fighting himself.

"Chloe," said Forest, laughing at his own mental image.

"What?"

"Thank you for all the stress management tips, but I think but-terfly tapping is dumb."

"Then it's not for you." She didn't even look offended.

"I think I need to go for a run," he said, remembering when he'd been able to chase anxiety away with exercise.

"That is a great idea! Running forces measured breathing and releases endorphins!"

Forest shook his head. He and Chloe looked at things so very differently, but he couldn't say she'd ever been wrong.

The streets were dark with a rain that had come through, and his feet made a soothing rhythm that pulled his brain into following along until he couldn't remember the last thought he'd had. He tried to think of the last time he'd run on streets instead of a treadmill—probably before Vera and Olly. He had condensed his time down to essentials, and the extra five minutes it took to change to outside gear had been designated as wasted.

He inhaled and felt the relief of wet air and the soft scent of asphalt. He cut across a park and enjoyed the challenge of damp turf sticking to his feet and slowing him down. The burn of exertion felt like it was flattening out the mountain he'd made of the lawsuit. It was a challenge, and he hated it, but Chloe was right—he had money and lawyers at his disposal. No one would be taking Olly away.

The thought of Chloe made his heart falter, and he pushed a little harder, trying to move faster than whatever emotion was coming next.

He hadn't meant to kiss her, but he couldn't say he regretted it. A relationship with the nanny was a disaster in the making. How was he supposed to take a risk on a relationship for himself when Olly had to come first, and Chloe was the one thing that was making Olly happy?

He would talk to her. He would say it had been a mistake. She valued honesty, and it was the truth—he couldn't afford to take the risk.

Forest slipped quietly in the side door and checked the time on his watch. His heart rate was now elevated but not racing, and he no longer felt like he was going to jump out of his skin. The light was on in the kitchen, and one side light in the den. He walked in further, dreading that Chloe would be waiting for him but still wishing she would be.

She was—of course—because Chloe cared about him. But she was also asleep. She was cuddled under the cashmere blanket she and Olly preferred when snuggling on the couch.

Her blonde lashes were pale on her cheeks, and he could see the soft smattering of freckles across the bridge of her nose. Over the past few weeks, her hair had faded from vibrant purple to a softer lavender. Reluctantly, he brushed a lock of hair away from her face. What was he supposed to do?

"Chloe," he whispered, but she didn't move. "Time for bed."

"OK," she said sleepily back, but it was a tone he recognized from Olly as not really being awake.

Gingerly, he bent down and scooped her up. She snuggled into his shoulder with something that might have almost been a word and wrapped her arms around his neck with a heavy sigh.

For a long moment, Forest stood there breathing in the scent of Chloe like she was oxygen. Then he carried her into her room and laid her down gently on the bed. It took all his willpower not to lie down next to her, but he forced himself to turn around and walk out the door.

13

*Chloe*

# THE GALA

Forest was avoiding her. Which was upsetting. It was probably because they'd been making out before he'd had a panic attack, and then she'd fallen asleep on the couch. She felt like she ought to attack the subject head-on, but Olly kept following them around, and Forest wouldn't make eye contact. He seemed to be frowning at everything, including the TV, which he'd turned to the news.

Olly made happy noises as he ate his banana slices, and Chloe smiled at him. He didn't seem to notice anything was wrong.

"Unca Roan!" chirped Olly.

"Not today, bud," said Forest, looking up from making tea. Chloe noticed that he was also making a cup for her. She took that as a good sign.

"Unca Roan!"

"We can call him later," said Forest.

Olly shook his head, looking frustrated.

"Unca Roan!" he yelled, pointing at the TV.

Chloe looked up at the TV on the wall and blinked in surprise at the crawl that read VETERAN'S CHARITY GALA SCENE OF DRIVE-BY SHOOTING. A woman in a one-shouldered red dress that gave Chloe an absolute pang of capitalistic jealousy was speaking to a news reporter. Behind her, a dark-haired man with one arm bandaged was surveying everything.

"Holy shit," said Forest, grabbing for the remote to turn up the sound.

"Hollyship," muttered Olly under his breath, sounding smug.

"We are working with the police, of course," said the woman. "But the Victory Mission serves veterans, and we take this attack as a targeted assault on our community. We are fortunate that a team from Valkyrie Security was in attendance as guests and acted swiftly to prevent the worst from happening. We ask for your prayers for the Hoskins family during this difficult time."

The man behind her touched her arm lightly.

"Thank you," said the woman, moving off. "We will make additional statements later."

The reporters clamored for Ms. Kaye and Mr. Valkyrie's attention, but neither he or the girl responded.

"That's the girl he said he was bringing to Thanksgiving," said Forest, sounding shocked.

"Lady!" said Olly happily, going back to his banana.

The clip cut back to the reporter at the desk who gave a synopsis of the late-night drive-by shooting, which had left local lawyer Howard Hoskins in the ICU, and finished with the information that Rowan Valkyrie had been personally responsible for saving Mr. Hoskins from a hail of bullets.

"Hail of bullets?" repeated Forest, turning to Chloe.

"I don't know," said Chloe. "Google it."

Forest was already reaching for his phone. There was a string of muttered swear words as he flipped through screens. Then he paused to read an incoming text.

"Grant Ichikawa says to tell Rowan the firm sincerely appreciates him. What the——" Forest cut off, clearly biting back swear words. He looked at her as if expecting her to have a plan.

"Uh… Call Rowan?" offered Chloe. "Sorry, I have no frame of reference for this."

"I guess I will do that." He glanced at Olly. "Maybe in my office. Be right back."

"Lady," said Olly, still looking at the TV. They showed a brief snippet of the girl in the red dress again. "Hollyship."

Chloe smothered a laugh. Forest would *not* be amused once he figured out what Olly was saying, and she didn't want to encourage him.

"Let's just try PBS Kids," she said, tentatively picking up the remote and hoping she could push the right buttons.

"Magic School Bus!" chirped Olly.

"I hope so," agreed Chloe.

She supposed she was late to the party, but she and Olly loved PBS Kids and devoured every episode of the Magic School Bus. According to her family, PBS was a heathen channel with a liberal agenda that tried to indoctrinate children. Now, having actually watched it, she thought being kind and learning about science and the alphabet was a level of indoctrination she was comfortable with. The Magic School Bus was too old for Olly to follow, but he was fascinated by Miss Frizzle and her iguana. But this morning, Sesame Street was teaching the letter *P*.

Forest came out of the office a few minutes later, the phone pressed to his ear.

"Ash, you literally know everything that I know. He sounded fine when I talked to him. Don't freak out."

He paused to listen to his younger brother.

"No, I don't think this is like the time."

Chloe looked up in surprise. There had been another time?

"Yes, I know he probably got shot this time, too, but I saw him on the news. He was walking around and doing the thing. You know, the thing where he looks like Mr. Scary Security Guy. So it obviously wasn't that bad, or he wouldn't have been walking around last night and wouldn't be at home now."

Forest paused to nod at the phone.

"Yeah, I mean… I will call him later, but you can also call him. Why am I in the middle? Ha. Ha. Yes, I'm aware that I'm the middle child. You are hilarious. Yeah, OK, talk to you later."

Forest hung up and blatantly rolled his eyes.

"What? You don't like being in the middle?" asked Chloe, amused.

"I love my brother, but sometimes I swear he acts about as proficient as Olly. He is thirty-two. He is fully capable of doing his own communicating, and yet… Here's me doing it. I will let it slide from Rowan because I think if you get shot, you've earned the right to lay in bed and not make phone calls."

"Fair," agreed Chloe, nodding. She was amused by Forest's ranting, but mostly, she was just glad he was talking to her.

"But seriously! Ash can pick up the phone and text as well as anyone else. Why am I managing this?"

"Because you're his older brother, and you've always done it, and he thinks it's your job?"

"It's not my job!" barked Forest.

"Family assumptions about your role are hard to fight," said Chloe.

"On the plus side, I'm pretty sure Grant is going to handle the custody stuff pro bono because of Rowan, so that's working out for me. Apparently, poor Mr. Hoskins is still in the ICU, and Rowan and Vivian—that's the girl—had to wrangle cops and reporters all night. Sounds like a complete shi… bad show."

Chloe chuckled as Forest tried to divert his swearing.

"I really thought I'd broken this little linguistic habit," said Forest, shaking his head as he flipped the channel back to the news.

"It's probably stress," said Chloe.

Forest turned the volume on the news down to a murmur, returned to his tea, and sighed at the sight of what was probably very burned tea leaves. He poured the tea down the drain and started again.

"Why do you know all the stress stuff?" asked Forest, looking up at her. "Which one of your many jobs required stress management?"

Chloe laughed. "None of them. Breathing is part of meditation, which I studied, and my sister used to get panic attacks, so I spent time researching it."

"Why did she get panic attacks?"

"Probably because she had to be perfect all the time. When I started recognizing the same symptoms in myself, I started thinking about ways not to get married and get out of my parent's house."

Forest grunted and made a face. "Yeah, I guess you would know about busting out of the role your family assigned you."

"Yes," said Chloe. "It can be incredibly freeing but also very disturbing to your family."

"I don't want to disturb them," said Forest, shaking his head.

"Even at your own expense?" asked Chloe skeptically.

"Rowan has always put us first. Ash and I never questioned it when we were younger, but Rowan was always there for us in a way our parents never were. And Ash was always the baby that we took care of. I want Rowan to be happy and have a real life. Which is why his dating this girl is exciting, but I'm a little fuc... fudging nervous about it. On the other hand, she apparently said Olly was the cutest thing ever."

"Well, that goes in the plus column," said Chloe.

"Exactly. And I don't want Ash to think he can't count on me, but I would just like to maybe readjust some of our life patterns. I want Rowan to remember that he doesn't have to be the parent and could share some information. And I would like Ash to communicate for himself! That is not too much to ask."

"You're not wanting to change everything. You just want to re-inforce boundaries and relate as equal adults."

"Yeah."

"That's reasonable. You can ask for that."

"I can't ask for that."

"Why not?" asked Chloe, laughing.

"Because that would be very... I would have to say that. Out loud. It's very confrontational."

"Didn't you say you had to tell the President of Harborview that she was going to have to spend, like, half a billion dollars more than expected?"

"Yeah. Very unfortunate. Not related."

"Very confrontational."

"Nah. Just bad news. You're laughing at me."

"Yes, I am! How are they different?"

"Well, one person I don't give a crap about. I mean, I care. In the general, she's a fellow human way. But my brother's matter. I don't want to upset them over nothing. You know what? I'm just complaining. I shouldn't have said anything. It doesn't matter."

"Your feelings matter," said Chloe.

He paused as he came to the table with her tea mug in his hand, staring at her as if she'd grown three heads.

"Daddy, I love you," said Olly.

Forest blinked at him. "I love you too, bud."

"I'm gonna eat Legos."

"No," said Forest.

"Absolutely," said Chloe. "Then you will be made of Legos. You will be a Lego boy and have a yellow head. And hands that go like this." She made the Lego C-shaped hand claw hand.

"What?" demanded Forest as Olly laughed. "We do not eat Legos!" Olly laughed harder, which made Chloe laugh. Forest looked between the two of them. "Did he just... He said that just to make me freak out."

"Pretending is fun," said Chloe.

Forest sat down, shaking his head.

"Fine. Pretend all you want, but we still do not eat Legos."

Olly looked at Chloe for confirmation.

"He's right," said Chloe. "I tried it. I didn't turn into a Lego girl, and I was sad because it hurt my tummy."

Olly sighed gustily and shook his head.

"I was five," she said to Forest's questioning look.

"You set stuff on fire when you were a kid, didn't you?"

Chloe knew she must have looked shocked but couldn't stop herself.

"The macramé owl wall hanging," she whispered. How had he known? She'd wanted to make fire with the matches, and the owl had always seemed to be watching her.

"Ha! I set the macramé pot hanger on fire. Smelled horrible. If we had known each other when we were kids, we would have gotten along so well."

"My mom thought I was possessed by demons."

"Ash's first-grade teacher said we were Satan spawn and made Ash cry. Rowan flattened his tires, and I stole his windshield wipers. You would have fit in great."

Chloe laughed. "It wouldn't have worked out. I'm younger than Ash. I wouldn't have been able to keep up."

"Oh. How old are you?" asked Forest.

"I'm ancient." Forest looked puzzled. "I'm thirty."

Forest snorted. "Ah, yes. The *oh, crap, I turned thirty* syndrome. No wonder you freaked out and came home. You probably thought you had to be a grown-up."

"I didn't freak out. Although, I do think I should be a grown-up."

"Meh. It's overrated. I'm over here adulting the hell out of stuff, and let me tell you, it's less than fun."

"It's not fun to be childish. It's selfish and isolating. And being an adult isn't boring and sad. It's being responsible to and for other people. It requires connection and community. I think our culture fears getting old and equates that to being an adult, but most people don't actually know *how* to be a grown-up."

"You say the most profound things, and I have no idea what to do with them."

"I don't mean to. I'm think I'm just excited to have someone who wants to talk to me."

Forest grinned. "I know the feeling. People talk *at* me all day long and want me to solve their problems, but they don't actually want to know what I think. Probably just as well, come to think of it. Telling people what I really think might not be the best idea."

"I tell people what I think all the time," said Chloe.

"Yes, I'm aware," said Forest, drily, as he leaned over to clean up some of Olly's mess.

"You don't think I should?" asked Chloe, puzzled by his tone and trying to decipher if he was being sarcastic or not.

"I think you absolutely should," he said, looking up. "Honesty is rare."

"I don't regret last night," said Chloe, trying not to sound belligerent.

"Neither do I," he said, glancing at Olly. "I'm just… worried. Olly…"

"Has to come first," said Chloe, recognizing the source of his worry. Forest's shoulders dropped in relief.

"Yeah," he said.

Chloe understood that, but she thought fear of the unknown was keeping them from something potentially extraordinary.

"OK," she said, trying to accept him in the place that he was at and not be disappointed.

Forest sighed and looked like he was about to say something.

"I have to poo," said Olly.

"Uh…" said Forest, jumping up and trying to grab Olly, who was still strapped into his booster seat. Olly, startled to be yanked up in the air but still wearing his seat, kicked his feet and squirmed.

"Agh!" Forest fumbled for the snap buckle while Olly made squawking noises. Chloe didn't know whether to get up and help or if she would just be in the way. She suspected that would be the latter, but sitting there and laughing at the pair seemed rude. Forest finally freed the toddler, and they ran toward the bathroom while Chloe leaned back in her chair and enjoyed her tea.

The news showed a story about a homeless encampment slated for cleaning due to an upcoming construction project. A Jordan and Sons truck was parked prominently in the background. Chloe didn't have a strong belief in psychic abilities, but the sight of her family's logo gave her a strong sense of foreboding. She reached for the remote to turn up the volume, but the scene returned to the studio and the perky weather girl talking about snow on the passes. Chloe sighed. She hoped her conversation with her mother had been enough to settle things with her family, but she still had the dangling feeling of things left undone.

## 14

*Chloe*

# SENSE OF SELF

Monday arrived with a slew of Halloween ads in the mail centered around the implied desire to be someone else. Chloe found them jarring and wished there were ads about being more herself. She looked at Olly, who was wearing his pirate costume and building a Lego boat.

"You like me to be me, don't you, Olly?"

Olly looked up. "No."

"Who should I be, then?" asked Chloe, surprised.

"Chloe."

"Ah," said Chloe, nodding. "I see that you have mastered the Zen sense of self."

He ignored this comment and continued to shove the blocks together. Amused, Chloe looked up from perusing the junk mail and caught sight of herself in the mirror on the far side of the playroom. Her hair had faded to a pale pastel purple, and her blonde roots were showing. One of the circulars showed a Tinkerbell costume similar to the one Forest had purchased for her. The model was wearing a blonde wig. Chloe thought that if she fringed her bangs more and rinsed out the dye, her hair would better match the fairy than a wig. She still wasn't sure how Forest had convinced her to get the costume. He'd just seemed so excited to give Olly the full Halloween experience.

"Well, maybe I'll be Tinkerbell instead of Chloe for a day," said

Chloe.

"OK!" said Olly cheerfully.

"We'll work on that after we go to the playground."

Olly looked up, keying in on the word *playground*. He loved the Treetops Play Center, but Chloe wasn't as sure—she found it fraught with invisible social boundary lines. However, Chloe gathered her courage, the diaper bag, and Olly into the truck and forged ahead anyway. The point was to help Olly move, exercise, and connect with his body. What other people thought about her was irrelevant.

When they arrived, Chloe looked nervously around. There were a lot of moms and other nannies at the tot playground. Most of them were parked along the walls on their phones. Chloe had a book about Vera's illness that she could be reading, but she didn't want to leave Olly all alone. And to be honest, while understanding what had happened to Vera was helpful, from the book Chloe now understood that not only did Olly *not* have Lupus and it was only a *possibility* that he had inherited even the potential to get it. After skimming the book and talking to Olly's pediatrician Chloe had moved on to other books that seemed more helpful on how to raise children with healthy immune systems. She just wasn't sure how to communicate to Forest that his child was fine.

Only one adult was on the equipment with the children. The woman was hanging upside down from one of the thick ropes, and her daughter was pulling up her shirt to give sloppy tummy tubas. They were both laughing uproariously. Olly was fascinated and sidled their direction.

The mom righted herself and helped her daughter onto the rope where the little girl hung with all four limbs dangling down. They both had long black hair, and to Chloe's eye, they looked Korean— although Seattle was a melting pot, so no one could really be sure. Olly tried to climb up on the rope, too but then looked up at Chloe.

"Chloe? Help, please?"

"Mmm, OK," said Chloe, hoping she wouldn't sway the rope

too much. Fortunately, the little girl looked excited to have another kid on the rope with her. Olly and the little girl draped themselves floppily over the rope and eyed each other.

"Heh," said the mom, pulling out her phone to take a picture of the little girl. "They look like sloths."

Chloe laughed in surprise. "They do!"

"Hi, I'm Daisy. That's Norah."

"I'm Chloe, and that's Olly." Chloe hesitated. She would like a new friend, but there wasn't any point in concealing the truth. "I'm the nanny."

Daisy looked her over. "Already gotten the *mommies are better* attitude from the stroller brigade?"

"Yes," said Chloe. "I don't need to make friends with everyone, but I didn't realize that small talk was not allowed if you are a nanny."

"Yeah, I'm a POC divorced working mom who still uses a cracked iPhone seven. I'm not sure I'm even ranking at nanny in this neighborhood. I'd go somewhere else, but this is the most convenient play area, and I refuse to be bullied around by snooty rich bitches."

"I offer fist bumps of solidarity," said Chloe, holding up a fist.

Daisy laughed and tapped her knuckles against Chloe's.

"Chloe!" crowed Olly. He had managed to sit up and balance on the rope.

"You are doing so awesome!" said Chloe appreciatively.

Norah tried to copy Olly but slid sideways until she was hanging upside down.

"Doing OK, Norah?" asked Daisy, bending down to see her daughter's face.

"Yes," said Norah with a giggle. Her dark hair was sticking to her face.

Olly looked impressed with Norah's maneuvering and tried to copy her but fell off and tumbled onto the rubber-matted floor with an oof. Norah landed next to him, and they laughed together.

"Olly, this is Norah," said Chloe. "Can you say hello?"

Olly hid his face in his hands.

"Yeah, that's where Norah is, too," said Daisy pragmatically. "It's a developmental stage. She just turned four."

"Olly won't be four until February."

Olly and Norah climbed to the feet, burbled something in baby to each other, and then ran toward the tiny slide.

"But now they're best friends, so… clearly introductions are overrated," said Daisy, and Chloe chuckled.

By the time tot hours were ending, she and Daisy had exchanged limited life stories and phone numbers, and Chloe felt a tentative wave of hope that she had found a friend outside of her old college acquaintances.

"What else are you doing to burn toddler energy?" asked Daisy. "The days are getting so short that outdoor time isn't working out for us."

"Well, in the mornings, Olly and I usually play Legos and practice kung fu," said Chloe.

"Olly does kung fu?" asked Daisy, puzzled and interested.

"Well, I do kung fu. Olly generally sort of dances. But that's a great starting point for learning."

"I used to take Tae kwon do in college. I miss it," said Daisy. "But finding the time or money for a me hobby is a little difficult. My deadbeat ex is suing me for custody."

"Oh! Did you have a panic attack?"

"No, but I cried a lot. I also filed for a restraining order after he slashed my tires, so I don't think he's going to get custody, but with all the lawyer fees, money is kind of tight."

"Well, if you've got a free morning or afternoon, you and Norah could come do kung fu with us. I'm not a master or anything, but I can teach you the basics. Although—full disclosure—Olly will also force you to play Legos."

"I'd love to! Maybe on Friday? I have a work-from-home day,

and I usually take a little bit of a long lunch."

"Perfect! I'll text you the address?"

After the play center, Chloe also managed a trip to the library and then a stop to pick up color-removing shampoo. Then they climbed into their swimsuits for adventures in shampooing Chloe's hair, which mostly turned into playing with the plastic ducks on the bathroom floor while Chloe did all the shampooing. But at least she could keep an eye on him while she was in the shower.

She and Olly were working on drawing letters when Forest came home. Olly's hand control wasn't there yet, but he wanted to write things like the adults, so she drew the shape with her finger and he copied it with a crayon in one chubby fist.

They both heard the garage door open, and Olly jumped to his feet and grabbed the paper. He ran toward the door just as it swung open.

"Daddy!" he yelled, holding up the paper.

"Oh!" exclaimed Forest, dropping his bag immediately. "Look at that! That's your name!"

He picked up Oliver, and they looked at the paper together. "O-L-I-V-E-R. Did you do that by yourself?"

"Yes," said Olly.

"He really did," said Chloe, following Olliver into the kitchen. "He's even remembering some of the letter shapes."

"Ah!" Forest jumped back in shock, and both Olly and Chloe stared at him in confusion. "What... What did you do to your hair?" he demanded, waving at Chloe's white-blonde locks.

"I washed the purple out," said Chloe.

"But purple is your hair."

"Uh... you do know that hair doesn't come that way naturally, right?" asked Chloe, raising an eyebrow.

"Yes! I mean... I don't know about blonde."

"Well, it's my real hair color, and since I'm being Tinkerbell for Halloween, I thought it would work."

"Oh. Right. I just wasn't prepared. It doesn't look that bad." Then he winced as if he realized how that sounded only after he'd said it.

"Gee, thanks," said Chloe, laughing. "Olly, do you like my hair?"

"No," said Olly.

"Tough crowd. What color do you think my hair should be?"

Olly looked like he was thinking deeply.

"Blue."

"OK, we'll do blue after Halloween."

"Blonde is OK," said Forest. "I really didn't mean... "

Chloe began to laugh. "This is so hilarious. If I'd dyed my hair when I was a teenager, my family would have accused me of doing drugs, and now you're horrified at a natural color."

Forest sighed, and Chloe laughed harder, Olly giggling along in delight.

"I'm sorry. The blonde looks nice. I mean that. I just wasn't prepared."

"Next time, I'll warn you," she said, still chuckling.

Olly began to wiggle to get down.

"Daddy, go outside."

"Uh..." Forest looked at the gloomy clouds out the window.

"We went to the play center earlier," said Chloe, knowing that Forest was convinced that Olly would get sick if he went out in the cold.

"Ugh," said Forest. "So many germs."

"Well, the book I'm reading on the immune system said that staying overly germ-free can be bad. It sounds counter-intuitive, but exposure to germs as children helps build stronger, healthier immune systems. It also said that as we move into more urban living, we're losing some important outdoor benefits like light exposure."

"The book..." Forest looked perplexed.

"You gave me that book on Lupus, and that was really great, for people who have it—who knew they should avoid garlic?" Chloe took a look at Forest's face trying to gauge if this was the time to be saying these things to him. She wasn't sure how receptive he would be.

"But since Olly doesn't actually have Lupus, I needed I needed more information about Olly specifically." She paused. She thought this was the part where he could freak out. "So I called his pediatrician because you signed the thing that said I could authorize care. And she said that Olly only has the *possibility* of a genetic pre-disposition to Lupus. But there is no test for it."

"We don't know," began Forest. "He could develop it at any time! There's no way of knowing!"

"That is the frustrating part," agreed Chloe. "But it was very reassuring for me to hear from the doctor that he is fine and perfectly normal for his age."

"Well, yeah," said Forest. "I mean, he's fine now. But at any minute, it could flare up."

"Not really," said Chloe. "The doctor and the book agree that Lupus is part genetic and part environmental triggers and we don't even know if he inherited the genetic trait. The doctor said the best thing to do is keep him healthy and avoid potential triggers."

"Oh," said Forest.

Chloe knew the pediatrician had told him that, too, but she suspected Forest had only heard don't let Olly go outside and keep away from all germs. Forest looked like he was struggling, but he hadn't freaked out yet, so she forged ahead.

"So, we're definitely doing the right thing with sun hats and sunscreen to help him avoid any sunburn triggers. But after that we just need to avoid overly stressing his immune system and I got a book about the immune system so I could be more proactive."

"Proactive? How?"

Forest looked perplexed. She suspected that it hadn't occurred to Forest that protecting Olly from illness wasn't the same as making him healthier and stronger.

"Just anything to help boost his immune system. I don't want to go overboard, but with your budget, I don't see any reason not to do simple things. Keep a healthy variety in his diet, lots of fiber to keep his gut microbiome happy, reduce chemicals and microplastics. Stuff like that. But this book also indicates the importance of exposure to dirt and germs. Turns out that cleaner isn't always better. And exercise is super important, so I like Olly to be outside for at least a portion of the day. He needs to run, wiggle, and touch dirt."

She waited for Forest to argue and try to go back to his Olly-in-a-bubble plan. Instead, Forest's brow furrowed as if he was trying to absorb her words.

"My plan is to give him the healthiest immune system I can and protect him from as many of the triggers as possible." Chloe tried to sum up her approach in one sentence.

"Your plan…" repeated Forest, slowly. Then his expression seemed to clear. "You're moving toward a goal instead of away."

"Well, yes," said Chloe, uncertain of his tone.

"I really appreciate that you're doing all of that. Thank you."

Chloe smiled involuntarily. Sometimes, he surprised her.

"You're welcome, but I do it because I want what's best for Olly."

Forest's smile was magical, and Chloe tried not to melt into a puddle. It was so frustrating that one smile from him had such sway on her.

"Well…" said Forest, looking thoughtful. "Well, it was dry when I came in. Maybe… No, I probably have to get dinner started."

"The meal kit said soup. I could do the prep while you guys go play."

Both Forest and Olly's faces lit up.

"OK," said Forest, "let me get changed, and then you and I can play outside for a few minutes."

Twenty minutes later, they were running around the back-yard waving sticks while Chloe chopped vegetables. It was an odd sensation. She'd always avoided cooking for other people because she'd vowed she wouldn't fall into traditional gender roles. But she hadn't thought twice about cooking for Forest and Olly. They needed to be fed. Not just with food, but in the way that Forest had meant on that first day in the elevator—to know they were worthy of being cared for. And she wanted Forest and Olly to spend time together, so someone had to start dinner. Was it a gender role or simply a job that needed to be done?

She had just finished the last carrot when Forest and Olly returned, beaming and stomping mud off their boots. Forest got Olly out of his outdoor gear, and they came into the kitchen in their stocking feet.

"Oh, look at all those yummy carrots," said Forest, stealing one for himself and Olly.

"Yummy," said Olly, chomping his, which made Forest grin.

"OK," Forest said, making shooing gestures at Chloe. "My turn. You go take a break."

"Cool. Want to go read books, Olly?"

"Chloe," protested Forest with a laugh.

"What?"

"This is your time. You're off the clock. You can do your own thing. I can manage dinner and Olly."

"But Olly and I got new books," said Chloe. "We haven't had a chance to read them. I was looking forward to it."

"OK, but don't let us monopolize all your time," said Forest.

Chloe looked down at Olly. "Daddy likes to hog all the book reading."

"I'm not hogging it!"

"Hogging!" agreed Olly.

Chloe giggled and grabbed Olly's hand. They snuggled on the couch and read books until dinner. It wasn't until Olly went to bed that Chloe realized she still hadn't tried on her Tinkerbell costume.

## 15
# *Chloe*

## NEW TERRITORY

"OK," said Chloe, dragging herself off the couch. "I'm going to try on that stupid costume to see if it fits."

"You don't have to wear the costume," said Forest.

"I..." She looked at Forest. "I want to dress up. We weren't allowed to when I was a kid, and they don't do Halloween overseas like we do. But I'm feeling conflicted because I have spent a lot of time learning to accept myself, so dressing up to be someone else seems like backtracking."

"Chloe, it's Halloween. Not a statement on your core identity."

"You're not dressing up."

"Unless my costume can be Tired Dad, I don't think I have the energy to dress up. Maybe next year. I used to love doing it when we were kids. You're right that other countries don't do Halloween like we do, so I haven't had a proper Halloween in a long time, either. I've been looking forward to Olly being old enough to dress up."

"All right," said Chloe, feeling more at ease. "I'm doing it."

"You really don't have to."

"No! I'm doing it!"

"Whatever you want to do," said Forest.

"I'll be right back."

Chloe marched determinedly into her room and pulled the dress off the hanger. She wiggled into it and put her hair up in a bun. Then slid her arms through the loops on the fairy wings.

She turned to look at herself in the mirror and then stood and stared. It had been a long time since she'd *tried* to dress sexy. Sexy felt like a foreign country she no longer had a map to reach. But in her Tinkerbell dress, Chloe thought she looked like she'd gotten her passport fully stamped. Was that good? She believed sex was good. Sexy was, therefore, also good. Only... Chloe had no idea what to do with it. How did other women inhabit this landscape so easily? Or forget other women—how had *she* done this before?

Chloe finally realized that she was uncomfortable because she felt unskilled. That was a good place to be. That meant she could practice her way out of the feeling. The risk of being unskilled was only to her ego, and that was not a precious object. She could practice on Forest. He was safe and would give her an honest opinion.

She went back out to the living room.

"OK, don't laugh," said Chloe.

Forest was fixing himself a drink at the bar, his back to her.

"I'm not going to laugh," he said, even as he chuckled.

Chloe went a little closer and waited for him to turn around. She clasped her hands behind her back. He was drinking as he turned, and he stopped—the glass still at his mouth.

He finally took one long swallow and reached back to set the glass on the bar. Then, he crossed the room in two swift strides. Chloe blinked up at him in surprise.

"Second date," he said.

"What?"

"People kiss on second dates too."

"Oh," said Chloe. "Yes, that's true."

His hand curved around her cheek as he hesitated, and then Chloe went up on her tiptoes and pressed her lips to his. Chloe forgot where her toes were. Everything was zing-pow and bourbon-flavored sweetness.

"Oh," said Chloe, breathing out in shock. "I like second dates."

"Yeah," agreed Forest, pushing her wings off before wrapping his arms around her.

The intensity of his hug took them backward, and with a surprised squawk, she ended up underneath him on the couch.

"That didn't go quite as I planned," he said, looking embarrassed.

"Planning can be overrated," she said, curling a leg over his hip.

"You know when you put it like that…" he said, pressing in for another kiss.

Delighted to have his agreement, Chloe ran her hand over his neck and into his hair as they kissed. She'd been longing to touch it. She wanted to feel the strands against her palm. The texture was as silky and spiky as she'd expected, only better. She tugged at the hem of his shirt, wanting to fulfill the next item on her wish list and touch his skin. He groaned as she used her palms to run the entire length of his back.

"God, I want to taste every inch of you," he murmured as he nibbled along her neck.

"Yes, I would like that," said Chloe, trying to enunciate her consent clearly. "And then I want to ride you like this was the rodeo."

He burst out laughing and propped himself up on his elbows to look down at her. He brushed some of her hair out of her face.

"Anything else I should know about?" he asked, putting a delicate kiss on the tip of her nose.

"Well, like I said, I don't really do plans, but I thought I should be clear to make sure we were on the same page."

"We're on the same page," he said. "But, um… We need…" He made vague hand gestures, and Chloe stared at him, entirely at a loss. "Protection." He finally blurted out.

"Oh!" exclaimed Chloe, her eyes going wide. "Yes! Uh…"

She looked around as if condoms would suddenly appear themselves.

"I used to be better at this," she muttered, and Forest laughed.

"So did I. Come on, Tinkerbell." He stood up and grabbed her by the hand, pulling her upright. He headed up the stairs, and she followed him with a giggle and they made it upstairs before he stopped to kiss her again. They stumbled toward his room, trying to kiss and walk at the same time. Chloe couldn't help giggling again as he pushed her up against the wall. It halted all forward progress but allowed her to unbutton his shirt a little further. She spread her hands across his chest as his hands pushed her skirt up.

Chloe tilted her head, inviting him to kiss her along her neck. His lips made her sigh, and his hands were causing waves of heat. He palmed both her ass cheeks and pressed his mouth to hers. Every inch of him was against every inch of her, and it was glorious.

"Mm." He made a noise that was half a laugh, and she blinked up at him in confusion. He was grinning a deliciously wicked smile, but she didn't know what it meant. "I forgot about your underwear."

"What underwear?" she asked.

"Exactly."

"I told you they were unnecessary," she said. "In fact, I think we should take yours off."

"Oh, we should definitely do that."

They half fell through his bedroom door, laughing as they simultaneously tried to remove each other's clothes. He managed to get the Tinkerbell dress over her head and onto the floor, leaving her naked before she'd gotten more than his shirt off.

"Damn," he said, sucking in air. "I don't even... Why are you so sexy?"

"Because," she said, putting her hand on her hip. "I'm a woman." She looked down at herself and realized the fairy wings had left residual elements. She turned around and looked over her shoulder in an attempt to see her own ass. "Also, I'm covered in glitter."

She looked to see if he appreciated the finer points of her philosophy and saw that his pants had come off.

"What you are, is a damn goddess," said Forest, which made Chloe feel more than a little bit worshipped.

The condoms were in his dresser and were managed in a

matter-of-fact manner that made Chloe feel that her friends, with tales of pouty boys who wouldn't wear protection, had been dating selfish man-babies. But she didn't have much time to ponder that because soon she was lost to the sensation of Forest's hands on her body,

Chloe groaned as he entered her. She had been worried that she wouldn't remember how to do sex properly, but she was realizing that remembering didn't do her any good. Sex with Forest was all new. The weight of him, the angles, the smell, the soft and the hard, and the rhythm were all new things to be learned and explored.

She nibbled along his shoulder, licking the line of his tattoo, making him laugh and groan.

"Wait a minute," he said, panting a little. He stopped moving, and Chloe growled unhappily. "I think there was a to-do item."

To-do item? Was the man on drugs? This was not the time for a checklist. What was he—

Chloe made an involuntary squeak of surprise as he grabbed her and rolled. She ended up on top of him. Slowly, Chloe put her hands on his chest and pushed upward.

"There's my goddess," he said with a grin. "Now…" He bucked, and Chloe gasped at the impact and pressure. "What was that about a rodeo?"

"Yay!"

She supposed *yay* was not what she was supposed to say during sex, but she couldn't help herself. Forest made her so happy. He grinned up at her, and Chloe tapped her fingers on his chest and then stroked him gently before flexing and driving downward with her hips.

"Oh, fuck me," groaned Forest, his eyes closing, and Chloe giggled in delight.

"Yes," she agreed.

Forest might be all new, but she still had *some* ideas about what to do with him. Together, they explored each other until their rhythm was perfect. Chloe could feel her legs trembling, but she felt like she was radiating joy. Forest had a firm grip on her hip and one on her ass, and it was everything. She pushed harder on his chest and closed her eyes, losing herself in the moment and to Forest as her orgasm overtook her.

"Oh, fucking God," he groaned as he bucked one final time and then pulled her down to kiss her as he came.

Chloe felt him remove the condom and toss It into the bedside trash, but he was back moments later to wrap his arms around her. Chloe felt floating and grounded all at the same time, anchored and drifting on an endless sea of happiness.

It might have been an eye-blink or hours later that Chloe finally focused on something that wasn't the golden haze of sex and Forest, and it was green glowing numbers. He had a clock on his dresser. It was after midnight. She tried to turn that into something that meant anything and then decided that she probably should go back to her room to keep the morning routine as normal as possible. She didn't want to because being snuggled up next to Forest was much better than being alone in her bed. But… she didn't want Olly to be confused about the sleeping arrangements.

Chloe hesitantly turned over, preparing to make a stealthy exit, but Forest made a grumbly, complaining noise and rolled with her. He flailed under the covers, and she was enveloped in his arms and the comforter in what was possibly the most comfortable spoon of all time.

With a sigh, Chloe gave in. She would just have to sneak out in the morning.

## 16
*Forest*

# WALK OF ZERO SHAME

The next morning should have been a trip to Panic City. Instead, Forest woke up in the best mood of all time. Chloe looked like a little angel curled up next to him with one foot sticking out of the comforter, tempting all under-the-bed monsters with her delicious toes. He tugged the covers over her and brushed a kiss onto her forehead before sliding out of bed to hit the shower.

He smelled like sex and the peculiar Chloe smell that he thought was her rose lotion combined with the incense she sometimes burned. He didn't want to wash it off, but it seemed polite to the rest of humanity not to rub his good fortune in their noses.

He stood under the rainfall shower head and tried to feel bad about last night.

It was a losing battle.

Every time he got even halfway close to admitting that it was the wrong decision, he remembered how she had looked in her Tinkerbell costume. The look on her face as she told him she was doing additional reading to form a plan and keep Olly healthy. The way she looked at him with such sweetness or the feeling of her mouth on his. How was he supposed to think it could bad idea? They would just have to be discrete around Olly. That was all. Grown-up activities would have to stay in the after-hours realm.

He heard the bathroom door open and saw a naked Chloe hurrying across the cold tile floor. He reached out a hand and pulled her into the steamy shower and his arms.

"Oh," she said, smiling up at him. "So warm."

"Hi," he said, planting a kiss on her. It was wet and sloppy from the shower and made her laugh, but he didn't care and trailed more kisses down her neck.

"Forest," she protested, giggling.

"Yes?" he asked, pulling back in case she actually wanted something.

"We need to talk."

"OK," he said and consciously didn't move his arms from around her, even though he suddenly felt incredibly exposed.

"I don't want... Olly shouldn't..." She looked nervous, which she rarely did. Anxiety was his thing.

"We should tell Olly absolutely nothing, and we should not do anything couple-y in front of him," he said.

She sagged in his arms. "OK, great. I was worried we wouldn't be on the same page. I was already worried about him being upset when I leave. I don't want to add to it."

Forest froze. "When you leave?"

"Well, you seemed pretty set on finding a super nanny, so I try not to promise Olly that I'll be around for things I won't be."

"Right," said Forest. "I mean... That's sensible. But it's not like the agency has found anyone." Probably. They had sent him emails. He just hadn't read them.

"OK. Great. So we're adults doing adult stuff, and we keep that for when Olly isn't around?"

"Right," he agreed. "That's what I was thinking."

Chloe looked back to her sunshiney self, but Forest felt a pang of doubt. Was she really thinking about leaving? She *had* said she wasn't sure about living in the U.S.

"Speaking of Olly plans, are we still doing the Halloween thing with your brother? Olly is really excited to show Unca Roan his costume."

"You mean his sword?" corrected Forest drily, and Chloe laughed.

"Yes, that is what I mean."

"Yeah, it's on my calendar. Do you want to meet me there, or should I swing back here and grab you guys?"

"Grab us. I think it will be more fun to ride together."

"OK, I will grab you," said Forest making it a double entendre and running his hand down her back to help himself to a handful of her ass.

"Oh, no! I'm being grabbed!" Chloe pretended to flail but only rubbed herself against him harder.

"Are you sure you were in movies?" he demanded, laughing. "That is the worst acting of all time."

"I did stunts! Jumping off stuff and kicking things. All my acting is physical." This time, she gave a shimmy that slid all of her against all of him and made him groan. He supposed that the tender dance of flirtation was erotic to someone, but he had to admit that Chloe waving him in like she was air traffic control on a jumbo jet was such a relief. He was not confused about what she wanted, and it made everything less stressful.

He kissed her more seriously this time, and she responded with equal heat. Her hands skimmed his body, alternating between the light drag of her fingertips and the hard press of her palms. She twisted in his arms to nibble on his earlobe, and he groaned and slapped his other hand down onto her ass. She giggled—pleased with his response—and tongued his entire ear.

Forest could not get over how much he loved Chloe's ass. That was the kind of thing that didn't get said out loud, but that didn't change the fact that having her ass in his hand made him feel like a damn king. He lifted her onto the tiny ledge that was supposed to hold the soap. It never had and never would because the clutter and soap scum drove him insane, and instead, he had a basket on the bench along the far wall for that kind of thing, but that just meant that it was a pristinely clean surface to hold Chloe while he fucked her.

She moaned and arched as he thrust into her. The shower filled with steam, but the water only hit his back. The steam made everything hot, slippery, and wet in the best way. Chloe locked her legs around his hips and tried to get in a kiss between thrusts, biting at his bottom lip but then giving up to gasp in pleasure. Her head tilted back, eyes closing, and he licked a bead of water off her neck. Watching her pleasure made him so fucking hot.

Some part of him recognized that they weren't using a condom and that this kind of behavior that had led to Olly's existence, but another part said that Olly was perfect, and so was Chloe, so the other part of his brain could shut the hell up.

"Oh, Forest," she gasped, grabbing for his neck. "Forest, you feel so good."

His first thought was that damn right he felt good—he felt amazing. Then he realized she meant that he felt good *to her*.

He captured her mouth with his. Forest had no words for how she made him feel, and he doubted he could have said them anyway. All he had was his body, and he hoped that could communicate for him.

Chloe's fingers dug into his shoulders, and her breath quickened. "Yes, Forest, oh, God, yes."

He could feel himself reaching his moment as well and pushed harder. She gave a little whimper of happiness and clenched around him, grabbing on tight.

"Oh, yes!"

Her orgasm echoed off the tile, and he laughed and then groaned as he realized what had to happen.

"Chloe," he gasped. "I need to pull out."

She made an unhappy noise but let go with her legs. It was barely in time as he came on her thighs. She promptly pulled him back tight to her and kissed him.

"Mmmm," he moaned, letting his tongue tangle with hers.

She slid off the ledge and onto her feet but promptly grabbed onto him again.

"Rubber legs," she said with a chuckle.

"I know the feeling," he agreed breathlessly, holding her tight.

It took longer than usual to get out of the shower, and for once, Forest didn't give two shits whether or not he was on schedule.

He and Chloe made their way out to the bedroom, but it was slow because they kept stopping to kiss. Forest dug through his underwear drawer while Chloe went to pick up her Tinkerbell dress.

"Eeee," said Chloe, clutching her towel tighter.

"What?" asked Forest, looking around as he pulled on pants.

"Olly and I have talked about how he has to stay in his room until the number on the clock has a seven in front, but it's after seven!" Chloe pointed at the clock on the dresser.

"Shit," said Forest and hurried to the bedroom door. His son did have a propensity to make a break for the Legos at the earliest possible moment. Forest cracked the door and looked down the hall—Olly's door was still closed.

He kept his eyes on Olly's room and waved to Chloe. She scooted out into the hallway. Forest couldn't remember the last time he'd snuck a girl into or out of his room, and the sight of a damp Chloe tiptoeing away in his towel made him chuckle.

She turned around and glared at him, making him laugh harder.

She marched back and shook her finger at him, giving a silent telling-off. He leaned in and nibbled her fingertip. She refused to give in and glared harder, so he went for a more salacious effect and sucked her finger, ending on a flicking lick. She blushed and giggled in delight.

"Chloe!" yelled Olly from inside his room. Chloe squeaked in terror and sprinted towards her room. Forest ran down the hall and grabbed the doorknob to Olly's room, holding it closed until Chloe was in her room. He could feel Oliver fumbling with it on the other side. When she was safely out of sight, he let it go.

"Hey bud," said Forest as Olly banged open the door. Olly was wearing his pirate hat, footie pajamas, and waving his sword.

"Daddy! Hello-pirate-een!"

"Yeah! Halloween! We're going to see Uncle Rowan today and go Trick-or-Treating!"

"Yay!"

By the time he got Olly dressed and out to the kitchen, Chloe was also dressed and waiting for them. Goodbyes were somewhat awkward because he almost kissed Chloe after smooching the top of Olly's head. Chloe gave him a stern WTF look, and he managed to abort. Then he'd gone off to work feeling robbed of a kiss and confused about why he'd done it.

Ash called as he sat down at his computer, and Forest picked up instead of pushing him to voicemail. Unlike Rowan and Forest, Ash never seemed to mind actually calling people. Forest wasn't sure there was any conversation that couldn't have been an email or text.

"Hey!" said Ash, sounding cheerful.

"Hey," said Forest. "What's up?"

"Well, you never called me and told me how Rowan was."

"Uh… and your fingers are broken? Why didn't you just call him?"

"I didn't want to bug him while he was recuperating."

"If you had texted this call, I would send you an eye roll right now."

Ash laughed.

"Rowan's fine," said Forest. "Chloe, Olly, and I are going to see him later today at his office. He's got a thing for families at four. So, yeah, he's fine. He's dating that girl, though. In case you really did miss the memo."

"What girl?"

"The girl from the news!"

"The hot chick in the red dress? I mean, cool, but what happened to the girl from work?"

"And now there's a facepalm emoji," said Forest, leaning his head into his hand. "What girl from work?"

"The one the guys at Rowan's work were all excited about. She spent the night at his place and they were happy for him. They said her name, but I don't remember it."

"You never remember names," said Forest, tiredly.

"I really don't. But I thought it was good because I knew they all hated what's her face—that chick he lived with for a while. Well, I mean, they didn't *hate her*, but they definitely thought she brought the party down. And they were excited about this new girl. I guess I can get behind hot news girl. But isn't she a little young for him?"

When Ash rambled it reminded Forest of their mother and he always wanted to roll his eyes.

"Yes, but we are not saying shit about it because he sounds really happy, and also, apparently, she punched some killer guy in the face."

"Well, hot chicks who punch stuff, that sounds like a good match for him. And he deserves someone who makes him happy."

"Yeah, of course. But I'm withholding judgment until I actually get to talk to her more."

"Wait, you've actually met her?"

"Just for a minute when I picked Olly up from Rowan's. She works for Hoskins, Branch, and Kato. Mr. Hoskins owns the building, so she's Rowan's building rep."

"Oh. Then I think maybe she is the same girl that Mark and Teddy were excited about. They met at work, right?"

Ash's convoluted statement of vicarious approval actually made Forest feel better. Mark was Rowan's Vice-President and a level-headed individual. It was a good sign if Vivian had the sign-off of the Valkyrie Security employees.

"I think so. Like I said, she was nice. But I'm not sure two minutes of chat time is making me prepared to have her at Thanksgiving."

"She's coming to Thanksgiving?"

"Oh, my God," said Forest. "Have you not been paying attention?"

"I've been busy!"

"Doing what? I swear you spend half your time at parties."

"It's called networking!"

"Whatever."

"Sorry, but not all of us want to put in sixty hours a week."

"Hey, I am trying very hard not to put in sixty hours, but sky-scrapers don't build themselves."

"Yeah, from what I hear, you're not building skyscrapers. You're kicking homeless people out of their camps."

"That is the city. We will build if we get the go-ahead, but I have made it very clear that we will not make anyone leave. That is on their plate, and I'm not moving one damn load of dirt until I think it's safe for everyone, including the people that are living there now. And also, fuck you."

"I... Sorry," said Ash. "That was a low blow. I'm just short on sleep and grumpy."

"And I believe that networking is work. I'm just jealous. What's got you staying up late? Anyone fun?"

Ash snorted.

"I wish. Just work. I've got three projects set to launch next month, and I'm trying to get everything finalized before then. Ever since Emma and I broke up, I've been getting a lot more unreturned phone calls, and I'm... I guess I'm a little stressed."

"Yeah," said Forest, nodding. "It's like that steady background hum of freak out, right? Ever since Vera's parents dropped that cus-tody suit on me—"

"What?" Ash yelled so loudly that Forest had to pull the phone away from his ear. "When did that happen? What? Why? What? Is it serious? What do we do?"

"*We* don't do anything," said Forest. "I had a panic attack, and then I handed the problem over to the lawyer Vivian set me up with at Hoskins, Branch, and Kato. And now I go running every day so I don't have a heart attack."

And also have sex with Chloe. Which was a way more fun way to relieve stress, but he wasn't going to tell Ash that.

"Well, but, is it… what does the lawyer say?"

"Grant charges me like five hundred bucks every fifteen minutes, so I try not to make him say much of anything. But he handled Olly's paperwork when I got him citizenship, and Grant says because they didn't contest the custody when Vera died, that they don't have a shot. He's already filed some stuff and chortles with smug noises whenever he gets something from the judge. It's going well. He says we'll get a proper ruling in January, but Olly will stay right where he's at unless something unexpected happens."

"Oh, thank God. Seriously, you couldn't call and tell me that? Were you saving that for the Christmas letter?"

"Uh, well, when I said on text that I had to go deal with the lawsuit stuff, what did you think I meant?" This was a new level of air-headedness, even for Ash. Ash didn't always track what happened with Forest and Rowan, but he usually read the family text thread.

"I don't know. You're always dealing with public hearings and whatever. I can't pay attention to all of your things."

"I am now red face emoji," said Forest. "Strong side-eye and eye roll."

"All at once? Wow. That's got to be a new record for me. Hey, speaking of your random bullshit that I can't pay attention to because it sounds like infrastructure blah blah blah, do you want in on one of my projects?"

"What?"

"I've got one that sounds like you."

"Infrastructure blah blah blah?"

"Yeah, also soft assets, equipment tracking, lidar, more blah, blah."

"That does sound like me, actually," admitted Forest, thinking that his brother's inattentiveness sounded more like stress than flightiness.

"I'll bring you a packet," said Ash.

"Sure, whatever," said Forest. "Do you want to come over for dinner on the weekend? Olly would love to see you."

"Yeah, maybe? Kind of depends on how much networking I have to do. I want my slate of investor prospects filled out before I go live."

"Tell me again about not working sixty hours a week? At least I'm off on the weekends."

"Yeah, I know. It's just this launch. I'll be back to normal by the time we get to December. Mostly. Probably anyway."

"Uh-huh," said Forest, thinking he would call Ash on the weekend and make him come over. The kid probably needed an evening off. "OK, well, I will look at your packet of crap, but now I have to do some of my sixty hours. Was there anything else you want me to catch you up on? Should I just read you the text thread?"

"I can read it myself," said Ash. "Eye roll emoji back at you."

Forest shook his head. He felt like he was getting a preview of Olly's teenage years.

"Uh-huh. OK, well, love you, bud. I'll see you later."

There was a brief silence on the phone, and Forest realized that *I love you, bud* was what he always said to Olly before leaving. He couldn't remember the last time he'd said that to his brothers. It had just come out.

"Love you too," said Ash, and Forest could hear the smile in his voice. "See you later."

## 17

# *Chloe*

# HALLOWEEN

Chloe helped Olly disentangle his sword and got him pointed in the right direction while Forest held the elevator door open. Chloe took Olly's free hand they walked into the lobby of the Hoskins building. From the outside, it looked like a very concrete, blocky tower of boring, and Chloe had reservations that such a building could host a decent Halloween event. Chloe had to admit that she might have been blaming the building for her own nerves. She and Forest had agreed to keep things out of sight for Oliver, but she didn't know how to behave when meeting his brother.

"Oh," said Chloe, blinking at the interior. The entire lobby was festooned with orange and black, and there were at least twenty booths of games and trick-or-treat options.

"Hey!" exclaimed a man striding toward them. Chloe recognized him from the news story, but his resemblance to Forest and Olly was enough that Chloe felt that she would have known they were related without being told. "You made it!"

"Unca Roan!" shrieked Olly and sprinted toward him.

Rowan barely broke stride, bending down to scoop up the toddler and throwing him high in the air, just like Forest did. For some reason, she found that reassuring. If Forest's relatives treated Olly well, it would probably be an OK day.

"I got a sword!" Olly held out his sword to his uncle for inspection.

"That is an awesome sword," said Rowan, admiring the foam weapon. "You make a great pirate!"

"What do pirates say?" asked Forest.

"Arrrrr!" yelled Olly, which made Chloe laugh every time, and she was happy to see it had the same effect on Rowan.

"What? Are there pirates in the building? What will we do!" demanded a woman, and Rowan turned to look at her, his face lighting up.

Vivian was a petite, auburn-haired woman with her hair in a messy bun with pencils sticking out of it and a purple dress decorated with drawings of science implements. Chloe and Oliver both gasped.

"Miss Frizzle!" yelled Oliver, and Vivian laughed.

"Yes! See," she said, poking Rowan's side, "I told you people would get it."

"Miss Frizzle?" repeated Forest.

"The Magic School Bus!" exclaimed Chloe.

"Oh! Right. I just thought it was just a weird dress. Sorry," said Forest, grimacing apologetically.

Rowan looked like he was about to say something when the elevator dinged, and the doors opened again. A young man about Chloe's age exited, his head buried in a folder. He had sandy brown hair and was wearing a suit that Chloe suspected was expensive because it appeared to fit him just right. He glanced up briefly, and Chloe recognized him from her brief introduction the night Forest had come to get her. He made a beeline for them.

"What's Ash doing here?" asked Forest, sounding puzzled.

"I don't know. He just texted a minute ago and said he was dropping in."

"OK," Ash said, flapping the folder shut and looking up. "I have…" He trailed off, seeming to take in the scene. "Your lobby doesn't usually look like this, does it?" He looked around in confusion and then at Chloe and Vivian. "And I don't think Miss Frizzle and Tinkerbell are supposed to go together?"

Rowan sighed deeply and turned to Chloe and Vivian. "My brothers are nice people. Not very observant, but I swear they're nice."

Vivian and Chloe both laughed.

"Oh. It's Halloween," said Ash, looking around again.

"I have a sword!" yelled Olly.

"Yeah, you do! Come here, Cap'n!" Ash shoved his folder at Forest and reached out for Olly. Olly dove for him, and Chloe smiled at their mutual enthusiasm. Ash hugged Olly and then looked again at Chloe.

"Oh, Chloe is Tinkerbell and goes with Captain Hook here. Got it." Then he turned to Forest, a mischievous twinkle in his eye. "Does that make you a Lost Boy?"

Chloe tensed. In her family, that would have started a fight. But Forest only snorted in amusement.

"Perpetually," said Forest drily.

"Ash, Forest," said Rowan, "this is Vivian. Viv, these are my brothers."

"Nice to meet you," said Ash, shifting Olly over to one side so he could shake Vivian's hand. "And Chloe, it's nice to see you again. I think you had different hair last time?"

"I washed the purple out. This is my real hair color. Olly has voted for blue. So we're going to do that next week."

"Olly gets a vote?" asked Ash, looking like he didn't think it was a good idea.

"Well, I like to let him practice decision-making when there are no wrong answers," said Chloe, shrugging off his judgment.

"I never thought about it like that," said Rowan thoughtfully, "but providing only correct options is a strategy I use with clients all the time. Choice is important, but I need them to pick something that doesn't endanger them."

"Self-determination is key to long-term happiness," said Chloe.

"And they've done studies that indicate that feeling powerless is one of the key ingredients in creating trauma and PTSD."

"Ah," said Rowan and Vivian at the same time, both nodding.

"That aligns with what I've read," added Vivian.

"Oh, my God," said Ash. "Now there are three of them that are going to nerd out on whatever study they've read this week."

"Oh, whatever," said Forest, tucking Ash's folder into the diaper bag. "Like you're not going to tell everyone about the latest cool technology coming out of the UW in a minute."

"Bionic eyeballs!" exclaimed Ash, grinning.

"OK, but bionic eyeballs sound really cool," said Vivian.

"They are!" said Ash.

"It's always cool," said Rowan. "It's just always more than you wanted to know."

Chloe tensed again, waiting for Ash to get angry and preparing to snatch Olly away from what would surely be an argument.

"What? You don't want to hear me regurgitate everything I've been reading for the last two weeks? I am offended. I will now take my nephew and storm off to the nearest booth that is giving out candy!"

Both Rowan and Forest chuckled as Ash tucked Olly under one arm and took an overly giant step toward the nearest booth.

"Yeah, make sure Olly actually gets some of that candy," said Forest.

"I know where there are adult beverages," said Rowan. "You know, as long as Ash is taking Olly."

"What was that?" asked Ash, coming back quickly.

"My firm is hosting the adult rest-stop booth," said Vivian. "We're next to the Valkyrie Nerf gun shooting range."

Forest and Ash looked at each other.

"The Nerf gun shooting range?" asked Forest, grinning ear to ear.

"In case that was of interest to anyone," said Rowan in mock innocence.

"I can't believe your guns are winning over my alcohol," said Vivian.

"In this specific audience group," said Rowan, "I had no doubts."

Chloe smiled at the brothers, feeling confused and relieved. None of the interactions of the last few minutes would have been possible in her family. It was only now that she saw them all together that the frizz of anxiety in her stomach eased. She realized that she had been anxious because it had been a family gathering, and in her previous experiences, those were cause for fear, shame, and anxiety.

"Candy, Unca Ash!" said Olly, tugging Ash's suit lapel.

"Of course, big man!" said Ash. "OK, candy first. We've got to get our pirate some treasure," said Ash. "And then Nerf guns and *then* drinks."

"Ash," said Forest, laughing. "Chloe and I were going to take him."

"But... I want to take him trick-or-treating," protested Ash, looking embarrassed.

"Olly is so lucky," said Chloe, blushing as everyone looked at her. "He has so many people who love him."

"Candyyyyyyyyy," said Olly, struggling to get down.

"There are twenty-three booths," said Vivian. "The last two are mine and Rowan's. That means that each brother gets seven booths, with rendezvous points at booths eight and fifteen, and then we all converge on Nerf guns and booze in thirty minutes."

"Synchronize your watches," said Rowan, and Forest and Ash both automatically looked at their watches. "And Team One – Ash and Olly – is go!"

"Candy!" Ash yelled, taking off, Olly giggling and scrambling to keep up.

Forest watched them go and laughed. Chloe thought it was the first time she'd heard him laugh off Olly leaving without any hint of worry.

"Yeah," said Rowan, watching them go. "Olly *is* pretty lucky." He turned to Chloe and smiled. "So, do you and Forest want to be Team Two or Team Three?"

"Anchor leg," said Chloe promptly.

"Then we will see you at booth fifteen. Ms. Kaye?" He offered Vivian his arm, and Vivian took it with a smile that said more clearly than any words that she was in love with Rowan.

"Ohhhhhh," said Forest when they were out of hearing range. "My brother is in so much trouble."

"What do you mean?" asked Chloe.

"She has his number, speaks his language, has him wrapped around her little finger, whatever metaphor you want to use, she's got it."

"And he's got her," said Chloe. "Didn't you see that smile? He is the sun, the moon, and the stars for her."

Forest shook his head. "Over the moon, the pair of them. I love it. Ash and I were starting to worry that he would never really... you know... live for himself. This makes me happy."

The expression on Forest's face made her heart hurt at how genuinely Forest was thrilled for his brother. Her eyes welled up with tears from emotions that were too big to be contained.

He turned to look at her and looked startled. "What did I do? Are you all right? Why are you crying?"

Chloe laughed and brushed a tear off her cheek. "I'm fine. You love each other so much. It's beautiful."

He muttered what might have been a swear word and fumbled in the diaper bag until he came out with a Kleenex. "You're going to ruin all your glitter."

"Yes," she said, leaning in and letting him dab her cheeks.

"We're not beautiful," he said firmly.

"Yes, you are," she said, taking the Kleenex to blot her nose.

"Why are you weird?" he demanded, shaking his head, and Chloe laughed.

"Recognizing the beauty of a loving family is not weird," she said.

"Our family is messed up," he said impatiently. "Our dad beat us. Our Mom was an alcoholic and barely talks to us. We are *not* beautiful."

"Yes, you are. You fight over who gets to spend time with Olly. And you text each other every day. And you celebrate each other's happiness. And you would do anything for each other."

Forest blushed, and he looked down at his feet.

"We just want..."

"You love each other," said Chloe. "And that is beautiful. My family has never had any of that. Everything was always transactional for them. There was a lot of talk about unconditional love, but their love always came with strings. We had to look right. Act right. Or suffer the consequences. And my suffering was always deserved. It was because I was born sinful and wrong, and I wasn't even trying to get better."

Forest looked up sharply, his expression hardening.

"You are not wrong," he snapped. "You are... weird. But there is nothing wrong with that."

"Yes, I know," said Chloe, smiling at him.

"I'm sorry if I say that too often."

Chloe chuckled. "You say it, but you never expect me to change."

"I don't want you to," he said, looking unexpectedly stubborn. It was an expression that reminded her of Olly, and Chloe felt the breath catch in her throat. Why did he have to be so wonderful?

"I like me the way I am," said Chloe.

"Well, then that makes two of us. Should we go wait at booth fifteen?"

"We should at least *find* booth fifteen," said Chloe, looking doubtfully at the overwhelming array of Halloween in front of them.

"Mmm... I'm betting Vivian arranged this circus and judging from her instantly conceived three-pronged assault on booth twenty-three, I'm going to guess it's organized in a logical and co-herent manner."

Chloe chuckled. "Miss Frizzle is probably an apt alter-ego."

"Ah, yes, see? They all have big numbers on the front, like house numbers. Odds on one side, evens on the other. This way, Tinkerbell."

He grabbed Chloe's hand and pulled her through the crowd. Chloe followed willingly but felt a strange bubble of elated confusion inside. She wished she had a little more silence to examine the feeling, but everything was a buzz of voices and a blur of color. When they finally collected Olly from Rowan and Vivian, he was having the time of his life and excited to teach them how to Trick-or-Treat properly. His method was to arrive, push his way to the front, and bellow *Trick-or-Treat* as loudly as possible, sometimes with an *Arr, matey* that he'd learned from Ash. Fortunately, this was received with universal approval, and candy rained down upon him like mana from heaven.

When they got to the Valkyrie "booth," Chloe realized it took up one whole section of the lobby and was essentially an obstacle course with various cardboard targets. Forest looked almost as thrilled as Olly, and they both promptly disappeared to go play with Ash and the Valkyrie team, who divvied up Ash, Forest, and Olly like they were picking teams at recess.

"Did a fight almost break out over your brothers?" asked Vivian, standing on the sidelines beside Chloe as Rowan approached, taking off his jacket.

"Yes. Forest has better aim, but Olly is a handicap. But on the other hand, you have Olly, so who cares if you're winning or losing?"

Chloe laughed at the accuracy of that statement.

"And you can use him as a human shield," Rowan added in a pragmatic tone.

"What?" gasped Vivian. "No!"

But Chloe nodded. Obviously, Rowan would never allow anyone

to shoot Olly, so, therefore, hiding behind Olly was safe. It made a loving uncle sort of sense.

"Which team are you going to be on?" asked Chloe, and Rowan chuckled evilly.

"I'm my own team. Everyone's going down. Except for Olly. Back in a few. Save me a drink."

He kissed Vivian and then headed for the weapons shack.

"I feel like this is… I have no siblings. I have no idea what this is," said Vivian.

"It's love," said Chloe.

"Is it?" asked Vivian skeptically.

"Well, if they didn't feel safe with each other, they wouldn't compete at Rowan's game," said Chloe, remembering how her brothers had stopped playing football once Terrence had started playing in high school. The reward for winning was the same as losing—getting their faces pounded into the grass—so what was the point?

"And Forest would absolutely, never in a million years, let Olly within a hundred feet of this if he thought there was any chance of him getting hurt. The extent of their competition is a measure of how much they trust each other. Safety and trust are the cornerstones of love."

Vivian stared at her for a long moment. "I don't think I could have extended that concept to this activity without you pointing it out. Rowan does make me feel very safe and sometimes we do like to compete. I hadn't considered that."

Chloe felt complimented. "Forest also makes me feel safe. And he didn't look up my skirt in the elevator when he had to lift me up. He's very trustworthy."

"Rowan definitely looked up my skirt, but I wanted him to," said Vivian, to which Chloe nodded.

"Sometimes that's what you want. But I'd just met Forest, and I wasn't wearing any underwear, so I didn't want that."

"Sure," agreed Vivian, nodding. "Want to get a drink?"

"OK," said Chloe, surprised to find that she did want something. "I think I would enjoy a small amount of wine."

"Which is exactly what you will get," said Vivian. "Because we're using tiny glasses. This way."

The Valkyrie brothers came back eventually. Or at least Ash and Rowan did. Forest was letting Olly play with a bow and arrow on the obstacle course. Vivian was called away, and Chloe had to admit that she felt a little nervous to be left with Forest's brothers.

"Forest says you lived in Vietnam?" asked Ash, twisting open a water bottle.

"Yes," said Chloe, relieved to have an easy getting-to-know-you topic.

"This must be a bit of a change-up," said Rowan, taking a glass of wine from someone. Chloe suspected Vivian had sent them because it was a real-sized glass.

"Yes," said Chloe. "But change is inevitable, and I'm finding being with Forest and Olly is making that easier to embrace."

"Oh," said Ash. "Really? I'm not going to say that Forest doesn't have his good points, but being flexible and capable of change is not really something I associate with him."

"He saves it for work," said Chloe.

"Ha!" exclaimed Rowan. And Chloe and Ash both looked at him in surprise. "Sorry, that just makes a lot of sense. He tries to control everything else because he knows he can't control the job. I get that."

Chloe nodded.

"But wouldn't that make him try to control you, too?" asked Ash, staring at Chloe as if she were an enigma.

"I'm uncontrollable. And he did at first, but now he really only gets upset about my underwear."

"I... What?" asked Rowan.

"I only have five pairs of underwear, and it upsets him. Do you both have more than five pairs?"

"Yes," said Rowan.

"I don't even…" Ash seemed at a loss for words. "Lots more. I have lots more. I could easily not do laundry for a month. Not that I do laundry."

Chloe blinked. "Oh."

## 18

*Forest*

## SUGAR CRASH

Forest heaved Olly onto his shoulders and surprisingly had to work at it a little bit. Little man was getting heavier. He walked back over to where Chole was standing between Rowan and Asher. Her white blonde hair was still unexpected, but damn it, she looked so hot in her Tinkerbell dress that he didn't care what color her hair was. Although, she was puckering her lips as if she was most displeased about something. Forest felt a little nervous, wondering what his brothers could have said to her.

"Forest," she said when he got closer. "They both own more underwear than me."

Forest could not stop himself from flailing in utter disbelief. The movement caused Olly to grab onto his hair and laugh.

"Everyone owns more underwear than you!" he said, raising his hand to steady Olly.

Rowan was attempting to hide a laugh in his drink. Ash was just grinning.

"Well, they both have a lot of money. Maybe it's just a rich person thing."

"No, Chloe, rich, poor, and everyone in between—they *all* own more underwear than you. Everyone, literally everyone in the world, owns more underwear than you," said Forest.

"I don't think that's true. And maybe it's just because they're men."

"OK, fine. Let's ask Vivian," said Forest, looking around for Rowan's new girlfriend.

"That is not a fair comparison," said Rowan. "Viv will tell you herself that she owns enough underwear for eight people."

"Really?" Chloe looked startled. "Why?"

"She says it's a form of self-expression."

"Oh, that's fun," said Chloe, looking like that was a legitimate reason.

"Yes, it is," agreed Rowan, whole-heartedly.

Ash made eye contact with Forest for a minor eye-roll, but they both grinned.

"Chloe," said Olly. "Drink?"

"No, thank you, I don't want a drink," she said, deliberately mis-interpreting him. Olly made an annoyed noise, and Forest bit his tongue to keep from speaking for Olly. It was one of Chloe's meth-ods, and the first week had resulted in near meltdowns from both Forest and Olly until they realized what she wanted was more words.

"I want a drink," said Olly.

"Oh, *you* want a drink," said Chloe. "What goes with that ques-tion? Where is our friend, Mr. Please?"

"Please," sighed Olly disgustedly.

"Yes, of course!" replied Chloe as if Olly had truly been polite. She reached up, and Olly tumbled over Forest's shoulder into her arms.

She nommed his head in loud kisses, and he giggled before squirming to get down.

"Be right back," she said, and the pair tromped off toward the water table that Rowan's team had set up just off the obstacle course.

"Mr. Please," said Rowan, looking after them. He shook his head and laughed. "Chloe is a quirky girl."

"She's really smart," snapped Forest, his hackles rising.

Rowan looked around, surprise clearly on his face. "That wasn't an insult. I think she's great."

Ash laughed. "I'm not saying she's not awesome, but she's uh… You know she's kind of complete weirdo, right?"

"I know she's different," said Forest uncomfortably. "But she is so great with Olly. She has him trying all new foods. And I swear he's tripled his vocabulary. And it's… it's just been so much easier with her here."

"We can tell," said Rowan. "You were starting to get a little tense there for a bit. You've definitely eased down about eighty-two notches."

"Yeah, well, when I've got someone I can count on, life gets magically easier," said Forest with an awkward shrug.

"Funny how that works," said Rowan, nodding sympathetically.

"I know she's a little weird," said Forest. "But—" He wasn't sure how to say that once they knew her they'd love all of her oddities like he did.

"She's not weird," protested Rowan, and Forest wanted to hug him. "She just does things her own way. That makes her a strong person. Swimming upstream is hard. Whatever you do, don't try to make her change."

Forest laughed. "Are you kidding? I doubt that I could. Although, I swear to God, if she doesn't do it soon, I am buying her more underwear."

"Go for it," said Rowan.

"I don't know," said Ash. "That's a little personal. Might not be the best employer decision."

"Nope," said Rowan, firmly. "I think he should do it."

Ash gave him a puzzled look, but Rowan only smiled in return. Forest suspected Rowan was instigating trouble, which he occasionally did when it hit him in the funny bone. Ash was probably right— it wasn't proper. On the other hand, he doubted that Chloe would ever consider that, even if they hadn't been sleeping together.

"Hey," said Ash. "Changing the topic. Do check out the paperwork I gave you when I get a chance. This is the pre-public period, so not many people have looked at it. I'm not shopping it yet. But if you want in let me know. Also, he's looking for test cases. You could get extra shares if you sign up for that."

"Yeah, I glanced at it," said Forest nodding. "Asset management algorithms. Sounds magical, boring as fuck, and also exactly what I need. Sign me up. I'll figure out a number when I talk to accounting."

Ash grinned. "Awesome. OK, I'm going to try to weasel my way into the Chang Investment Christmas party. Be right back."

"Is it really what you need?" asked Rowan when Ash was out of earshot.

"Yes," said Forest. "You have no fucking clue how much time and money go into tracking assets in the construction and public works fields. So yes, find me a way to do it better. I'm all for it. And if this kid's software or genius plan or whatever it is becomes a real thing, then trust me, I won't be the only one buying it, and I'll be making a fuck ton of money as an investor. But honestly, it wouldn't matter if it was a good idea or not. Ash is freaking out about not being able to land investors. This break-up has him feeling like he's under a microscope. If he needs investors, then… what else am I going to do?"

Rowan nodded. "Yeah, that's where I'm at. But I wasn't sure if you'd picked up his vibe."

"You mean, his *ahhhhhh my world might be ending* vibe? As an expert in anxiety, yes, I did notice that subtle aura."

"How is your anxiety, by the way? Any more panic attacks?"

"I'm fine," said Forest eyeing his brother. "Grant is handling the legal stuff, and everything is under control. You don't have to worry about me."

"I do worry about you," said Rowan. "I worry about both of you."

"Yeah, before or after getting shot?"

"Sometimes both," said Rowan.

"Really, who could tell?"

"What's that supposed to mean?"

"I'm just saying that sometimes you parent up a little hard. I need my brother. I don't need a parent who keeps things from me for my own good." He put air quotes around *own good.* "That's the shit I do for Olly. You didn't tell me about Viv. You didn't tell me about getting shot. You think I don't worry about you, too?"

Rowan took a breath and then paused. Forest braced for impact and tried not to sweat through his shirt. He couldn't believe he'd actually said any of that.

"You know what? You're right. I'm not really used to talking to you guys. Partially because of how we grew up, but also because we've spent a lot of the last decade on separate continents."

"Which also applies to me," said Forest. "I'm not saying I don't have room for work, but it's frustrating to be kept out of your life when you're right here and...."

"And you would like to relate like adults?" asked Rowan.

"Yeah?"

"I hear you. I'll work on it."

They stared at each other.

"OK, this feels weird, and I'm uncomfortable with this amount of emotional honesty," complained Forest. Surprised, Rowan let out a loud chuckle and threw his arm around Forest's shoulders.

"Work in progress," said Rowan, squeezing Forest hard enough to lift him up onto his toes. "Besides, Chloe seems like she's the kind of person who's emotionally honest at all times, so you'd better get used to it if you're going to have that in your house."

"Uh, yeah," said Forest, laughing. "She will honest the crap out of anything. It's abnormal."

Forest hesitated. Was this the moment to mention that he and Chloe were sliding well past proper employee boundaries? How insane was Rowan going to think he was? Or maybe he should save that until he and Chloe were more definitive about what they were doing? Which, of course, brought up the question of what the hell they were doing—a question he didn't have an answer for. Forest decided to put that on hold. He'd said what he wanted, and it felt like Rowan had heard him. There was no reason to push his luck.

The afternoon passed in a golden glow, and Forest felt he couldn't have loved his brothers more. Even if they were annoying jackasses, who shot him twelve times with Nerf guns. It felt like the perfect day as he buckled Olly and Chloe into the truck and headed home.

"Rowan and Vivian seemed really happy," said Chloe, sounding reflective as she stared out the passenger window at the surrounding cars.

"They really did," said Forest. Talking longer with Vivian had been reassuring. She seemed incredibly down-to-earth. Just what Rowan needed. "I really liked her."

"Did you like Vivian?" Chloe asked, turning to look at Olly in his car seat.

"Miss Frizzle!" chirped Olly, waving his lollipop.

Chloe chuckled. "I hope Auntie Vivian doesn't mind being called Miss Frizzle. I have the feeling that's going to stick for a while."

"I think *Auntie Vivian* might be a little premature," said Forest. "I mean, they just started dating."

"Yeah, but it's serious," said Chloe. "I mean, maybe they won't get married. I don't know how they feel about the institution, but after you move in with someone, you have to take them seriously as a partner whether they're married or not."

Forest pulled up at a stop light.

"What?" he said, turning to look at Chloe.

"What?" she repeated, looking confused as he felt.

"They don't live together," he said.

"Um… Yes, they do."

"No."

"Yes?"

"No."

"Vivian said she was excited about Christmas tree shopping this year but hoped the remodel was done in time, and Rowan swore it would be. And Rowan said he'd bought a smoker set up because Vivian wanted to smoke the turkey for Thanksgiving, but he was thinking about cooking a second one so that everyone had enough leftovers."

"But that's just…" Forest hesitated. He thought it was just the kind of appropriation that girlfriends did of their boyfriends' spaces.

"And Vivian told Rowan to remind her to send photos of the event to Howard and Nadine when they got home."

That was harder to argue with.

"Rowan can't move in with her. They just started dating."

"Well, trauma bonding is a thing," said Chloe with a shrug. "And after you face down killers with someone, I imagine that moving in with them doesn't sound particularly daunting."

"But Rowan is…"

Chloe looked at him, waiting for him to say what Rowan was.

"Sensible. He doesn't rush into things. He lived with that Melissa chick for about two years and barely mentioned her to us."

"Well, he probably wasn't in love with her the way he is with Vivian. And I agree. I don't think he seems like the kind of person who rushes into things he's not confident in. Which tells me he feels very confident in Vivian."

Forest mulled that over as he pulled into their driveway.

"I don't think I'm comfortable with this. Maybe we shouldn't go to Thanksgiving."

"What?" asked Chloe, looking at him like he'd grown a second head.

"This is too fast. It's not right."

"It's too fast for you," said Chloe tartly. "It's just the right speed for them."

"I don't want Olly to get attached to someone who isn't going to be there long-term."

"You don't want Olly to get attached, or *you* don't want to get attached?" asked Chloe.

"What? No. I don't even know Vivian. Rowan can date whoever he wants, but I don't have to have them in Olly's life."

"Two minutes ago, you really liked her," said Chloe.

"But this is too fast," said Forest, shaking his head.

"Forest, if you don't go to Thanksgiving, Rowan will know it's because of Vivian and not only will you be in a fight with your brother, you will be wrong."

"You don't know what you're talking about! You don't know my family!"

Chloe looked like she was going to argue, and then she stopped with a sigh.

"You're right. I have just met your family. You know them best."

"And?" demanded Forest, angrily punching the button to open the garage door.

"And nothing. I don't need to argue about your feelings and hypothetical scenarios about how people may or may not react. You know what you're feeling, and neither of us can know the future."

Forest stared at her in disbelief. "You can't just..."

She was doing the Chloe thing where she stared at him and waited for him to stick his foot in his mouth.

"You can't just *not* argue."

"I believe that I am in charge of my actions, so yes, I am choosing not to argue."

"You have to argue!"

"Forest, do you *want* me to argue with you?"

"I want you to admit that I'm right!"

"You're right."

"You didn't mean that!"

Suddenly, Olly gave a sob and began to cry.

"Shit!"

Forest hurried to park the truck and turned to look at Olly.

"It's OK, bud. What happened?"

"Chloe!" wailed Oliver, holding out his arms for Chloe and straining against the seatbelt. Chloe got out and opened the back door to pull him out of his car seat.

"It's OK, Olly," she said, unbuckling him.

"What happened?" demanded Forest, looking for reasons for the tears. The lollipop was on the floor, and Forest pulled it up, annoyed at the mess and the minuscule reason to cry.

"It's fine," said Chloe. "Just too much sugar and yelling."

Olly wrapped his arms around Chloe, and she took him out of the truck. Forest sat in the driver's seat and felt like he'd been kicked in the gut. A text popped through on the family text thread from Rowan.

I'M REALLY GLAD YOU GUYS HIT IT OFF WITH VIVIAN. I PROBABLY SHOULD HAVE MENTIONED THAT SHE MOVED IN WITH ME, BUT IT FELT LIKE A WEIRD THING TO ANNOUNCE OUT OF THE BLUE. I GUESS I DON'T HAVE MUCH PRACTICE WITH INTRODUCING YOU TO MY GIRLFRIENDS. LIVING IN THE SAME TOWN IS KIND OF NEW TERRITORY.

Forest stared at the text. He sensed Rowan was trying to be responsive to their conversation earlier. Ash's response came through almost instantly.

OK, THANKS FOR CLARIFYING BECAUSE I WAS TRYING TO FIGURE OUT HOW TO ASK ABOUT THE LIVING SITUATION WITHOUT ASKING.

Ash's text had a string of laughing emojis at the end, and he followed it almost immediately with a second message.

FOR THE RECORD, I THINK VIV IS AWESOME. NO CLUE HOW YOU GOT THAT LUCKY, BUT TWO THUMBS UP.

Forest read Ash's second text and knew that he should be putting in his own message. His thumb hovered as he tried to compose a politely disapproving text. Then he remembered how Vivian and Rowan had looked at each other, and he swiped out a different message.

OLLY MAY BE CALLING HER MISS FRIZZLE PERMANENTLY. TELL

HER SORRY IN ADVANCE.

Ash sent more laughing faces and a Miss Frizzle GIF.

I THINK OLLY CAN CALL HER WHATEVER HE WANTS. SHE JUST SPENT FIVE MINUTES TELLING ME HOW HE WAS THE MOST ADORABLE THING ON THE PLANET. AND THEN FOLLOWED THAT UP WITH HOW LUCKY I WAS TO HAVE SUCH NICE BROTHERS. I KNOW I'M LUCKY, BUT YOU GUYS HELP ME LOOK GOOD. THANKS.

Forest sank even further into the driver's seat. Why was he such an ass?

Rowan sent another text. This one was a photo of Chloe, Vivian, and Olly.

Ash immediately responded with a picture of one of Rowan, Vivian, and Olly. And then a moment later, one of Chloe, Forest, and Olly. Olly was beaming. He looked happy. More than that—like it was the best day of his life. Forest sent a picture of Ash and Olly to complete the family set.

WE NEED TO GET ONE OF EVERYBODY AT THANKSGIVING.

Forest hit send without thinking about it. And then stared at his phone. Vivian and Chloe, Rowan and Ash. That was everybody that mattered to Olly, and it had happened so fast. Slowly, he climbed out of the truck and went into the house. The Halloween candy was on the counter, and Olly and Chloe's shoes were in the shoe rack. He put his shoes next to them and went to find where they'd gone. He found them in Olly's bathroom. Olly was in the tub, and Chloe was kneeling beside it, scrubbing his hair.

"I told Rowan we need to get a photo with everyone at Thanksgiving," he said.

Chloe looked up at him with a thoughtful expression.

"It would be nice to have a family photo," said Chloe. "And Olly and I would like to add more photos to the digital frame in the living room."

"I'll do it tonight," said Forest. "I've got loads on my phone."

She went back to scrubbing, and Olly splashed his favorite tank from Uncle Rowan in the bathwater.

"I ruined the day, didn't I?" Forest felt like shit. "I didn't mean to yell."

"It's a moment, Forest. One moment. What counts are the moments that come next."

"Daddy! My tank is underwater."

"It's a submarine tank," said Forest. Olly looked at his tank like he'd never seen it before.

"Subtank!"

Chloe laughed. Forest knelt next to her on the tile floor and grabbed a yellow ducky from the pail of toys. "Ahhhh! Here comes the duck!"

"Duck!" yelled Olly, splashing in a big wave that doused Forest in water.

Olly's eyes were huge, and he felt Chloe tense beside him. Forest sputtered and wiped his eyes. He couldn't help laughing – it was ridiculous.

"Daddy is all wet!" Olly sounded horrified.

Forest laughed harder.

"Bath time for Daddy!" said Forest, and finally, Olly began to laugh too.

"Bath time for Chloe?" asked Olly, looking devious.

"No! No, no, no," said Chloe, leaning back.

Olly looked at Forest, who grinned.

"Yes!" whispered Forest. Then he scooped a handful of water and flung it at Chloe. Olly roared his approval and splashed mightily.

"Ahhhhh!" Chloe dissolved in laughter as they drenched her, too. She leaned in and splashed back. Soon, the bathroom was covered in water, and Olly's hair was more or less rinsed.

"OK, OK, OK. No more splashing," said Forest, still laughing. "I'm getting the towels."

Dinner that night was order-in, and they ate in a blanket fort in the family room in jammies and sweats. At bedtime, Olly declared the day to be the best day ever.

"It was an adventure," Forest agreed, tucking him in.

## 19

## *Chloe*

# FEELING CASSEROLES

Chloe held Olly's hand as they walked out of the Treetops play center, but he refused to let go of Norah with his other hand. Together, they created a daisy chain with Daisy in the lead.

The days since Halloween had ticked by, and Chloe was awash in a sea of unexpected happiness. Her nights with Forest were glorious perfection; her friendship with Daisy and Norah had deepened, and the entire world seemed tinted a rosy pink of joy. Chloe tried to meditate and keep herself apart from it—at least a little. She wasn't unaware that Forest's knee-jerk reaction to Vivian also applied to her. She also couldn't help thinking that Vivian was quantitatively perfect, and if Forest objected to her, then Chloe didn't stand a chance. But knowing that didn't seem to make a difference to her heart.

Daisy looked back at them with a grin, well aware that they were a ridiculous little group and enjoying it. She led them toward the parking lot, making *S* curves and going around the bollards to make the kids laugh.

"OK," said Daisy. "We're in the parking lot, so everyone, keep holding on to your buddy."

She turned back to the parking lot just as a Lexus screeched to stop in front of them.

"Shit!" swore Daisy and turned back to Chloe. "We need to go back inside."

"Do you think you can get away with this?" demanded a man

jumping out of the driver's seat. "Do you think I was going to do nothing?"

He wore a suit, but spit was flying out of his mouth, and he was a horrible shade of red. He looked unhinged.

"We need to go inside," said Daisy, panic written across her face. She grabbed for Norah, but the toddler dodged.

"Daddy?"

"I am not going to let you do this!" snarled the man. He had one hand outstretched, reaching for Daisy. Chloe let go of Olly's hand, aware that he looked surprised as she passed him.

"Stop!" barked Chloe, striding forward. "Turn around. Get back in the car."

She pointed at the vehicle and stood in between Daisy and the man. He hesitated but then tried to dodge her. Chloe side-stepped and stood in front of him again.

"Chloe," gasped Daisy. "No!"

The man swung his hand back, clearly intending to slap Chloe.

"OK," said Chloe, accepting what the universe had brought her. She brought her arm up and blocked the slap. Letting the energy flow through her, Chloe brought his hand around in a smooth circle, caught it in her opposite hand, and pulled him forward. The weight shift caused him to stumble toward her, and she lashed out, kicking him in the stomach. He folded around her foot with a sharp oof and sprawled face-first onto the pavement as Chloe retracted her foot.

Chloe stepped back, waiting for him to get up again. But he just lay there in a heap. None of her stunt fights had ended this quickly. Possibly, stuntmen were tougher than abusive ex-husbands. She stared down at him, trying to decide what to think. All that came to mind was that she'd miss-timed the kick a fraction. She should have been slightly faster.

"I am calling the police," said Daisy loudly and clearly. Chloe glanced around and saw that Daisy had Norah and Olly behind her and was holding out her phone, clearly already dialing. "Hello, yes, my ex-husband just attacked me and a friend in the Star Center parking lot. His name is David Avett. I have a restraining order against him."

On the ground, David rolled onto his side, gasping for air. Daisy continued to give the police information.

"Your desire to protect yourself against assaults on your ego is causing you to lash out," said Chloe. He looked up at her, his eyes watering as he tried to find air. "I suggest you meditate on this."

He managed to make it to all fours and then to his feet and stumbled away to his car.

"Well," said Chloe with a shrug as he peeled out of the parking lot, "I tried."

Daisy gave a high-pitched giggle. "You tried what? Giving him meditation tips?"

"It can't hurt," said Chloe. "He clearly needs it. Is everyone OK?"

Olly stood slightly apart from them, looking confused. Norah clung to Daisy's leg, looking teary. Chloe recognized the confusion and fear on the child's face. It felt more real to her than the anger in David's.

"That was scary, huh, Norah?" asked Chloe. Norah pressed her face into Daisy's leg. Chloe looked over at Olly. "Olly, are you OK? Did you get scared?"

"Kick!" he exclaimed, throwing one leg in the air. Chloe couldn't tell if he was excited, scared, or impressed.

"Yeah, I did kick the angry man," said Chloe. "I don't let people hurt my friends." Olly nodded and stuck his finger in his nose.

"Uh, maybe we can try this tissue," said Chloe, pulling one out of her pocket. She tried to reduce her disposable paper product use, but Olly was a walking booger machine. He grunted and twisted, trying to avoid her face swiping.

"The police are on their way," said Daisy, who also looked teary-eyed. "We'll have to make statements."

"I'm hungry," said Olly.

"No problem," said Chloe. "I've got snacks in the car."

Officially, the police advised her that she had acted recklessly. Unofficially, the officer who reviewed the security footage laughed and said she'd done a good job. But whether or not she had done the right thing, it still took an hour to finish the statements.

"Chloe," said Daisy as the police car pulled away. "Are you all right?"

"Yes, of course," said Chloe.

"You seem really calm."

"Oh, I got a bit of an adrenaline rush, but I'm OK. We walked around enough afterward, so I'm fine."

"You got assaulted by my dickhead ex-husband!"

"Well, yes, but I'm pretty sure that was scarier for you and Norah," said Chloe. "To me, he's just an asshole I kicked one time."

Daisy gave a hysterical chuckle. "How can you be so calm about it?"

"Violence is not a solution, but it can be an appropriate response to a given situation. It's regrettable, but I'm fine. I find that it's really the emotional aspect of violence that is more traumatizing."

Daisy took a deep breath. "I'm not sure I can separate them."

Chloe nodded. "I understand that. But I didn't act out of anger or fear. I acted out of love for you, Norah, and Olly."

"You've really thought about this," said Daisy.

"Yes. Kung Fu is an art form with the inherent promise of violence, which is against the teachings of Buddhism. I have thought about it a great deal. It is my intention to never use my training in anger or with the express desire to inflict pain on someone. But I'm not required to let someone else hurt me or my loved ones."

Abruptly, Daisy threw her arms around Chloe. "You're a really good friend," said Daisy. "Thank you for including Norah and me as your loved ones."

Chloe hugged her back and felt a bloom of happiness in her

chest. "I'm glad I could help. I hope he gets arrested."

"Actually, I think he might," said Daisy with a laugh. "The judge ruled against him in the custody case and said he had to pay my lawyer fees. That's probably why he was so mad. But honestly, this might actually be the thing that gets him put in jail."

"Well, I hope his actions get the consequences they deserve," said Chloe.

She hugged Daisy goodbye and then got in the truck.

"How are we doing, Olly?" she asked, looking in the rearview mirror at Olly in the car seat.

Olly didn't answer. He was too busy dipping another pretzel into his hummus cup. His fingers, face, and shirt were covered in the chickpea goo.

"Ready to go home?"

"Yup."

Chloe nodded. So far, Olly didn't seem traumatized about the incident, but tonight at bedtime, she would be sure to ask if he wanted to talk about anything. She was almost all the way home when her phone rang. She stared at the screen, surprised to see her parent's number.

"Hello?"

"Chloe?" asked her mother cautiously.

"Hi, Mom," said Chloe. She paused, but her mother didn't speak. "Did you need something?"

"Well, I need your address because I want to bring you... well, I want to bring you a casserole."

"I don't want a casserole, Mom," said Chloe firmly.

"But you have to feed your family," protested her mother.

"I don't, actually," said Chloe. "That isn't one of my responsibilities."

"Yes, but..."

Chloe heard the agitation in her mother's voice. This wasn't about a casserole.

"Mom, do you want to see me? You don't need to bring food to do that."

"I told your father I talked to you," said her mother. This time, her distress was clearer.

Chloe realized every muscle in her neck and jaw was tense and tried to force them to relax.

"And he said that if you were back, we could give you all your things."

"What things?" asked Chloe, puzzled.

"Your baby things and your hope chest. I put them in the attic."

Chloe blinked back unexpected tears. All the girls in the family had a trunk of trousseau items that they had expected to take into marriage. She had assumed that her parents had gotten rid of them. The fact that her mother had put hers in the attic spoke of at least a flicker of hope that Chloe might come home someday.

"And I thought maybe I could give them to you?" her mother's voice sounded breathlessly childish. It was a common vocal affection among women in their fundamentalist world, but Chloe also heard the waver of nerves. Her mother had probably been told to get rid of Chloe's things and was trying very hard not to throw them out and covering up her mission with a casserole. It broke Chloe's heart.

"OK," said Chloe. "Do you have a pen? I'll give you the address. But please come before five." Chloe didn't want to have to introduce Forest to her parents. The fact that Forest hadn't figured out that she was related to Jordan and Sons was probably for the best. He got annoyed whenever she mentioned her family, and she didn't want to sour their business relationship.

"Of course," said her mother. If anyone would understand about timing things around the lives of men, it would be her mother.

Her mother arrived at four in a truck that Chloe didn't recognize and climbed out of the passenger side. Chloe tried not to wince at the sight of her mother. She looked older, grayer, and more faded than Chloe even remembered. The driver's side door slammed, and a woman in jeans and a cardigan got out.

"Crystal!" exclaimed Chloe in surprise. Crystal looked like the Pinterest version of bland, conservative perfection. Hair and make-up were carefully done, but not over the top. Everything was restrained. Chloe scanned the truck and saw children peeking from the windows.

"Oh! You're blue," said Crystal in shock, and Chloe belatedly remembered her hair.

"This week, yes," agreed Chloe. "And a nose ring." She pointed to her nose—just in case Crystal had missed it—then regretted it. It was an old pattern to bait her family. She didn't need to do that. She was here to make new patterns.

"Those are... common in the Bible," said Crystal, valiantly.

"Hey, look at me, I'm historically accurate," said Chloe.

Crystal stared at her, and Chloe could practically feel the energy Crystal was expending to *not* say something.

"It was a joke," said Chloe, taking a breath to accept that she was not what Crystal was hoping for in a sister and respect the effort it took not to comment.

Her older sister smiled and held out her arms for a hug. Chloe hurried to give it to her.

"I came to help, Mom," said Crystal, her tone urgent as if to explain away her visit with a legitimate reason.

"Of course," said Chloe.

"Let me get into the truck bed first," said her mother, veering away from Chloe as if things were too intense.

"Um..." said Chloe, who had been expecting a hug.

"It was kind of hard to get out the door today," whispered Crystal. "Dad put Terrence in charge last year, so he could, you know, try to step back."

That had always been the plan, but Chloe thought it a bad one. Her father didn't give up control easily, if at all, and he had never really trained Terrence.

"But I don't think it's been going that well. Anyway, I think there was some sort of disagreement before we left. I could hear Terrence yelling. I didn't take the kids in. James doesn't like them to be around when Terrence is in a mood."

Chloe nodded because she knew that was what was expected. Whispers were how information was passed in her family, but now that she'd been away, she found her sister's hushed tone grated across her nerves. Whatever the news was—it shouldn't be quiet. The actions of men should not be kept as closely guarded secrets, women should not be forced into holding their emotions for them, and children should never *need* to be protected from them.

"OK," called their mother, and Chloe and Crystal went around to the back of the truck. Her mother had pushed the trunk to the edge of the bed, but it was an evident strain on the older woman.

"Mom," protested Chloe, "what are you doing? Crystal and I will do that."

"Well, I wanted to get it on the furniture pads to protect the truck bed. You know how your father is about his truck, and I don't want to mess up James's truck either."

"James will be fine, Mom," said Crystal firmly.

Chloe just nodded, not trusting herself to say anything else.

"Mom, you come down. I'll get up and shove it your way," said Crystal.

Her mother climbed down, and Chloe tried not to clutch at her. Her mother's long skirt was impractical, and it made Chloe nervous to see her mother climbing around in it.

"Oh, who is this?" asked their mother, ignoring Crystal and Chloe as she spotted Olly standing uncertainly by the garage door. Her mother's long braid swung forward as she bent down to smile at Olly, and, with a visceral clarity, Chloe remembered the weight and swing of her own hair when she'd worn it that way. She also remembered how naked her neck felt when she'd chopped it off. How free. And how safe, knowing that no one would ever grab her by it again.

Chloe held out her hand, and Olly ran over to hide behind her leg.

"This is Oliver."

"Oh, aren't you a handsome and strong little man," cooed Crystal.

Olly remained silent. "He's funny and clever," said Chloe, ruffling his curls and choosing non-gendered words to lodge in Olly's brain. He smiled up at her and held out his arms. Chloe obligingly picked him up, and he snuggled into her neck. Crystal and their mom made *awwwww* faces, and Chloe gritted her teeth. She loved Olly, but their admiration for that love was felt like weaponized gender conformity.

"OK, well, I've got space in the garage if we want to unload the trunk there," said Chloe, gesturing to Forest's parking spot. She assumed that she could move it once they were gone.

"Truck?" asked Olly, picking up his head, and Chloe laughed.

"Trunnnnnk," she said, enunciating the N more clearly. Olly looked disgusted, and everyone else laughed. But he watched with interest as Chloe and the other two women unloaded the wooden trunk onto the garage floor. It was a lovely, light cherry wood with darkened hinges and curved top. It was prettier than she remembered. And smaller. It had seemed massive when she was younger.

When they were done, her mother ran to the truck and returned with a silver food storage bag.

"He's precious," said her mother, pressing a Hot and Cold bag into her hands but looking at Olly. "You know, it's not too late. God works in mysterious ways. You could still have children."

"I might do that," agreed Chloe. "The universe is infinite."

"It's a tuna casserole," said her mother.

Chloe looked down at the bag and thought that sometimes the universe did feel like tuna casserole—warm, soft, occasionally delicious, periodically stinky.

"Thank you very much," said Chloe. "I appreciate your effort and the gesture."

She hugged her Mom, and maybe it was her imagination, but she thought her mom actually looked happy. Crystal hugged her next.

"Dad said he would burn the trunk," Crystal whispered. "This cost Mom a lot."

Chloe hugged her tighter but didn't respond.

## 20
## *Forest*

# WORKING THROUGH STUFF

Forest stared at the trunk in his parking spot. He'd found Chloe and Olly rooting around in it when he'd pulled up to the garage. Chloe had looked embarrassed and said she'd meant to have it moved by the time he'd gotten home. Chloe so rarely looked embarrassed that alarm bells had promptly gone off.

"OK, you went to the play center with Daisy—she's the one who works at a non-profit or something?" He was relieved at the existence of Daisy. Everything he'd heard about her sounded normal and nice.

"Yes."

"OK, but can we skip to the part about the trunk in my parking spot?"

"No, that's an important part, but I'm trying not to talk about it in front of Olly."

They both looked at Olly. He was playing with the measuring cups he'd found inside the trunk and banging them on the concrete floor.

"Olly's fine, right?" asked Forest cautiously. He hated the play center. Everyone was so snobby. Whatever she was going to say was probably going to piss him off that someone had been mean to her.

"Yes. Completely fine, but it made us late for naps. So Olly might be grumpy."

They looked at Olly again. He was trying to balance the

measuring cups on his head. They slid off, and Olly laughed at the clatter.

"That place has so many germs. Are we sure there isn't some other play center you can go to?"

"Not unless put in an indoor playground in the backyard!" exclaimed Chloe, throwing up her hands.

Forest thought that over. He actually did have the space for a covered play area. He wondered how much that would run him. He should ask one of the compliance guys about what kind of code he was facing in this neighborhood.

"You can't do it within the next month, anyway," snapped Chloe, reading his thoughts. "And Olly needs to run around all the time." Forest nodded in acknowledgment.

"So, play center thing we're not talking about, and then you came home, and your mom dropped off a trunk?" he asked, looking back at the hope chest. He knew that Chloe had felt ambivalent about her conversation with her mom. He was not sure that this additional interaction was better.

"Yes," said Chloe.

"But you don't believe in owning stuff," said Forest.

"I don't," Chloe agreed, staring at the chest with him.

"Then why did you let her bring it?"

"Because my Dad wanted to burn it, and the fact that she saved it is a massive gesture and something that she had to fight for. I wanted to honor that gift. I'll donate it. Ooh! If I can donate it to Daisy's organization! Or if I can't, she'll know who I can call."

Her words were cheerful, but Chloe's hand caressed the lid, and he saw the sadness in the gesture. Forest sighed and tugged at his beard, realizing that, once again, he'd managed to sound like a complete dick.

"I'm not saying you can't keep it. I might have sounded like that, but that's not what I meant. It just doesn't look like anything that you'd want. It's beautiful. I like the wood."

"I do like the trunk. My grandfather made them all. I already looked at the things inside. There's a quilt I'll keep. My sisters and I made it. Well, mostly my sisters. My sewing skills are abysmal. I thought it would make me sad, but honestly, I barely remember anything in there. It's like it all belonged to a stranger." Her eyebrows pulled together in confusion. "It's so odd, but once upon a time, I was very proud of that trunk. It was a representation of me as a woman."

"No," said Forest in flat refusal. "It's pretty, but I can't think of anything that represents you less."

Chloe chuckled. "It's true. I didn't grow up to be like anyone thought I would—including me. But I no longer hate that old me." Her fingers trailed along the top of the trunk. "It makes me sad that my family can't like me now, and I thought this would make me more... I thought it would be more traumatic to have it here, but this trunk is just furniture."

Impulsively, Forest put his arms around her. "Then keep it. If it represents something that you've made peace with, keep it. Don't feel like you have to give everything away. You should have your own things."

Chloe looked around for Olly, and Forest felt a little guilty that he had managed to break his own rules about being affectionate in front of Olly. But Olly was looking inside the trunk for what else could make noise. With Olly occupied, Chloe leaned into Forest.

"No. If I go back to Asia, there's no way I'll be able to ship it. And moving it, no matter where I end up, will be a pain. I don't think it fits the shape of my life anymore."

"Well, think about it," said Forest, stepping back, feeling rejected. Why did she keep bringing up leaving?

"Yes, I will," said Chloe. She put the measuring cups back in the trunk and took the cookbook out of Olly's hands before carefully shutting the lid. "Lego time!" said Chloe, and Olly sprinted toward the house. Forest and Chloe followed more slowly. "But if—"

Chloe cut off as Forest's phone jangled. Forest groaned when he saw the name.

"Jim?" asked Chloe, looking amused.

"I wish. It's one of my PMs who I promised five minutes to and then ducked out on." He sighed. "Go ahead without me. I'll be right there."

Chloe nodded.

"Hey, Tessa," he said, picking up.

"Hi!" Her voice sounded higher than normal. "I am so sorry for calling after hours, but I really need to consult with you, and I swear I'll be fast."

"It's fine, Tessa," said Forest, putting his earpiece in and dropping his phone into his pants pocket. "What's the problem?"

"It's the Sound Transit job," said Tessa, and Forest reflexively sighed as he stripped off his jacket and hung it on the mirror of the truck.

"That is on pause until the City stops trying to force us to do their dirty work. We are in the business of building, but that in no way encompasses bulldozing a homeless encampment. I will not be kicking people while they're down."

He glanced inside the trunk. It seemed full of household goods. He picked up a sketchbook. It was old, but full of Chloe's trademark doodles. She had a knack for art deco-looking designs. She left them on stray pieces of paper all over the house. Apparently, it was a long-running habit.

"I'm with you," said Tessa. "And I got all the speeches from legal. That's not the problem."

"Then what is it?" asked Forest, squatting down and experimentally hefting the trunk. It seemed heavy but manageable.

"Well, we've got two sub-contractors inked for the job. They're qualifying us for the OMWBE requirement."

"Right," said Forest, heaving the trunk upward. "Signage firm is woman-owned, and Johnson and Sons are veteran-owned."

"Yes. And we've used Johnson and Sons for various projects in the last three or four years. They've been reliable."

Forest walked the trunk toward the now vacated section of the garage where the truck had lived. He heard the hesitation in Tessa's voice, and he understood.

"They have *been* reliable," he supplied. "But this year, they've been inconsistent, and their work has been subpar."

"The oldest son took over," said Tessa. "Terrence. He has a temper, and I don't think he's settled into the role yet. Anyway, he's been leaving me a lot of messages wanting to know when we're starting the project. I've explained to him that we're waiting on the city, but he says that we're forcing labor problems on him and wants us to either compensate for the time they're *not* working or put them on another job."

"Uh, no," said Forest, setting the trunk down. "As you just pointed out, they're not as reliable as they were, so I'm not going to be moving them to something else, and, no, I'm not paying them for not working. That stuff is covered in our contract." He sat down on the trunk and unbuttoned his sleeves to roll them up. "We will move on the project when the City does their part and not before."

"I tried saying that, but honestly, he's kind of aggressive."

"Oh, hell no," said Forest. "Sorry. But no. If you feel like he is threatening you, we will rip that contract up. That is unacceptable."

"I don't feel threatened," said Tessa. "He's just loud and unpleasant in my immediate vicinity."

"He's creating a hostile work environment," said Forest. "Please make a note of his calls and keep the voicemails on file. Tell him the answer is no, that's coming from the top, and if he keeps going, you'll be referring the matter to legal. If you don't want to talk to him, that's fine, Jim or I can make the call."

Tessa sighed. "They're a small business and I kind of get the impression they're having cash flow problems. I don't want to make life hard for them."

"Yeah, well, he's got no problem making life hard for you. I'm sorry for their problems, and maybe if they were more reliable, we could work something out, but they don't get to take their issues out on the rest of us."

Tessa sighed again. "Yeah. You're right. Thanks, boss. I appreciate the back-up."

"Meh," said Forest, straightening up. "It's what I'm here for. See you tomorrow."

"See you tomorrow!" Tessa sounded more cheerful now, and Forest signed off feeling that he'd at least managed to help someone for the day. He pulled his car into the garage and then headed into the house. Forest took his shoes and looked up just in time to see Chloe checking him out. He grinned at her, and she blushed and shook her head.

"I like your tattoos," she said, then buried her head in the fridge.

Forest couldn't help laughing as he came into the kitchen.

"I moved the trunk so I could park," he said reaching around her to grab a water and nibbled a little kiss on the back of her neck. She gave a little sigh and turned her face up for a real kiss, her body leaning into his. Every day, keeping up the pretense of mere friendliness became harder.

"Daddy!" yelled Olly coming around the kitchen island, holding out one of his Lego creations. It was in two parts, and Forest knew it was his job to put it back together. Reluctantly, he stepped away from Chloe.

"Thanks for moving it," she said, going to the island. "And if nothing else, we got a tuna casserole out of it."

"Oh, yay," said Forest sarcastically as he handed the Legos back to Olly.

"Not hitting your yum button?" she asked over her shoulder.

"I hate casseroles," said Forest, wincing at the unexpected vehemence in his voice. Chloe turned to face him in surprise. "It was kind of your mom," he said awkwardly. "But when I was ten, there was a lady down the street who'd make us a casserole once a week. I thought it was nice until Rowan said it was because she knew Mom wouldn't feed us. Casserole hits me in the charity button. That's when I started to watch cooking shows. I knew Rowan would be leaving when he turned eighteen, and I wanted to make sure Ash and I didn't have to rely on the neighbor."

Chloe put her hand up to her chest as if the story physically hurt her, and her bottom lip trembled.

"Oh, no, don't look like that," said Forest, cupping his hands around her face. "That wasn't supposed to make you cry."

"You don't have to eat the casserole!" sniffed Chloe.

He leaned in for a soft kiss, and a small body cannoned into their legs. Chloe let out an *oof* and clutched at Forest. Every time their bodies connected, it was like fireworks, and he held onto her longer than he knew he should.

"Up," demanded Olly, holding out his arms. Forest picked him up, giving Chloe a grimace. Chloe stepped back, but Olly grabbed at her. "Hugs!" he chirped, squeezing both of them by the neck so that their faces were as close as if they were still kissing.

"And kisses," said Chloe, trying not to laugh as Olly gave them both sloppy three-year-old kisses.

When Olly finally let them go, Chloe pulled the casserole out of the warmer bag, and as the tinfoil dish slid out onto the counter, a three-by-five index card fluttered onto the floor.

"What's this?" asked Forest, picking it up and reading the message.

Chloe glanced over at it and rolled her eyes. "That is Luke chapter fifteen, and I forget the verse."

"Huh?"

"It's the end of the parable of the Prodigal Son."

"Is this supposed to be some sort of... what is this?"

"She's trying to say that if I come home, I will be welcomed back," said Chloe. "Which is lovely but untrue. The prodigal son got a party, but even if I apologized and went to church every day for the next five years, I would still be watched with suspicion. Nothing ever gets forgotten in my family. My father still won't speak to his brother over something that happened ten years before I was born."

Forest looked at the card in disbelief, feeling rage on Chloe's behalf. How dare they try to guilt her into going back?

"This is really inappropriate," he said. "You have nothing to apologize for, and I resent her sliding it in to be ambushed by later." He wanted to add that her family sounded abusive as fuck, but didn't.

"I would have been surprised if it didn't come with a Bible verse," said Chloe with a shrug. "It's fine." She paused and then looked at him, her eyes twinkling. "Do you want to drop the casserole in the trash or light it on fire out on the BBQ?"

"Oh. Uh... Now I feel like I'm wasting food, and that's not OK."

"BBQ it is," said Chloe. "Come on, Olly! We're going to light things on fire!"

"Fire!" yelled Olly, and Forest laughed, then realized she was serious.

"No," he said, following her to the outdoor kitchen. She carried the silver tray aloft like a priestess going to a ceremonial sacrifice. "Burning food is... You're right. Your mom was trying to be nice, and that's what's important. Burning it is a waste. It's childish."

"Yes, it is," she agreed, opening the lid to the BBQ and placing the tuna casserole in the center of the grill. "Do you know why it's childish?"

"Because it's not rational to waste food?"

"That is correct. And when you were ten, you ate every single one of those casseroles, didn't you?"

"Yes, of course. We couldn't afford not to. Mom would go out on a date, get drunk, or just not feel like cooking, and Rowan would have to make something. So those stupid casseroles..."

His throat suddenly stopped working, and he stopped to blink tears out of his eyes.

"I hate casseroles," he said thickly.

"When you were ten," said Chloe. "But you had to be an adult and make the rational decision." She opened the cupboard by the BBQ and found a bottle of lighter fluid. She doused it over the casserole, and he watched in horror. She pulled out a box of matches next and handed it to him. Then she picked up Olly and stepped back.

"Tonight, you get to make the childish decision. This is not for you now. This is for all the times ten-year-old you had to eat casseroles from a very nice lady who wasn't your mom. This is for all the times your mother couldn't give you what you needed."

Forest looked at the box of matches in his hand. Slowly, he pulled one out.

"I just wanted her to be like other moms," he said. "They made their kids dinner. Why couldn't she? But no. She always said she couldn't manage such pedantries. Pedantries. Who the hell says pedantries? We were kids. Rowan should never have had to be responsible for us. That lady—I wish I remembered her name. I would call her up and thank her. I really would. She should never have had to feed us."

Angrily, he struck the match. It flickered in his fingers.

"I hate casseroles," he said again and tossed the match.

The tuna casserole went up like a Roman candle. Flames shot eight feet in the air and sparked along the grill.

"Jesus!" exclaimed Forest, jumping back.

"Wow!" exclaimed Olly, and Chloe laughed a little manically.

For a moment, Forest had visions of tuna casserole sparked house fires, but then it settled down to a steady dancing flame, and the three of them stood watching the casserole burn. It was strangely satisfying.

## 21
## *Forest*

# THANKSGIVING

Forest exhaled a pale stream of cigar smoke and then laughed. "Chloe will probably tell me I'm polluting my body or something."

"You are," said Rowan. "And it's great."

They stared across Rowan's backyard to the boats on Lake Union. Inside, the detritus of Thanksgiving littered the table. Vivian and Chloe had declared their intention to walk off some of their calories and had taken Olly with them, leaving the Valkyries to clean up. Rowan was ignoring the mess in favor of cigars and whiskey on the deck under glorious heat lamps. It had truly been one of the best Thanksgivings of Forest's life. It had been the stuff of Hallmark cards and sappy fifties movies. They were one argyle sweater away from turning into a Norman Rockwell painting.

"The remodel turned out nice," said Forest, looking around. "I saw the pictures. I could barely tell it was the same building."

"Your people did great work," said Rowan. "I thought Vivian was going to cry about the closet."

Forest looked over, worried. "Did they screw it up?"

"No, she loves it so, so, so much, and I'm not far behind her. It's got dedicated space for her lingerie *and* our guns."

"Ah," said Forest. "Well... whatever makes you happy." He glanced at Ash, who looked as taken aback as Forest.

"Yeah, it was really nice of them to redo the layout for the gun safe. I've never had a custom closet before, and I have to say that I had no idea what a game-changer they are. It seemed nice when I discussed it with the designer, but now I'm a closet convert. One of my absolute favorite parts of the house. Having a specific place for everything is luxury at its finest."

"And here I was thinking luxury was all the food I just crammed into my face," said Ash, blowing out a stream of smoke and sinking down into his chair with a happy sigh.

"So much food. I may never move again," agreed Forest.

"Will Vivian be mad at you?" asked Asher, glancing over his shoulder into the dining room.

"No, I saved her a cigar," said Rowan, wafting smoke like a happy dragon.

"I meant about the cleaning."

"We're getting there," said Rowan. "We're just taking our time, and honestly, my cleaning OCD usually kicks in before hers. So, no, really not."

"So living together is going OK?" asked Ash.

"Going great," said Rowan, looking surprised. "Why?"

"I don't know. I was just wondering how living with someone would go. Emma and I never actually pulled the trigger on that. Which made breaking up pretty easy, but lately, I've been wondering how people *ever* manage it."

Rowan laughed. "Well, it helps that I've spent a bunch of time living with complete assholes. After the military, everyone seems easier to live with."

Forest and Ash both chuckled.

"And it probably helps that I wake up happy to see her every day. Why don't you ask Forest? He's the one who's moved a complete stranger into his house."

"OK," said Ash. "Forest, how's it going with Chloe?"

"We burned a casserole," said Forest and then wished he hadn't, but it was on his mind.

"Just order out," said Ash, looking puzzled.

"Why the fuck would you make a casserole in the first place?" asked Rowan sourly.

"No, Chloe's mom made us a tuna casserole because... Whatever. But later, Chloe and I took it out to the BBQ and set it on fire."

Rowan began to laugh until it filled up his chest and echoed across the backyard.

"She used a lot of lighter fluid, and the fireball was, like, eight feet high."

Rowan laughed harder but managed to clink his glass off Forest's.

"Oh, God," he said, wiping his eyes. "I would have paid to have seen that."

"I don't understand," said Ash, smiling but perplexed. "What's wrong with casseroles? Viv made that yummy green bean casserole today, and you both ate it."

"That is not the same thing at all," said Forest. "That was a side dish made with love. It was delicious, and I ate way too much of it."

Rowan nodded his agreement.

"Then I don't understand," said Ash. "I always liked the ones Mom made us when we were kids. What's wrong with a casserole?"

"Mom never made us any casseroles," said Forest, and Rowan made an abrupt half-cough, half-shushing noise. Forest looked at his older brother in confusion.

"It doesn't matter," said Rowan. "Forest and I just don't like casseroles. Let's go—" Rowan began to stand up, but Forest glared at him and refused to budge.

"Mom never made any casseroles," said Forest.

Rowan made an unhappy grunt but settled back into his chair.

"The nice lady down the street, whose name has been on the tip of my brain all week, made them for us," said Forest.

"What? She did? Why?" asked Ash.

"Mrs. Steenburgen," said Rowan.

"Thanks. That's been driving me nuts."

"Why did she make us casseroles?" asked Ash.

"Because she knew Mom wasn't going to feed us," said Forest.

"You always say the worst shit about Mom," snapped Ash. "Mom fed us."

"Rowan fed us," said Forest. "He did the majority of the cooking. Mrs. Steenburgen knew it, and she made us casseroles. That's why I hate them. I resented having to rely on someone else, and I was embarrassed that she knew how shitty a job Mom was doing."

"Mom fed us," reiterated Ash angrily. "I remember tons of times when she made me pancakes or other stuff."

"I remember that too, bud," said Rowan soothingly.

"And I remember that she would make them on days when we were supposed to be in school, but she said she wanted company, and it was going to be a *fun* day," said Forest.

"Forest," said Rowan reprovingly.

"Why do you let him believe her bullshit?" demanded Forest.

"Why do you have to ruin his good memories?" Rowan shot back angrily. "Why shouldn't he believe nice things about Mom?"

"Because they aren't true!"

"For him they are!"

"No! She was the same damn woman. She was a shitty parent."

"Not for him."

"And why the fuck does he get to be so lucky?" barked Forest, and instantly regretted it. "I'm sorry," he said, standing up. "I shouldn't have said that. I'm going to go clean something."

He went back inside and began to angrily clear the table.

Chloe and Vivian came back in. He could hear them in the front hall, but he continued to load the dishwasher. Chloe popped into the kitchen with a big smile, her now blue hair fluttering around her face. He wasn't used to the blue yet—it made her look like a punk fairy. Chloe wrinkled her nose and looked at him searchingly.

"What happened?"

"Rowan wants to leave my brother the illusion that Mom was a good parent, and I want to rip all of his good memories away because I'm a horrible human being," said Forest.

"Ah," said Chloe. "And what does Ash want?"

Forest paused. "Uh... I don't know?"

"OK," Chloe took a plate out of his hands. "So you should probably go find out."

"No, I said mean things. I can't just go back out there."

"What are you going to do then? Not talk to them for the rest of the time we're here? Stop being weird. Use your words. Go talk to them."

"I don't know what to say!"

"It doesn't matter," said Chloe. "Just be honest."

"I always say the wrong thing!"

"You already did that. Now you can go explain yourself and tell them how you feel."

"My brother is a Marine. I don't think they talk about their feelings."

"I'm not here," said Vivian's voice from the hall. "But yes, they do."

Chloe tried unsuccessfully to smother a laugh behind her hand.

"Oh, fine," said Forest, shaking his head and stomping towards the deck.

His bravado lasted all the way until he got outside. Rowan was still sitting in his chair, but his glass of whiskey looked emptier, and Ash had walked down to the fire pit.

"You're just enough older than he is," said Rowan. "You remember things more clearly, but he remembers Mom being fun."

"You did that," said Forest. "He remembers it as fun because you protected him, and he doesn't even acknowledge it."

"And maybe if I'd been better at protecting both of you, you wouldn't be so angry. I don't need to be acknowledged, Forest. I need you to be OK. Otherwise, what the fuck was the point?"

Forest was surprised into silence.

"I'm fine," he said after a moment. "Well, not really. I have periodic panic attacks, I'm afraid of Olly dying, I'm sleeping with my nanny, it's the best decision I've made lately, and, yeah... I'm a train wreck. But on the other hand, I've got more money than I know what to do with, and Olly can sing the alphabet song, and he's not even four. I must be doing something right."

Rowan looked up at him, a wry smile on his face.

"You never get to comment on how fast Vivian and I got together again."

Forest laughed tiredly. "Yeah, yeah. Fine. For the record, I didn't use to be this angry. I think having Olly made it worse. Every time I make dinner, I can't help thinking that it's not that hard."

"Promise me that's true. Vivian wants kids."

"Yes!" exclaimed Forest, giving a fist pump.

"Calm down. We're not doing anything for at least a year, and I haven't even proposed yet."

Forest still couldn't keep the grin off his face, and Rowan shook his head.

"OK," Forest said, feeling guilty, "I do have to admit that sometimes it *is* that hard, and I order out."

"Yeah, of course," said Rowan, "I'm told by the procreating set that this is normal."

"But if I can do it, you can do it," said Forest confidently as he flopped back in his chair. "My point is that every time I do something that I consider baseline parenting—not even *A* level—I realize all over again just how crappy a parent Mom was, and I get more angry."

"She had reasons," said Ash.

Forest looked up in surprise, realizing that Ash had returned.

"And this is why she won't come to family events." Ash gestured between Forest and Rowan with his glass. It also looked a good deal emptier. Forest wondered how much of their honesty was being helped along by whiskey.

"Yeah, all my fault. Hashtag sorry, not sorry," said Forest.

"I didn't say you. I said *this*. She knows she was bad at parenting. She was escaping an abusive relationship, and she was self-medicating."

"She's an alcoholic," said Forest bluntly.

"No, she has depression, anxiety, and PTSD from our dipshit father, which, yeah, she treated with alcohol."

Forest wanted to yell out some angry response, but instead, he took a breath and tried to absorb what Ash had said.

"I can acknowledge that she had issues," said Forest, slowly, "but it doesn't change the facts about our childhood."

"Those aren't the only facts," said Ash, impatiently. "I remember pancakes. You remember them, too. It was fun. You don't get to hate them now. Or maybe you do, but you don't get to make *me* hate them."

"Pancakes and casseroles," muttered Forest, rubbing his hand through his beard. How was he supposed to reconcile these things?

He looked over his shoulder and saw Chloe and Vivian playing with Olly in the living room. There was a heated foam sword battle going on. Olly was grinning like a fiend. A sharp memory of playing superheroes in bed sheet capes flitted through his mind. Their mom had swooped them from couch to chair, helping them fly.

"You're right," he said and winced when he saw Ash try to hide his surprise. "What I'm feeling are things I'm trying to deal with. I shouldn't try to make you feel them, too. But what's been really hard for me is the lack of acknowledgment from Mom. Or, frankly, from you."

"You get plenty of acknowledgment from him," said Ash bitterly, gesturing to Rowan. "I get it. You two know *so* much better. But I don't want to trash talk Mom! She doesn't want to come to anything because she knows damn well that you two are sitting there judging her! Do you know how much anxiety she gets just leaving the house? How many presents she's bought for Olly but then gets scared to send? Forest, you've had a panic attack. Why can't you empathize? I love Mom. I don't know how both of you can't."

"I love her," said Rowan. "Or I wouldn't have paid off her mortgage. Unfortunately, I have a tough time spending more than about an hour with her without wanting to put my fist through a wall."

"Thank you both for saying that," Forest said, breathing a sigh of relief.

"Uh," said Ash, glancing uncertainly at Rowan. "Was that sarcasm?"

"No, I've just spent a lot of time with Chloe, and I finally realized why she says it."

"Care to enlighten the rest of us?" asked Rowan.

"She says it because we can't reach understanding if we don't tell each other the truth. Ash feels shut out. I feel like everyone is gaslighting me. Rowan just wants everyone to be all right. It's fine. None of us are wrong. And it makes me feel so much better hearing what you're feeling. I'm sorry, Ash. I don't want to trash talk Mom, and I do remember pancakes. I remember superhero days and midnight sprinkler runs in the park."

Ash chuckled. "Those were the best."

"But please, can you remember that Rowan was the one who cooked us dinner?"

Ash glanced guiltily at Rowan. "I know Rowan took care of us."

Rowan made a frustrated noise.

"And I remember you cooking me dinner, too," said Ash. "I know that the two of you did everything for me. I'm sorry I couldn't ever help."

"You were six," said Rowan drily.

"What are you talking about? You used to carry all the beef jerky when we shoplifted at the 7-11."

"Forest!" gasped Rowan.

"What? Ash was the perfect wingman. He was so damn cute. No one ever suspected him. We got away with so much shit because of him. He was the best lookout, too."

"Two-foot taps means someone's coming," said Ash automatically.

"Oh, my God," said Rowan.

"What?" repeated Forest.

"Juvenile delinquents, the pair of you."

"Ash is worried he didn't contribute. Clearly, he's forgotten some key details, and I'm just saying he's an indispensable member of the team."

"Can we be a team if we all want different things?" asked Ash.

"We don't want different things," objected Rowan. "We want Team Valkyrie to succeed. But we're negotiating how to respect our various MOS as we move forward."

"Military Operational Specialty," Ash muttered toward Forest.

"Thanks. I was never going to get there," said Forest.

"We have different tactical specialties," said Rowan. "Forest has always had to keep an eye on reality because I will just put my head down and charge ahead regardless of what's going on, and Ash, you know you will wander off when left unsupervised."

Ash grinned. "There are a lot of shiny rocks and flowers out there. I get distracted."

"Yes, and that means that Forest is left trying to keep us connected. That's not easy when we're pulling him in opposite directions."

"I'm burned out," said Forest abruptly. "I know I used to be better at keeping everyone connected. But I'm burned out. Vera dying, taking care of Olly, and then managing the business... I'm at my limit. I don't want Mom here because it makes my fucking anxiety so high that I get headaches. I physically can't deal with her. I'm not saying it will always be that way, but that is where I'm at right now. If she wants to send a present for Olly or something... I guess that's fine."

"I think she just wants to see him. I forward her pictures sometimes." Ash grimaced like he expected Forest to be mad.

"Great. Perfect. Then I don't have to think about it."

Ash hesitated. "Uh... So what if I took him to see Mom?"

Forest's eye twitched. "Um... Maybe... Maybe set up a lunch or a play date with Chloe?"

"Yeah, OK. I could do that."

Forest breathed out a sigh of relief. That seemed like it might work out. "We can check with Chloe in a minute," he said.

"I'll try to help more," said Ash. "I know I've been a little absent lately."

"You've been busy," said Forest. "Your business is important."

Ash looked at Rowan, who gave one of his enigmatic smiles.

"OK," said Ash with an eye-roll. "Well, for the sake of Team Valkyrie, I think I will make a little more effort."

"You know," said Forest, "whatever else is going on—this *is* the team I count on."

"Team Valkyrie?" asked Rowan, lifting his glass, a smile stretching across his face.

"Goddamn, right," said Forest, grabbing his glass. "I wouldn't have made this far without both of you."

Ash held out his glass.

"To Team Valkyrie and being honest," said Rowan.

They clicked their glasses and drank.

"But if we're being honest," said Ash, "can we talk about exactly *how much* time you're spending with Chloe?"

"All of it," said Rowan. "He's sleeping with her."

Forest groaned and sank down in his chair as Ash chortled gleefully.

"Honestly," said Forest, "if I ever wonder how Olly will turn out, I just look at you. You laugh the exact same, and you're an even bigger child than he is."

Ash made a face. "Bad news for Olly."

"What are you talking about? If Olly turns out like you, I'll be handing out cigars. God, if he turns out to be half like me, we'll all be in so much trouble."

"We'll be shelling out bail money, anyway," said Rowan.

"That horse had it coming," said Forest.

"I still don't think you should punch horses," said Ash.

"And that's why we hope Olly turns out like you," said Forest.

"I love how he managed to change the topic," said Ash.

"Mm-hmm," agreed Rowan around his cigar.

"Chloeeeeee," said Ash, stubbornly, sounding even more like Olly. "Spill the tea."

"I... She... It wasn't supposed to happen." Forest scratched his head. "I just... she's so..."

"I think it's great," said Rowan. "She's goofy as hell. Do you know what she told him today? He grabbed a rock off my path, and she said it was pretty but that it was a working rock and had to stay here."

"A working rock?" repeated Ash just as puzzled as Forest was.

"It was working at being a path," said Rowan with a grin. "I said the rock had been honorably discharged from duty and that he could take it home with him. They were both so pleased."

Forest groaned. "Just what I need—more rocks! Do you know how many rocks I end up carrying in my pockets?"

"My point is," said Rowan, chuckling, "that it's clear that he feels safe and loved with her. He's himself around her."

"She makes him shine," said Forest, looking through the glass again. Olly was sitting on Chloe's lap and laughing at Vivian as she waved two swords and did a victory dance. He still didn't understand how she did it, but Chloe made him and Olly feel both seen and accepted. Her kindness staggered him.

"She helped you set a casserole on fire," said Rowan. "I'm all for it. Buy that girl some underwear and make it permanent."

"She keeps talking about going back to Asia. She said she was thinking about it when she first moved in, but she keeps saying it like nothing has changed."

"Yeah, well, maybe that's because you haven't told her that things have changed," said Rowan.

"Uh... I think she's noticed," said Forest.

"But you haven't told her what the new plan is," said Rowan.

"I can't tell her the plan because I don't *know* the plan. This was never the plan to begin with! It's too fast."

"Didn't you just say how much Chloe appreciated honesty?" asked Ash.

That brought Forest up short. "Yeah?"

"So be honest. Tell her you don't know the plan, but you don't want her going anywhere."

"Yeah," said Forest. It sounded simple when Ash said it. "That *is* what I should do. Use my words. Stop being weird. Just tell her that."

"You should definitely listen to one of you," said Rowan, and Ash laughed.

"It's just that I tend to overthink things," said Forest.

"We know," said Rowan and Ash together.

"Oh, shut up," said Forest.

## 22
## Chloe

# FAMILY TIME

Chloe dropped her box of stuff on the intake counter and was pleased to see that the woman behind the desk looked excited about them. With Thanksgiving out of the way, Chloe had no more excuses to prevent dealing with her hope chest. Not that Forest had said a word about it. But she felt like the contents could at least be cleared out.

"Hey!" exclaimed Daisy, coming out into the lobby. "You came!"

"Well, it sounded like these items might be valued here," said Chloe.

"Oh, completely!" exclaimed the woman, rummaging through the box. "These are great. There's a complete sheet set!"

Chloe shrugged. If that was important to someone, then she felt happy.

"Want a tour?" asked Daisy.

"Yes, I would," said Chloe. She liked learning new things and wanted to show that she valued Daisy's work.

"How was your Thanksgiving?" asked Daisy as she held the door to the back area for Chloe.

"Amazing," said Chloe. "We went to Forest's older brother's place. Everyone was so happy and so nice."

Aside from the minor Valkyrie argument during clean-up, it had been a fantastic holiday. And even that argument had dissipated when the brothers had actually *talked* out their issues, which had apparently involved their mom. Chloe had been surprised by the request, but Chloe was happy to take Olly to meet his grandmother with Ash. After talking about it with Forest, Chloe thought their mother sounded safe enough for Olly in small doses, and she was looking forward to it. The party had broken up late with hugs, and Chloe had felt so welcomed and loved that she was still floating on the feeling days later.

"Oh, that's nice! I feel like my holidays always become a chore marathon with my Mom. Like I know how to fix a running toilet. I love my Mom, but why is this on my list now? I've started packing the cranberry sauce and my tool belt."

Chloe laughed. "Your Mom probably appreciates it a lot."

Daisy paused and seemed to consider that question. "Mmm... in a Korean Mom kind of way, yes, you're probably right. She did give me more *tteokbokki* than my sister."

"Oh, well, that says it all right there," said Chloe, and Daisy laughed.

They toured the building, saw Daisy's office, and chatted up a co-worker or two. Chloe felt like she was being shown off but couldn't figure out why anyone would do that. Chloe was neither impressive nor particularly useful to anyone.

"And this is our training room. Or lunch room. Or whatever we need it to be," said Daisy.

Chloe looked around the long open space. It had a linoleum floor with chairs and tables folded and stacked along the wall. Her eye landed on a poster near the door.

Ten Signs of Domestic Abuse.

"What we'd really love to have is a self-defense class," said Daisy.

Telling you that you never do anything right.

She remembered her father telling her that at least weekly.

"We don't want to advocate for violence, but we do want our clients to feel empowered," said Daisy.

"Yes," said Chloe. "Well, like I said, I don't believe violence is the answer. But it's important to learn to stand up for yourself, and sometimes violence should be met with an opposing force."

SHOWING EXTREME JEALOUSY OF YOUR FRIENDS OR TIME SPENT AWAY FROM THEM.

PREVENTING OR DISCOURAGING YOU FROM SPENDING TIME WITH OTHERS, PARTICULARLY FRIENDS, FAMILY MEMBERS, OR PEERS.

Going to school had always been fraught because they didn't approve of her spending time with all *those* people out in the world. Obviously, the poster didn't mean her family because keeping to other church members wasn't the same as isolating a child just to control them. Her brain stumbled over the thought. It wasn't? Was she sure about that?

INSULTING, DEMEANING, OR SHAMING YOU, ESPECIALLY IN FRONT OF OTHER PEOPLE.

How many times had her brothers said she was useless and stupid in front of other church members?

"Yes! Exactly," said Daisy, and Chloe tried to focus on the conversation. "But we're not sure how to build a curriculum for that. We're thinking about forming a committee."

PREVENTING YOU FROM MAKING YOUR OWN DECISIONS, INCLUDING ABOUT WORKING OR ATTENDING SCHOOL.

The fight when she'd signed up for college had been epic. Her father had refused to let her eat at the table, and since dinner was only eaten at the table then there had been no dinner. Crystal had smuggled her food.

CONTROLLING FINANCES IN THE HOUSEHOLD WITHOUT DISCUSSION, SUCH AS TAKING YOUR MONEY OR REFUSING TO PROVIDE MONEY FOR NECESSARY EXPENSES.

It had been such a struggle to get money for her college course books, even after she'd gotten scholarships for tuition. Dad wouldn't ever give it to her. Regina, of all people, had once given her twenty dollars toward a book, and Chloe had cried.

"If we formed a committee, do you think maybe you could

join?" asked Daisy.

"I would love to help with that," said Chloe.

INTIMIDATING YOU THROUGH THREATENING LOOKS OR ACTIONS.

INSULTING YOUR PARENTING OR THREATENING TO HARM OR TAKE AWAY YOUR CHILDREN OR PETS.

INTIMIDATING YOU WITH WEAPONS LIKE GUNS, KNIVES, BATS, OR MACE.

DESTROYING YOUR BELONGINGS OR YOUR HOME.

Each one reminded her of something her father or brothers had done. She got to the last one and thought of Crystal's parting whispers: Dad said he would burn the trunk. This cost Mom a lot.

A tear trickled down Chloe's face and then another. Her face felt hot, and she could feel her heart racing. She felt a hot wave of embarrassment, and she tried to sit with the feeling, but it made her want to run away.

"Chloe, are you all right?" asked Daisy, putting a hand on her shoulder.

"My Dad... does *all* of that," whispered Chloe, gesturing to the poster. "Everything on the list."

"Oh. OK. Uh... you don't still live with him, right?" asked Daisy, her voice seemed strained. "You live with Forest and Olly, right?"

"Yes. But I... I just thought he was a bad father." Tears were still trickling down her face, and Chloe swiped at them, but it didn't seem to matter. They just kept coming.

"He *is* a bad father," said Daisy. "If he does everything on the list, he's a terrible father."

"I am not a victim!" Chloe blurted out. Her voice was too loud and echoed off the linoleum. "I left. I ran away. I'm a bad daughter, but I am *not* a victim."

"You're a survivor," said Daisy, her eyes shining with tears.

Chloe stared at her in shock.

"I'm not abused."

"Yes? You were?" offered Daisy, looking uncertain. "But you

survived and escaped." She paused and then added more urgently. "You are *not* a bad daughter!"

"I'm not bad?" Chloe felt panicked, as though the entire world was trying to slip out from under her feet.

"No." Daisy was crying now, and her arms flailed like she wanted to hug Chloe. Chloe was fine with that—she liked hugs—so she leaned in with a sob.

"You're a good person," Daisy said fiercely as she hugged Chloe tightly. Chloe could feel Daisy's determination to embed that thought, and she found it reassuring.

"I know that," said Chloe. "I know that. I am..." She took a ragged breath. "I am the way I want to be. I am myself." She stood back and looked at Daisy again. "I thought I was the problem. I didn't... I just... I chose to be different because I can't be like them. I embrace that. But I thought I was the problem."

"That happens a lot," said Daisy. "They make you think that, but *they* are the ones who are wrong."

"I just thought everyone had to deal with that, and they were better at it than me," said Chloe, blotting her nose on her sleeve.

"Uh... no," said Daisy, firmly, rubbing Chloe's back. "Nope. Lots of people don't have even one of the things on the list."

"What?" demanded Chloe, eyeing the poster again. "None of them?"

"Yeah, believe it or not, healthy parents and partners are out there."

Chloe thought about Forest and how he encouraged her to see her friends or keep her hope chest. He was periodically insulting, but he'd apologized for the house chicken comment, and mostly, she thought he didn't do well with change. And he seemed to believe she was some sort of parenting genius for all the ways she got Olly to eat food. Forest had never threatened her. If anything, he went out of his way to make her feel safe. She thought about the way he treated Olly. Olly's safety was paramount to him. His desire to give his son love and stability was one of the things she most admired about Forest. She looked back at the poster. She could spot an item here or there from past relationships. She also realized that they had been the very reasons she had left those relationships.

"Daisy, I'm sleeping with Forest," said Chloe.

"Uh... OK. I was wondering but trying not to pry."

"He doesn't do anything on the list."

"That is great. Are the two of you, um, serious, I guess?"

"There are a lot of different ways to want someone. I didn't realize until right now that I think I want him in all the ways."

"Oh," said Daisy. "That's good, I think?"

"I don't make plans very well," said Chloe. "Or at all, really. And Forest is big on planning. Only, I'm not sure I'm part of his plan."

"Oh," said Daisy. "That is less good. What are you going to do?"

"I don't know," said Chloe as she took a slow breath. "I guess I will have to talk to him."

"Um, but if he doesn't... If he's not on your wavelength, what will you do?"

"I don't know. I guess I'll have to leave. Book a plane flight, I guess."

"Um... Or you'll call me, and we'll go out for drinks, and you can crash on my couch."

Chloe looked at Daisy. "That's probably a better plan. Thanks."

Chloe entered the house slowly. The kitchen wafted out the scent of garlic and an unfamiliar spice to greet her. Forest had been doing more Middle Eastern recipes lately. Chloe enjoyed it. Olly was suspicious, but once Forest had invited him to help cook—by throwing things into the pot—he'd become more excited about trying the new flavors.

"Hey," said Forest, coming out of the kitchen and wiping his hands on a towel. Olly followed behind him, looking excited. "You're home!"

She loved that he said *home* like she belonged here.

"How was Daisy? I think it's really great you made a new friend. Making adult friends is hard. Maybe I'm the only one who thinks that."

"No," said Chloe. "It's hard."

"Are you OK?" he asked nervously, seeming to pick up on her energy.

"I had kind of a hard day," said Chloe, not wanting to verbalize her feelings yet but unsure what to say instead. "Some new thoughts I'm going to have to meditate on. I'm really happy to be home, though."

"OK. Uh. I don't want to make you think extra, but..." He glanced toward the living room.

"Think about what?" asked Chloe, puzzled.

"Well, we're going Christmas tree hunting this weekend, right? So... uh... I had to move things to make room for the tree and..."

He grabbed her by the hand and pulled her to the living room. There, under the streamlined floating shelves that the designer had clearly meant to be minimalist and chic, was her old-fashioned hope chest.

Chloe stared at it and tried not to cry. She clutched onto Forest's hand more tightly and was relieved when he didn't pull away.

"It's cold out in the garage, which can be bad for wood. And I thought it fit nicely there. You're going to cry, aren't you?"

"Maybe." A tear trickled down her cheek. "Yes."

"Good crying or bad crying?" he asked nervously.

"You think it fits there?" she asked, looking at her handmade trunk among the sleek furnishings.

"Yes. And I thought," he cleared his throat nervously, "if you decided to stay, then it would already be where you wanted it. No moving required."

She took a moment to think over his words. He was saying that the decision to stay or go was hers, but the trunk was saying what his feelings were.

"You want me to stay?" she asked hesitantly. Forest's hand shifted around hers. She couldn't tell if her hand or his was sweating.

"Yes. Do you want to?"

Chloe couldn't trust herself with words, so she nodded to show she did. Inch by inch, he gathered her to him until his arms were wrapped around her, and she could breathe in the scent of him and the heat of his body. She felt battered by the day, but with his arms around her, she felt protected and safe. For one long moment, everything was quiet, warm, and perfect.

"Daddy is hogging Chloe," said Olly distinctly.

"Yes, I am," said Forest, looking down at Olly.

"Ugh," said Olly disgustedly, and Chloe couldn't help giggling as he tried to wiggle between them.

Forest shook his head and laughed and then kissed her. "Fine," he said to Olly. "You win. For now."

"Hollyship," said Olly smugly.

"He keeps saying that," said Forest, looking puzzled. "What does it even mean?"

"Who knows?" Chloe replied with a smile as she ruffled Olly's hair.

23

*Forest*

# COMING TOGETHER

Forest checked his email as he got in the elevator. His Christmas plans were coming along. He and Chloe had agreed to partially cater and partially cook Christmas breakfast themselves. He, Chloe, and Olly would be getting a tree on the weekend, and then he had paid for a decorator because he knew he didn't have the ornament selection to get whatever tree they got. Chloe kept making faces about wasteful spending, but he'd promised to keep whatever ornaments were purchased this year and re-use them. Forest thought negotiating with Chloe would annoy half the guys he knew, but the very fact that she was there to negotiate with him was a goddamn miracle.

There was a new desk in the area in front of his office. Forest stared at it as he walked by. Puzzled, he was still staring as he opened his office door.

"Great," said Jim, looking up from laying out the usual array of folders on Forest's desk. "You're here."

"Yeah, I'm here, but there's a new desk out there—"

"Yeah, it's for your new assistant."

"Amir's not leaving, is he? No! He's just gotten good! I can't go through training again!"

"No, Amir's staying. He's now your primary assistant and in charge of training your secondary assistant."

"What? I don't need two assistants."

"Yes, you do. You're a bottleneck because you can't make it to all of your meetings and answer emails. I've been compensating by speaking to you directly, but we just put on three new project managers, soo... that's about to stop working. Amir and I decided that we're going to put the secondary assistant on emails, and then there will be three daily email check-ins."

"But..." Forest clutched at his phone, deeply panicked at the idea that someone else would be reading his email.

"I already sent out a memo to make sure to CC the new assistant's email address on all communications to you. Initially, you will only respond to emails that *don't* CC that address. You'll ignore everything else and let the assistant respond."

That system sounded like it would work to filter out any private correspondence, but the panic didn't ebb.

"But what will I be doing, then?"

"All the same things, but hopefully with time to finish them all. Forest," said Jim, pausing and scrutinizing Forest's face, "are you OK?"

"No, I'm not fucking OK! I'm supposed to be able to do my job!"

"Yes? We're making it so you can do that."

"I can work later."

"No, you can't," said Jim, his brow furrowing. "You have to be home with Olly and Chloe."

"But... I... I..."

"Forest," said Jim, putting a hand on his shoulder, "your business is a success. This is what happens. Just like you can't monitor all the jobs or keep track of all the project managers, you don't have time in the day to do everything. You have to give up some control so everything can keep moving."

"But those are the fun parts," said Forest sadly. "Financing and lawyers and asset management are boring."

Jim grinned. "And we hope this carves out a little place to keep the fun. I know it's a change, and I know that freaks you out, but not all change is bad."

"Chloe says change is inevitable," muttered Forest.

"I sure like her," said Jim. "She's smart. And see? You like having Chloe around. That was a change, and it's worked out great!"

"Uh... we're dating now," Forest blurted out.

"Oh, thank God," said Jim. "I didn't want to have to tell you to go date your nanny, but I was going to. She does have those voodoo forces, though, so look out."

"I think they're Buddhist forces," said Forest.

"Same difference," said Jim. "She can make people eat kale. Don't mess around on her."

"I wouldn't!"

"Just saying," said Jim with a shrug. "OK, the top sign-offs are on the left. Accounting bullshit is on the right. Call Carol with questions on that. Amir will be in later to introduce you to Flora."

"Should I know something about Flora?" asked Forest nervously.

"She's my niece," said Jim.

"Oh! You couldn't lead with that?"

"She has dreadlocks and tattoos and used to work for Issaquah Public Works, where that was a problem."

"Cool," said Forest, feeling reassured. "I should have known you'd hire someone that would fit in. I was freaking out. Sorry."

"You know, I really do like working here," said Jim with a laugh.

"Are you sure? In case you hadn't noticed, I'm kind of an uptight weirdo, " Forest said.

"You are uptight, but it's about the stuff that matters."

"Jim," said Forest, "the last couple of months... I keep meaning to bring it up."

"What?" asked Jim.

"I think we should change your title to Vice President."

"And are we thinking about changing my paycheck, too?"

"Yes."

"Did it get mentioned that I really like working here?"

Forest grinned. "I heard that somewhere."

"Good. Catch you at the PM meeting at eleven," said Jim, giving a jaunty salute as he left.

Flora was as Jim had described and also had some of Jim's imperturbable demeanor, which Forest liked. It meant she wouldn't start panicking when something caught fire, either metaphorically or in reality.

He clocked out promptly at five, nodded to the instruction that he was not to answer any emails that came in until the following day and hurried home.

He found Chloe and Olly making snowflakes and a mess in the living room.

"You're home early," said Chloe, looking up with a smile.

"You'll never guess. Jim hired me a second assistant!"

Chloe burst out laughing. "He did not!"

"He did! And now I'm not supposed to answer any email after five. We're trying a thing. I thought maybe we could go out to dinner. What do you think?"

Forest had visions of the three of them at some place nice, with table cloths and cocktails. It would be so perfect.

"Oh! I know of this great Vietnamese place! One of my fellow nuns has a sister who lives here. She and her partner started their own restaurant in Bothell. I've been meaning to go and support them."

Forest looked at Chloe and Olly. Olly was bouncing up and down, and Forest was pretty sure there were boogers in his hair. Chloe had hummus smears on her sweatshirt, and her feet were bare. Chloe looked down at Olly and stuck her tongue out at him. Olly stuck his out, too.

Was he ever going to get one perfect night?

"What do you think?" she asked, looking hopefully.

Did he even want perfect?

"I think it sounds awesome," said Forest. "I don't know how

they'll top your fish sauce, but I'm in."

"Really? It's not fancy or anything. It's in a strip mall."

"I just want dinner with the two of you," said Forest. "Fancy might be an adult-only thing."

Chloe chuckled. "Well, it might not be fancy, but they probably deserve hummus-free guests. Give me a second to change."

An hour later, Forest had his sleeves rolled up and was trying to teach Olly to use chopsticks. It was a losing battle, and he didn't care. The table was covered with food, and the owners kept popping out to give them a new dish despite Forest's protests. But that was also a losing battle since the moment Olly had asked for fish sauce, their prized guest status had been cemented. Chloe's friend's sister, or whatever third-generation acquaintance once removed she was, had decided they were family. Olly threw down the chopsticks and grabbed a fried radish rice cake to shove in his face. Like many things on the table, Forest hadn't had them before, but he and Olly were trying all the dishes. The fried radish cakes were Olly's new favorite.

Karaoke was about to start in the main dining room, and Chloe had been convinced to try one of the house specialty cocktails. She looked pink-cheeked and happy. The atmosphere was bright and festive, as if the holidays had arrived early. Forest took out his phone, and Chloe eyed it skeptically.

"I'm not answering emails," he said. "I'm leaving five-star reviews."

"You can do that from your phone?"

"Yes, because I have a modern phone, an online presence, and thumbs," said Forest, grinning at her.

She stuck out her tongue at him, but he only laughed. He quickly snapped a few pics of the food to add to his review. Then he took one of Olly and Chloe, consciously switched it to Do Not Disturb, and dropped his phone into his pocket. It was harder work than he might have thought to get it out of his hand, but he didn't want to see any alerts or anything else that came through. He wanted to be fully in the moment.

He and Chloe held hands as they drove home, but it wasn't until they were pulling into the garage that she said anything.

"This evening was perfect," she said. "Thank you so much."

Forest glanced back at Olly in his car seat. Little man's eyes were nearly closed, and his round belly was sticking out of his shirt. He looked like the picture of contentment, and Forest knew precisely how he felt.

"I can't think of anything better," said Forest.

## 24
# Chloe

# STATUS SYMBOLS

Chloe yawned, stretched, and accidentally elbowed Forest in the face.

"Ow!" he said, laughing at the same time.

"Sorry!" exclaimed Chloe, rolling over to look at him. She still wasn't used to sleeping with someone. His California king-sized bed had loads of room for all their other activities—she didn't understand how they still collided on accident.

"You have pointy elbows," he complained, pulling her on top of him.

"Yes," she agreed. "I have them sharpened on a bi-weekly basis."

"Ah, that explains it."

She rested her head on his chest and drew a finger around one of his tattoos. He was silent, eyes closed, while she explored the coloring book of his chest. There were flowers, waves, a tiger, and, for some reason, a pyramid.

"You like my travelogue?" he asked without opening his eyes.

"Your travelogue?"

"I don't collect postcards. I collect tattoos. I read a book once about how the old-time sailors tattooed all their ports of call on themselves. These days, I don't travel much, but I will have to go somewhere because I've got the tattoo itch."

Chloe chuckled and tried to reconcile the tattoo-gathering Forest with the one who freaked out about emails and germs. Forest looked down at himself.

"Some of these seem a lifetime ago," he said, lifting one arm to inspect it. "Back when I thought it was OK to start fights or disappear for a week. Back when I didn't have anyone counting on me. Honestly, I don't know how Rowan—or anyone in the military, really—can go out there knowing lives are on the line. I get scared from signing off on monthly paychecks."

"They train for it," said Chloe. "There aren't a lot of training programs for what you're doing."

"Maybe I should have gone to college," said Forest, with half a laugh. "I was always too busy working, though."

Chloe was surprised to learn he hadn't gone to college, but knowing that reaffirmed her half-formed plan for her own future.

"I don't think they really have college classes either," said Chloe. "I've worked for start-ups in multiple countries, and every single time, it's been someone with a good idea and *some* experience. No one I know has ever had a class on how to start your own business or how to make it grow."

Forest stared at her like he usually did when she said something that warped his brain.

"Huh. I always thought I was behind all those college kids like Ash."

"Nope. They're behind you. You have all the knowledge on how to make a business function. I'm not saying they don't know anything, but you have experience actually doing it. The classes that do exist are usually put on by, like… government groups of some kind. They're the ones who have a vested interest in getting you to a point where you can employ people. I took a couple. I keep a list of things that would make a business work. I call it my start-up kit for when I got around to doing my business."

"What business?" demanded Forest. "Why is this the first time I'm hearing about it?"

"Because it's kind of niche, and it requires a permanent place to live or at least a place to make things. It's a someday in the future thing. I want to do custom tiles or decorative bricks. I think I could make some cool things."

"Uh... Yeah. You could. I have seen all your design doodles. They'd be totally hot in the Northwest Modern houses. You should do it."

"I'm not ready," said Chloe. "That's what coming home was supposed to be for. I was going to settle my life, decide where I would live, make peace with the past, and wrap up all the loose ends. And once the path was clear, then I could maybe think about it. But now I'm on this road, so who knows? I'm not in a hurry."

Forest was giving her another look.

"Or I'll just put in a covered play structure and a pottery studio in the backyard," said Forest. "Problem solved."

Chloe laughed. "What if it turns out that I hate it? Then you have a pottery studio in the backyard!"

Forest shrugged which moved his chest underneath her. She loved the feeling of skin against hers.

"Then I'll turn it into something else. Man den or whatever. Doesn't matter, it will be good for resale." He stroked her back in a long, lazy arc, and Chloe nearly lost the conversational thread in the steady rhythm.

"You have such a flexible view of structures," she murmured, closing her eyes.

"Construction sounds less daunting when I know I could have a crew here in an hour."

Chloe turned her face down and rested her cheek against his chest. "That would be very impetuous."

"Meh. It's not crazy when you know what you're doing."

"Mm," said Chloe, tapping his chest to indicate that she agreed. His left hand on her back was a luxurious line of warmth, while his right had a comforting grip on her hip.

"Huh. Maybe that's why I get so freaked out about some of the

Olly stuff. I have no fucking clue what I'm doing."

"You should meditate on that."

Forest laughed. "Meaning that you agree but aren't going to say it. The problem is the consequences for getting it wrong are so high."

"You should evaluate the truth of that statement," said Chloe. "Or at least your parameters for *getting it wrong.*" This time, she added a kiss to his chest in the hopes of softening the edges of the statement.

The grip on her hip became hard, and the next thing she knew, Forest had rolled her over, and she was staring up into his hazel eyes.

"Now you listen here," he said, sounding almost serious, "don't you be using your supernatural Buddhist forces on me. I will not be seduced into having epiphanies."

Chloe laughed in surprise, and he chuckled as he leaned down to kiss her neck. Chloe sighed in delight and looped her leg over his hip as his hands drifted over her. She ran her fingertips up his spine, relishing the feeling of his body. She flailed out a hand toward the bedside table where the condoms were kept.

"I will not be tricked into self-reflection," Forest murmured between kisses.

Chloe giggled and forgot that she had been about to do anything as Forest's tongue caressed her nipple. She loved his mouth. He tongued his away along her neck and back up to her mouth.

"Just a little growth?" she asked as she nibbled along his jaw.

"More than a little," he growled.

She groaned as he entered her. The immediacy of smells and sensations overwhelmed her, forcing her to focus on the moment in a way that nothing else could. His hands tangled in her hair, kissing her as they moved together. The taste of him made was a wonder, and she caught her breath in rising excitement.

"Forest," she moaned, and he chuckled breathlessly.

"Yeah, I know what you want."

He did know. That was the best part.

Forest took a firm hand on her ass. She loved his feather touches, but she also loved it when he just grabbed her. Sometimes, it was the contrast that made them both even better. He thrust harder, and Chloe clung to him, overwhelmed and happy about it.

Later, when they were in a sweaty tangle among the sheets, Forest abruptly laughed and leaned down to kiss her.

"I'm ten minutes late."

"OK?" Chloe looked up at him in confusion. He wasn't moving. "And I don't care."

"Oh. Well… That's good?"

He kissed her again. "Yes."

Forest left for work ten minutes late, kissing both her and Olly goodbye, still declaring he didn't care. Chloe didn't believe in Supernatural Buddhist forces, but she had to admit she liked a less frantic Forest.

Chloe waited until after morning kung fu, and Legos had been completed before getting herself and Olly dressed for the outside world. Olly was less than thrilled to be abandoning the Legos and didn't want to go, even if it was for a ride in the truck. So he and Chloe had a conversation about feeling mad. Well, Chloe tried talking, and Olly flopped on the floor like a dead fish.

"This is what your father should see," said Chloe. "He thinks I'm the child-whisperer, but this would ground him in reality."

After a while, Chloe picked him up and took Olly and his shoes to the truck in his floppy state. He sighed dramatically as she put him in the car seat.

"We need to go Christmas shopping," she told him. "You have to help me pick out Nerf guns for Daddy, Unca Roan, and Unca Ash."

He looked tentatively interested.

"And what do we think Auntie Vivian would like?" He looked puzzled. "Miss Frizzle."

"Iguana!"

Chloe chuckled. "Maybe. I was thinking more like a custom tea blend." Vivian had seemed excited to meet another pro-tea person at Thanksgiving, so Chloe thought something nice for her upcoming job switch might be in order.

It had been a long time since Chloe had been wealthy enough to buy anyone a present. She also knew that Forest would tell her she didn't need to purchase anything, but the Valkyrie family had been so kind to her that she wanted to get them something.

The toy store with Olly proved to be the challenge she had thought it would be, but a Lego bribe went a long way toward compliance. It also allowed her to discuss that the Nerf guns were a surprise. Not telling an adult about a surprise was OK, but keeping secrets from Daddy and Chloe was bad. She wasn't sure how much sank in, but she figured it was a good foundation for further safety conversations down the road.

The next stop was the tea shop, where Olly was fascinated by the scoops and jars. A state that did not extend to the purchasing process, and he was bored and fidgety by the time they exited the shop. They were in a trendy Ballard neighborhood, and Chloe was admiring the darling Nordic-style window paintings on the shop next door when Olly let out a squawk and yanked free of her hand.

"Olly!" Chloe sprinted after the toddler who had gone jungle feral and dodged her outstretched hand to cannon into a couple ahead of him.

There was a general outcry as the couple—on the verge of kissing—found themselves attacked from the rear and nearly fell into the Tesla parked at the curb.

"Olly!" gasped Chloe. "Oh, I am so sorry!"

The woman was laughing as she tried to regain her feet and stop herself from sliding down the hood of the car. The man, hampered by Olly hanging onto his legs, was attempting the same, but also not crush the girl.

"Unca Ash!" yelled Olly.

"Oh," said Chloe, with instant relief, as Ash managed to turn around. "Ash. Thank goodness he didn't just tackle a stranger."

"I think I wish he had," said Ash. "Olly-man! We have got to talk about your timing."

"Up, up, up!" Olly held up his arms, and Ash picked him up. "Surprise!"

"Yes, that was indeed a big surprise," agreed Ash as Chloe went to help the woman.

"Are you OK? I'm *so* sorry. Hi. I'm..." Chloe hesitated over what to call herself as she dusted off the woman's jacket. "I'm Chloe."

"Harper, meet my brother's girlfriend, Chloe, and his sneak attack, terrorist spawn, also known as my nephew Olly."

Chloe froze. She hadn't realized that Forest had told his brothers. That was a more sudden declaration of status than she was prepared for.

"Hi," said Harper, grinning. She was a dark-haired woman with a generous smile and a twinkle in her eye. "Well, I don't think I've ever been tackled by anyone cuter. Although, I also would have preferred less of a surprise."

"Christmas surprise!" announced Olly, looking unphased by the criticism.

"OK, no, that's not what Christmas surprise means," said Chloe, feeling a little crestfallen. Her gold star for parenting was not looking quite so shiny today.

"Oh, I think it is now," said Ash, laughing.

"Best day ever," said Olly, repeating one of his favorite phrases.

"Well, we know that Olly's having a good time. How about you, Chloe? How's your day going?" Ash asked, grinning maliciously.

"Well, it was fine until now," said Chloe with a sigh. "Are you sure you're OK, Harper? I really am sorry. He can be quite fast when he wants to be."

"It's the shock and awe strategy," said Ash. "He's a master at it. Gives him time to get a head start."

"Yes, I'm fine," said Harper, smiling. "But, um, I should probably get back to work."

"Oh," said Chloe, realizing she had probably interrupted a lunch date. "No, don't leave because of us. Olly and I were just picking up some Christmas presents."

"Christmas surprise!" repeated Olly, hugging Ash, who squeezed him back happily.

"And now we're headed back to the house for lunch. Although," she glanced up at Ash, "I have been meaning to call you about lunch with your mom."

"Uh... yeah. I'll text you. She can be hard to pin down to an actual date sometimes."

"Well, whenever," said Chloe. "Olly and I clearly don't mind being spontaneous."

Ash snorted. "Thanks. I'll keep that in mind. Here's your ninja assassin back." He handed Olly over, and Chloe swung him around to her back so he could ride piggyback. Ash looked amused by this maneuver, but it was more comfortable for both of them.

"OK, Olly, say goodbye to Unca Ash."

"Bye!" he chirped.

Chloe waved and headed back down the street toward the truck, but when she took a surreptitious glance back at Ash and Harper, she thought they didn't look as cozy as before.

"I hope we didn't cause that," she said, but Olly only burped into her ear.

# 25

## *Chloe*

# REMINDERS

Chloe chased Olly into the gym, and Forest laughed as Olly clambered up onto the weight bench, her phone clutched tightly in one hand.

"What's all this?" asked Forest, grinning.

"The pirate king over there thinks stealing Chloe's phone is funny."

Olly giggled, which made Chloe laugh. She really was such a pushover for his cute little face.

"Did you do that?" demanded Forest, scooping up Olly and taking the phone away from him but kissing Olly's cheek noisily.

"He has just been full of all the extra-ness today," said Chloe, taking a breath and remembering that she should tell him about their literal run-in with Ash.

"Ha!" exclaimed Forest, making a happy dance.

"Ha? What, ha?" Chloe was offended, although she wasn't sure what for.

"You make it look so easy! Olly Level Three is for advanced players only, and I might be having a little schadenfreude at seeing you sweat."

"I sweat all the time! Kids are hard!"

"Yes, they are. I don't know. Maybe you've just got more experience with kids than I do because of growing up with so many siblings."

"Oh," said Chloe, shaking her head. "No. I mean, yes. I babysat for my nieces and nephews, but I never want to treat Olly like that."

"What do you mean?"

"Well, I treated them like I was treated, and it wasn't… good. The fundamentalist homeschool movement emphasizes obedience and advocates for withholding affection and striking your child."

Forest instinctively pulled Olly tight to him and took a step back.

"Yes," said Chloe. "Exactly. When I started thinking about my future, I wasn't sure children were a good idea because I didn't want to raise anyone the way I was, but I didn't know how else to do it. So, I read a bunch of books on conscious parenting. It dove-tailed nicely with what I know about nutrition, my psychology books, and my meditation training."

She paused, wondering if this was the time to bring up the rest of her family history, but Forest relaxed and laughed.

"Ah, yes, I'm getting the picture. You've been studying humans. And now humaning is easier for you than other people."

"No, humaning is harder for me, so I'm trying to catch up. Caring for a three-year-old is nice because it allows me to practice mindfulness. Three-year-olds are about my skill level. Or maybe I'm up at level five, and that's why I can handle three."

Forest chuckled again. "Fair enough. But why don't you let me practice my level three, and you take a break. Olly and I can work out together. You want to work out with Daddy?"

"Kung fu!" yelled Olly, kicking out his leg.

"Yes, show Daddy your kicks," said Chloe. She was so pleased Olly was starting to show an interest in their morning routines. She couldn't wait until he started being able to do real moves.

"Absolutely," said Forest. "I want to see your kung fu." He gave Chloe a face that said he thought the idea of Olly kung fu was hilarious.

"And I am going to go practice thinking about nothing for a period of time," said Chloe.

"Have fun meditating."

Chloe went back out to the hallway, frowning. She felt like she was hoarding up a list of things she needed to talk to Forest about, but Olly kept being around, and she never wanted to ruin their time together with serious topics.

She was about to go back to her room when the doorbell rang. Inside the gym, she heard Forest make a frustrated noise.

"I've got it," she yelled in his direction.

"If it's another lawsuit, tell them I've never lived here, and you've never heard of me!" he yelled back.

"On it!" She couldn't help laughing but stopped as she approached the front door and saw the display of who was outside on the screen.

Her brother's distinct arched nose showed as he looked away toward the side-yard as if sizing up the rockery and landscaping.

Her heart began to pound with a frightening rapidity. She had to answer the door, or Terrence would ring again. What was she supposed to do? The universe had brought this to her. The universe and her own choices. She should never have allowed her mother to come to the house. She should have known that her family wouldn't let it lie.

Gathering her courage, she opened the door. Terrence turned to face her, looking her up and down before smiling.

"Chloe! It really is you!" He held out his arms as if for a hug, but Chloe didn't move. They had never been the kind of siblings who hugged, and she didn't feel like performing the ritual now.

"What are you doing here, Terrence?" she asked. She walked out onto the porch and shut the door behind her. The winter air was biting with a hint of frost, although it wasn't cold enough to snow yet. It had been dark for hours, even though it was only a little after six. She still wasn't used to the shortened Pacific Northwest winter hours.

"I heard you were in town. I can't visit my sister?" he asked, dropping his arms. He looked annoyed at her lack of appropriate response.

"I work here. You can't be here."

His car was parked in front of the house—a flashy two-door. It looked new and sporty. The kind of thing she remembered him looking at as a teenager. She wondered why he wasn't driving his truck.

"Mom and Crystal came by," he argued.

"To drop stuff off, and they called ahead of time. You haven't been invited."

"We're your family. We don't need an invite. Besides, I was wondering why you hadn't come to the house."

"Well, the last time I was there, Dad told me I was going to hell and said I wasn't welcome in their home," said Chloe drily. "I'm respecting his wishes."

"But you're living here now. And childcare is a great job!" The unspoken phrase *for a woman* hung in the air. "If you just came to Sunday dinner or, you know, even went to church with us, then I'm sure you'd be welcomed back."

Chloe sighed. "I will not be going to church. Please don't think that will happen."

"But you came back," he said, moving forward. Chloe sidestepped and went down the stairs to the drive. Intentionally walking back to his car. He followed with a huff of anger.

"And I called Mom out of respect for her. Nothing about my stance on your religion has changed. I'll be sticking with Buddhism, thanks."

"You're being stubborn, as usual," snapped Terrence, his voice biting at her back like a dog at someone's ankles. "It's like you go out of your way to make trouble."

Chloe sighed again. "You came to me, Terrence. I'm not going out of my way to do anything."

"Mom and Dad should have disciplined you more," he growled.

"You always got away with this crap. But now you're a thirty-year-old, childless whore, who has nothing. You are nothing."

Chloe felt the words like the weapons they were, but instead of making her angry or hurting like they had in the past, they made her tired. She hadn't wanted to see her brother again, and this was why. He was just like their father. But she could have controlled a visit with her parents by meeting somewhere in public. Terrence never felt as constrained by public opinion as their father.

She stopped by the driver's side of his car.

"Your anger must be really heavy," she said. "I hope someday you learn to put it down. You should go now."

She turned to go back inside and saw a shirtless Forest standing in the doorway with a look of such fury on his face that she was startled.

"I'll leave when you have damn well learned your lesson," barked Terrence and grabbed her arm, yanking her hard and throwing her back against his car. Chloe slammed into the metal with a jarring shock that made her gasp. She wanted to move. Her hands curled into fists, but she couldn't seem to bring them up. Everything felt so familiar that she felt trapped inside her own memories.

Whatever Terrence had been intending to do next was stopped by Forest. He charged down the stairs, grabbed Terrence, and threw him across the hood of the car. The metal made a strange sproing-ing noise like an out-of-tune gong as her brother's body made it flex. Terrence staggered upright and tried to throw a punch. Forest blocked, and for some reason, Chloe became aware of how his muscles moved the tattoos around on his chest. Forest punched Terrence twice, then grabbed him by the neck and bounced his head off the hood. Terrence slumped down onto the driveway, leaking blood out of his nose.

Forest pushed her toward the door.

"Forest—"

"Go inside. I'll be in once he leaves."

She backed toward the door of the house uncertainly, watching as Forest returned to her brother.

"Let me make this *very* clear," snarled Forest, towering over Terrence. "If you come near her again, you will end up in cement."

He hauled Terrence up by the shirt collar and dragged him over to the car door. Yanking it open, he flung Terrence into the driver's seat.

"Now get the fuck off my property."

Terrence scrambled to get his feet inside before Forest slammed the door on him. After a moment, the car's engine flared to life, and Terrence backed quickly down the drive and then raced out onto the street.

Forest turned back to her, and she stood rooted to the spot. Men got angry, and they stayed angry, lashing out at everything around them. All of her careful un-learning and training seemed to have evaporated in the presence of her childhood fears. Forest took a deep breath and shook himself all over as if trying to shed rage like a dog shed water. And then he was her Forest again.

"Are you OK?" he asked.

"No," she said. "I thought my brother was going to hit me again, and I froze!"

They stared at each other. Chloe didn't know what response she was supposed to be giving.

"Do you want a hug?" he said.

"Yes!" she gasped in relief.

"OK, we're hugging?"

"Yes, please."

She took a stumbling few steps forward and collided with him, wrapping her arms around him. The relief of feeling his skin against hers was something unexpected, and she gave a sob and turned her face into his chest. He held her tighter, burying a hand in her hair, cradling her more fully.

"It's OK, baby, don't cry. I've got you."

# 26
## *Forest*

# SECOND THOUGHTS

Chole was trying to hold in her feelings for Olly's sake, but Olly could clearly tell she was upset—he kept crawling into her lap. Forest tried to distract him, but it wasn't working. Forest didn't know who he was supposed to comfort first. Olly was his priority. Period. But he didn't know how to make Olly feel OK without first fixing Chloe.

And he had no idea how to fix Chloe.

"I'll make some tea," he said. That had worked before. He looked toward the kitchen and then back at Chloe. Olly was already up in her lap again, wrapping his arms around her neck.

Chloe exhaled in one long sigh and then hugged Olly back.

"I'm upset," she said to Olly, and Forest froze. What the hell was she doing? She couldn't talk to Olly about what had happened.

"Chloe, mad?" Olly suggested.

"Yes. Mad and sad. Remember when we talked about having feelings too big for our bodies? I feel like that. Everything feels too big."

Olly took her face in both his hands and planted a kiss mostly on her cheek, sort of on her eye. Chloe laughed.

"Thanks," she said wryly, wiping off the slobber. "That helps a lot."

"All better," chirped Olly, using the same phrase Forest did for kissing boo-boos and applying Band-Aids.

Chloe hugged him again, and when she let go, Olly slipped off her lap, obviously feeling like he'd managed the situation satisfactorily, and headed for the Lego bin.

"Nothing quite like toddler drool to make you feel grounded in your body," said Chloe reflectively.

Forest wondered if he needed some applied as well. He felt jacked and panicky. What if Terrence had actually hurt Chloe? What if Forest hadn't been home? Forest tried to concentrate on some sort of task to keep the panic at bay. He made tea and then dinner. He made it through book reading time but still felt itchy in his skin.

Forest gently shut Olly's door and breathed out a sigh of relief. He couldn't believe Olly had been so oblivious to the emotions that seemed to be swirling around. Chloe had been quiet through dinner, but Olly had chortled delightedly about the peas in his pasta. Or rather, he'd been happy to pick them out and make a pile. The satisfaction of piling them up was far superior to eating them. Even Chloe's usual tricks hadn't worked. Not that either of them had been putting in top-notch effort. If Olly had sensed anything, it was that his adults were unable to mount a proper defense and had taken full advantage.

Forest entered his bedroom and found Chloe sitting on the bed contemplating her hair brush.

"My blue is fading."

"What?"

"Nothing."

"Chloe… What happened tonight?"

"My brother came to the house and got mad that I wasn't doing what he wanted. Then he grabbed me, and instead of kicking him in the balls like I always swore I would—I froze. I'm very disappointed in myself."

"Are you telling me that your brother has hit you before?"

"All of my brothers," said Chloe with a shrug.

"What the actual fuck."

"I told you my parents are fundamentalists. Women are meant

to be subservient and obedient. My father is the head of the family, but all boys can discipline younger siblings, and I was the youngest. Not everyone was mean about it. I think most of them didn't know any better. But Terrence... He's just like my father."

"Chloe! That's not fundamentalism. That is abuse!" Forest couldn't believe she was being so calm about her family.

"Yes, I've recently had that realization."

"What do you mean *recently?*"

"Well, when I left home, I thought I was obviously defective. All my brothers and sisters could fit in and get along, but I never could. I was pretty naïve when I left, and leaving the country was eye-opening but also foreign. So, even when I saw other families being kind to each other, I assumed it was because they were from a different culture. I aspired to be like that, but I assumed my family was normal. Which they are. For their community. It didn't occur to me until I visited Daisy at her work that they were abusive, not religious. Well, they're religious and abusive. They're both."

"What does Daisy have to do with it?"

"She works at an organization that helps domestic abuse survivors. There was a checklist, and I checked all the boxes. I was... It was kind of upsetting."

Somewhere, he was aware that she was downplaying how upsetting that revelation must have been, but she was fine now, and he had to focus on immediate threats.

"They know where we live," Forest blurted out.

Chloe was silent.

"I mean... You told them where we live."

"I told my mom," said Chloe, her tone stilted.

"That wasn't your mom on the doorstep," said Forest angrily.

"I'm sorry," said Chloe stiffly.

"We can't have them here. You can't talk to them."

Chloe gave a long slow blink, and Forest could tell that he'd pissed her off.

"I will talk to who I choose," said Chloe. "I don't want to talk to them, but please don't start dictating my behavior."

"I'm not trying to dictate your behavior. I'm trying to protect my son from people who you have told me have no fucking problems hitting children."

"I would never let them hurt Olly," said Chloe.

"It's a risk," said Forest, gesturing emphatically with his hands. She had to see it. "They are a risk."

Chloe was silent for a long moment. "I think what you really mean is that *I* am a risk. If I wasn't here, this wouldn't be a problem in your life."

"Well… yeah. But that's not what I was trying to say."

"What were you trying to say then?"

"That they are a risk, and you can't talk to them! We can't have them around Olly." Chloe's head cocked to one side, and Forest felt like he was paddling a sinking boat. "It's my job to protect Olly," he added.

"He has to come first," said Chloe, but there was something tight in her voice that he didn't like. "I understand that." She paused, and Forest didn't know what he was supposed to say. Once again, she'd agreed with him, but he didn't feel like he'd won the argument.

"Um… This has been a really upsetting evening, and I think I will meditate for a while. Don't wait up."

Chloe stood up and walked toward the door. It wasn't until he heard the bedroom door close that he realized she wouldn't be coming back to bed. Or at least not to his bed.

# 27

## *Chloe*

# FOOTAGE

Chloe drove with only half her mind on the road. Last night had not gone well. Not only was she disappointed in herself for freezing, but she had been unable to clearly articulate her past or present to Forest. And Forest... Possibly worse than being disappointed in herself was that she felt let down by Forest.

Chloe stopped at a red light and rubbed her head.

Forest was being a butthead.

It was a very undignified, very un-Buddhist outlook. She could tell that he was freaking out about her past, but Chloe didn't understand how it was any different today than it had been yesterday. Yes, they were abusive. No, she didn't want to spend time with them. When he looked at her, it was as if all he saw was her family, and now she was the threat. And beyond that, he hadn't even... She wanted him to hold her and tell her everything would be all right like he had on the lawn. Instead, he'd just argued about how wrong she was for his life. It wasn't fair.

Chloe took a deep breath and steadied herself. Clinging to the idea that life *should* be fair only hurt her. It was a belief that put herself at the center of the universe and implied that she should get her way. And with only a microsecond of observation, Chloe could see that the universe did not operate to her desires. However, knowing that didn't stop her from having feelings about it.

Chloe took another breath and accepted that she felt hurt and rejected by Forest's attitude. She also acknowledged that she didn't *want* him to feel that way. But she could only control one person, and Forest wasn't it. At least Forest's assistant had texted, suggesting they come for lunch. That was probably a good sign.

She parked in the Valkyrie lot and saw that there seemed to be a lot more people milling about than usual. Olly was excited about seeing Daddy and tried to hop down unassisted, nearly giving Chloe a heart attack, but he aborted at the last moment and chose to climb down using the lowered step.

By the time she'd gotten the Olly supply bag situated and got a hold of Olly's hand, they were approaching the front door. Only then did Chloe realize that the people were chanting and waving signs. She slowed down, but the crowd seemed to envelop them. Olly began to panic and ran toward the front door, pulling Chloe with him. Then, a bright light shone on them. Someone else shoved something at her and yelled a question. Olly yelled and tried to climb up Chloe. Chloe snatched him off the ground and ran toward the front door, clutching Olly. Everyone was shouting. She couldn't understand what they were saying. The doors flung open, and two employees hurried out and began pushing reporters back. Olly clung to her tighter. When the lobby doors slammed shut behind her, Chloe stood panting and could feel that Olly's heart was beating like a hummingbird.

"You're Chloe?" asked a young Black woman striding forward. "Hi, I'm Flora." Her dreads were tied up in a vibrant hair scarf, and Chloe felt instantly relieved that someone normal was working among the khaki-pressed office staff.

"What was that?" gasped Chloe.

"Sorry, I tried to call and tell you not to come," said Flora. "There's been an incident."

"An incident? What does that mean? What were they yelling?"

"Last night. Some people set—"

Olly pulled his face away from where he'd been hiding in Chloe's neck. "Daddy?" he whispered, looking around.

Flora froze as if she just realized that Olly had ears. "Uh… The potential Sound Transit job site was disrupted by unknown persons."

"The potential Sound Transit site?" The words didn't make any sense to Chloe.

"Where the unhoused persons have been…" Flora's eyes flicked to Olly again. "Camping."

Chloe wanted to make people feel respected, but in this instance, the politically correct terms felt disingenuous and euphemistic. Chloe recognized that it was partially due to Olly's presence but didn't think Olly was listening to what they were saying. He was still freaked out by the volume and intensity of what they had just experienced.

"Disrupted?" She returned to Flora's first statement, trying to figure out what that term was disguising. "Are you trying to say someone attacked the homeless encampment?"

"Yes," said Flora, grimacing.

"That's horrible. Who was it?"

"We don't know, but the press and the picketers," Flora gestured to the gathering of vans and people outside, "are inclined to think Valkyrie is to blame."

"Daddy," Olly repeated before hiding his face against Chloe again.

"I'm sorry, sweetie. Daddy is busy," said Flora. "He's in a meeting with lawyers, Jim, and the head of Marketing."

Of course, he was. This was a PR nightmare for Forest.

"We can't go back out there," said Chloe, looking through the glass.

"If you give me your keys, I can have someone drive your car around and meet you at the back door."

"OK," said Chloe, fishing in her pocket. "It's the white F-150."

"Oh," said Flora, taking the keys as if she didn't know what to do with them. "You're driving a truck."

"Yeah?"

"Um…" Flora looked embarrassed. "I'm sorry. I don't know why, but I assumed you were driving a Subaru or a Prius."

"It's the hair," said Chloe. "It gives *I care about the environment* vibes. Which I do. But I also really like trucks. Plus, I mean, it *is* Seattle. The odds were in your favor."

Flora grinned. "Seattle culture is sort of granola-based, no matter how many tech bros invade."

"Live, laugh, hike. Also, recycle, protest, and vote blue."

Flora gave a startled laugh. "Accurate." She glanced out the window again. "Although, in this case, I wish we were a little less quick to protest."

"Want Daddy," muttered Olly, his voice muffled by her hair. Flora grimaced again but went to the security desk and passed off Chloe's keys.

Chloe kissed his head. "Daddy has to work, baby."

"You said we see Daddy," said Olly.

"I know," said Chloe, hugging him tighter. "But something happened, and now Daddy has to work. We're going to go home. We'll see Daddy when he comes home."

Olly didn't say anything, but she felt a sob build in his chest. Chloe rocked him and kissed his head again. "I texted," whispered Flora, returning. "He might be able to come out for a second."

But Forest didn't appear until she and Olly were about to leave by the loading dock at the back of the building. Chloe thought he looked stressed and angry as he took long strides to meet them.

"I'm sorry," he said, reaching out to wrap his arms around both of them. Olly grabbed onto Forest and hung on with toddler strength. When she was sure Forest had him, Chloe let go. Forest's eyes closed as he hugged his son.

"We were in the car, and I missed Flora's call," said Chloe. "I didn't know there was a…" Chloe wasn't even sure what to call it.

"Protest at my front door? Yeah. I've called Rowan for some

additional security at the house—they'll probably be there when you get home. I knew I should have put in a damn gate."

"Does anyone know what happened?" asked Chloe.

"No. The police are making inquiries. But with the cell footage all over the internet, it seems like the press and public aren't bothering with actually finding out the facts."

Chloe nodded like she knew what the footage was, figuring she'd look when she got back to the house.

"OK, bud," said Forest, peeling Olly away from him. "You've got to go home with Chloe now."

Olly didn't look happy but went back to Chloe without protest.

"Are you going to make it back for dinner or book reading time?" asked Chloe, and Forest began shaking his head before her question was even done.

"We're performing an internal review. I want to show with complete transparency that it wasn't us. We're accounting for the whereabouts of all trucks and equipment. I've got meetings with the mayor and then the head of SDOT in an hour, and a detective is showing up in a bit. I have no idea when I'll be back."

"OK," said Chloe, nodding. She could feel tension building in her own body as she saw the stress Forest was under. "Don't forget to breathe and try to stretch between meetings."

His expression looked torn between laughing and disbelief. "I will attempt to remember that."

"Yes, I know I'm weird," said Chloe, glaring at him. "But I'm also right."

Forest leaned down and kissed her over Olly's head. "Yes, you are." He rested his forehead against hers for a moment, and she felt him breathe out. And for that moment, everything felt right between them. None of the tension that had been there since Terrence's visit existed. It was just the three of them, and Chloe felt a sense of ease settle in her bones. Olly gave a sigh and relaxed, too.

Forest stepped back with obvious reluctance. "OK, drive

carefully. If you see anyone on our property, call Rowan and then call the cops. I gave him your number. Just... be safe."

"We'll be all right," said Chloe confidently, and Forest smiled back, but she didn't think he looked as certain as she felt.

Two of Rowan's employees were back at the house waiting for her. Teddy and José added a panic button and motion-activated lights to the drive. Olly recognized them from other babysitting adventures and was happy to see them, and they seemed equally delighted to tote Olly around and let him help carry tools. Which left Chloe free to run to the computer and look for the facts of the incident and the footage Flora had mentioned.

Chloe skimmed the article from KOMO 4. Flora's description of the incident as a disruption was being called an attack by eye-witnesses. Three people were hospitalized with burns and other injuries, and several more were treated on-site. The video attached to the article was labeled disturbing. Reluctantly, Chloe clicked on it.

The video started with a bang and the sound of someone breathing hard. Everything was shaky as the person ran.

"They can't do this! They can't do this!" Someone off-screen was sobbing the phrase on repeat.

"Shut up!" the person holding the camera snapped. The image steadied and swung back toward an orange light.

"That's one of those construction trucks," said someone off-screen. "I've seen it here before."

Chloe watched as a large white truck with a diamond plate tool-box in the back did a donut through a tent, sending a parked shopping cart skidding. People were running, screaming in all directions. Something flaming arced from the driver's side of the truck, and Chloe felt a sickening lurch in her stomach. There was something so indescribably familiar about the movement that she could predict where the flaming beer bottle would go.

"That was Bernice's tent," someone said behind the camera. "I don't know if she got out."

The camera panned along the rows of tents, and Chloe saw with horror that fire was spreading to all of them.

The video ended, and Chloe sat in chilled silence, feeling like her life had just ended.

## 28

*Forest*

# GONE GIRL

Tiredly, Forest dialed Chloe.

"Hey," she said, picking up on the first ring. She sounded anxious.

"Hey," he said gloomily.

"That is not the tone of things going well," she said cautiously.

"Well, for now, the cops and the city are willing to believe it wasn't us. But the detective..." Forest couldn't quite put his finger on what Detective Caine was. Suspicious as fuck, which was probably a hazard of the job, but Forest had felt like there was something else. She hadn't liked him, and he wasn't sure why. "She wants to talk to everyone involved in the project. I gave her free access. But that is not my current problem. Grant Ichikawa just called. Apparently, Olly's grandparents just filed for a continuance."

"What does that mean?" demanded Chloe.

"Grant thinks it's their lawyer, who is local, watching the news and seeing how this whole thing shakes out. If it turns out that I somehow endangered homeless people, suddenly the whole custody case stops being a slam dunk for me."

"But you didn't have anything to do with what happened," said Chloe weakly.

"Grant says the lawyer will try to imply a connection regardless." Forest sighed and rubbed the back of his head. "He said it would still be dealt with but wanted to stress that solving the issue would be the best defense."

"No pressure," said Chloe bitterly.

"Yeah, well, welcome to my day. Anyway, I wanted to tell you not to wait up tonight." He gathered up his courage. "I know we need to talk about stuff." He didn't know what else to say after that.

"Don't worry about it," said Chloe, and Forest felt relieved.

"Anyway, yeah, I'm going to be here until we get the asset location survey back. At the rate things are moving… maybe ten. I don't know."

"OK," said Chloe sadly. "Forest?"

"Yeah?"

"You know I would never do anything to endanger Olly, right?"

Forest's heart gave an odd lurch.

"Yeah, of course. I know it's not… You didn't do anything. It's just…"

He had to protect his son, and when Forest thought about her family, all he could see were red flags.

"It's just what the universe is," said Chloe, and Forest couldn't decipher her tone. "OK, um, I'll see you when… whenever."

"I'll be home as soon as I can," said Forest, not liking the feeling in his stomach.

"Of course," said Chloe.

Forest hung up and rubbed his forehead. There hadn't been a lot of words, but he still felt like they had been all the wrong ones. He felt sick to his stomach.

"Well," said Jim, walking in, "do you want the good news or the good news?"

"I will take the good news," Forest said nervously.

"The good news is that your brother's weird asset management investment now gets my whole-hearted seal of approval."

"What?"

"You invested in that project of Asher's and agreed to use us as a test dummy for that AI asset management software bullcrap?"

"Yeah?"

"Well, it turns out that now that we've got it installed, we've got geo-locating on every single one of our damn assets. I had to call the guy to figure out how to get the report, and then I matched it to what we have of our manual survey just to double-check, but yeah... everything is and was fucking in place and miles away from the encampment."

"Oh, wow," said Forest, sagging back into his chair. "You weren't kidding about the good news."

"We're not out of the woods yet. It still could have been a rogue employee or something, but... This will go a long way to proving it was *not* us."

"OK, well, let's get this info to the cops. And maybe see about a press release or press conference or something. Also, I called the homeless shelter to ask about donating. Maybe that's bad? I don't know the right move politically, but I feel terrible. I don't care if it was or wasn't us. I want to help somehow."

"Personally, I don't think it can hurt, but let's see what marketing thinks," said Jim with a shrug.

Forest nodded but privately decided to figure out a way to donate regardless. He didn't need his name on anything—it wasn't about getting credit.

He made it through another round of meetings and talked to Detective Caine again, who seemed moderately more understanding. But finally, at six, he found he had no one to talk to. Even the picketers and media had dissipated. With cautious relief, he climbed into his car and headed for home.

He had never been more relieved to see his house but was confused by the sight of Ash's Porsche in the driveway.

"Hey!" called Forest, coming in through the garage. "Chloe! Ash! Where is everyone?"

"Oh, thank God!" yelled Ash from the playroom. It was accompanied by the sound of Olly crying.

"Ash?" Forest kicked off his shoes and headed for the kitchen.

Ash met him there, carrying Olly. Olly was sobbing, his head buried in Ash's chest.

"I'm not playing Lego's right," said Ash. "He bumped his knee, and I think… I think I'm just not Chloe."

"Want Chloe!" Olly wailed as Ash bounced him reassuringly, but Ash looked almost as distressed as Olly.

"What's going on?" demanded Forest, reaching for Olly. "Where's Chloe?"

"I don't know!" said Ash, handing over Olly's limp form. "She called. She said it was an emergency. When I got here, Olly was down for his nap. She said that she had to go and that it was for the best. What did she mean, *for the best,* Forest? What the hell did you do?"

"Want Chloe," mumbled Olly. His little body felt hot and damp from tears and sweat. Forest began to get a sick feeling in the pit of his stomach again.

"Chloe will be back soon," said Forest, holding Olly tighter. But Ash glared at him.

"Don't say that," hissed Ash.

"If it was an emergency, then I'm sure she'll deal with it and be back soon," said Forest, striving to sound calm.

"She took her bag. And she left a note," whispered Ash, pointing to the counter where Forest could see a sealed envelope. "That is not what you do when you're coming back."

Forest felt a wave of heat cross his body that left him cold and clammy. He rocked Olly and tried to come up with some sort of rational explanation. Chloe wouldn't leave them. Not over something that hadn't even been a fight. Maybe he'd been a dick, but she wouldn't just leave.

Olly stopped crying as Forest rocked him but still clung to Forest.

"I have Bear," said Ash, patting his pockets and pulling out the flattened stuffed animal.

"Bear!" barked Olly, holding out a demanding arm without

moving his head from Forest's shoulder. Ash put the stuffie into Olly's outstretched hand, and Olly stuffed Bear's paw into his mouth, then took a deep breath.

"OK," said Forest, keeping his voice soothing for Olly, "one thing at a time. We'll just read the note. I'm sure Chloe just didn't want to call me during a crisis. I told her I wouldn't be home until ten the last time we talked. She didn't know your asset management software was going to come through for us."

"It did?" Ash looked startled.

"Yeah, I'm doubling my investment. Worth every damn dime. But let's just…" He edged around the long marble island and managed to pick up the letter without jostling Olly too much. He opened it and saw that it was an entire page of Chloe's blocky architectural script.

Dear Forest,

I have been sitting here trying to capture my feelings, and it is not going well. I started this letter at least eight times. I need to say what I know, think, and feel, and it's too many things at once. I'll do my best to keep it simple, but I'm not sure I know how.

One – I love you.

Two – I think you love me.

Three - I will never be perfect, but perfect is what you want. From my past to my hair, I know I will never match your checklist.

And maybe if it was just you and me, that would be all right. Perhaps you could learn to accept that I'm imperfect. Or maybe I could learn to be all right with always disappointing you. But you're right—my family is dangerous, and being with me is putting you and Olly at risk. My name is Chloe Jordan.

She'd underlined her last name.

I know you probably never put it together, but my father

IS EZRA JORDAN, THE OWNER OF JORDAN AND SONS. AND AFTER VIEWING THE NEWS STORY TODAY, I'M VERY CERTAIN THAT MY BROTHER TERRENCE IS THE ONE THAT BURNED DOWN THE ENCAMPMENT. AND AS SOON AS THE PRESS FINDS OUT I'M YOUR NANNY, IT WILL NOT MATTER WHAT YOU SAY. THE LINE BETWEEN JORDAN AND SONS AND VALKYRIE DEVELOPMENT WILL BE TOO STRONG, AND THEY WILL BLAME YOU. AND I CANNOT AND WILL NOT PUT YOU AT RISK LIKE THAT. WE NEVER HAD A FORMAL CONTRACT, SO THERE IS NO PAPER TRAIL. IF YOU DON'T MENTION ME TO ANYONE, IT WILL PROBABLY BE ALL RIGHT. I WILL DEAL WITH MY FAMILY AND DO MY BEST TO PROTECT YOU. I LOVE YOU AND OLLY VERY MUCH, AND I ONLY WISH I HAD THE CHANCE TO SAY A PROPER GOODBYE.

There was a large water splash next to the line, and Forest had no trouble recognizing that Chloe had been crying when she'd written it.

BEING IN YOUR LIFE HAS BEEN WONDERFUL. I CANNOT EXPRESS MY GRATITUDE FOR BEING ALLOWED TO BE PART OF YOUR FAMILY FOR EVEN THE SHORT TIME WE HAVE BEEN TOGETHER. I WILL HOLD YOU AND OLLY IN MY HEART AND PRAY THAT YOU FIND THE LOVE YOU DESERVE.

LOVE ALWAYS AND FOREVER,

CHLOE

## 29
# *Chloe*

# PART OF THE SOLUTION

"Olly?" asked Norah, handing Chloe a foam brick. The little girl was wearing a pint-sized space helmet with no visor.

"Sorry, Norah," said Chloe sadly. "Olly didn't come today." Norah looked perplexed by this nonsensical answer.

Chloe's resolve to do the right thing had lasted all the way through getting out of the house. Ash had been confused, but Chloe didn't think she could explain without crying all over him, so she'd just run out before he could ask any questions. But now that she was at Daisy's, Chloe felt her determination faltering. She didn't have a plan beyond leaving Forest and Olly, but that wasn't really going to solve the problem, was it?

"OK," said Daisy, coming back with tea and shoving the mug aggressively into Chloe's hand. "I think I have the gist. Your brother swung by the house and attempted to..." she glanced at Norah, "act like my ex and Forest bounced his head off the hood of a car."

"I'm having conflicted feelings about his attractiveness in that moment," said Chloe. "It is not Buddhist to find that sexy."

"Yeah, well, my mom still puts up a Christmas tree."

"What?"

"That's not Buddhist either, but sometimes the heart wants what the heart wants," said Daisy. "My mom wants an excessive capitalistic display that smells like pine, and you want Forest going full Viking warrior."

Chloe felt a guilty grin spread over her face. "I mean…" Then she realized that while she wanted that very much, she couldn't have it, and a wave of sadness broke over her heart. "It doesn't matter," she said with a sigh.

"OK," said Daisy, "Sorry. But after that, we think your brother got into his truck and attacked that encampment?"

"Yes," said Chloe. "Sometimes in the summers, we would go to a church rally and camp by the Gorge. He would sneak off with the guys, drink beer, and do donuts. I've seen him do that exact same maneuver hundreds of times. It was him."

"Yeah, but *he drives like my brother* isn't exactly evidence," said Daisy.

"I saw his truck on the news a few weeks ago. He was parked down by the encampment. I think he took off the magnetic sign with the company name this time, though."

"OK, well, that's something the police could investigate."

"I need more than that," said Chloe. "I need this to go away. Forest was right—my family is a threat—and he wouldn't be in this mess if I wasn't with him."

"Uhhhh… Let's back that wagon train up," said Daisy.

She paused to take a small plastic hammer off the armchair before handing it to Norah and sitting down. Norah began to whack various things in her toy kitchen with the hammer.

"Your brother, if he was the one who did that, is a psycho with zero regard for human life. No offense."

"None taken."

"But you are not now, or have you ever been, responsible for his actions."

"I'm not responsible, but because he's my brother, being associated with me is a risk. And I can understand why Forest wouldn't want that risk in his life."

"Did Forest actually tell you to leave?" demanded Daisy, narrowing her eyes.

"No, he said he didn't want me talking to my family."

"Well, I'm not siding with him, but everything you've said about them sounds abusive and psycho. I think going no contact might be a boundary worth considering."

"I agree. But that ship has sailed. Where we are now is on the shores of trying to figure out how to convince the police that my brother did it before I buy a ticket back to Vietnam."

"I'm really not sure Vietnam is the answer."

"I can't stay here," said Chloe. "It's too expensive, and I will cry all the time. I already miss Olly." Chloe's voice cracked, and she took a hasty gulp of tea.

Daisy's face said that she was struggling not to sympathy-cry.

"OK, well, what about if we back-burner Vietnam for the moment," said Daisy, sniffing. "But it doesn't sound like you've talked to Forest. Maybe he doesn't want you to leave?"

"If you asked him, I'm sure he would say that," said Chloe. "That's why I'm not asking him. He gets very linear about things. He thinks there are perfect solutions and perfectly right answers to things. And I know that perfection does not exist. Sometimes, the only way to solve a problem is to prevent the problem to begin with. If I remove myself from the equation, he doesn't have to worry about finding a solution to my family. He won't have to deal with them at all."

Daisy frowned. "But…"

Chloe waited for Daisy to speak.

"I'm obviously not great at picking out guys. I stayed with David way too long. But when you talk about Forest, you tell me how supportive he is."

"He wasn't last night," said Chloe sourly. "After Olly went to bed and I tried to talk to him, all he wanted to do was talk about how much of a threat I was."

"Your family is not your fault," said Daisy emphatically.

Chloe sighed again. "It doesn't matter if they are or not. My family is putting his family and business at risk, and I will not let that happen. Also, Terrence could have killed someone. Something has to be done."

"Do you think that anyone else in your family knows what happened?"

"If he didn't take at least one of my brothers with him, I'd be shocked."

"Well, what I tell everyone who comes in, and what my lawyer told me, was to record everything. Maybe you could call your mom and ask her? If she knew, that might be enough to take to the cops."

Chloe rubbed her temples. "Vietnam sounds more wonderful with every passing minute."

Daisy laughed. "Yeah, I hear that. But—"

"Uh-oh," said Norah, and both Daisy and Chloe froze before turning to look at the child. There was the *tone*.

"Norah, sweetie, did you have an accident?" asked Daisy, setting her tea on the side table.

"No," said Norah, although her face and increasingly dark backside told a different tale.

"I'll be right back," said Daisy with a sigh. "But while I'm cleaning up whatever disaster just occurred in my child's pants, please reconsider the Vietnam plan. There have to be other options. And I'm still not sure you shouldn't talk to Forest." Daisy scooped up Norah and trudged toward the bedrooms at the back of the house.

Chloe slumped down on the couch. If Vietnam wasn't the answer, then what was?

She looked at the mantle above the painted brick fireplace and smiled at the crowded family portrait showing Daisy and Norah with Daisy's parents and sister. Chloe remembered painful family portraits from her childhood, with her hair in braids and long-sleeve dress causing her to itch and tug at the collar. They had been miserable experiences. Chloe remembered wishing she could blend into the backdrop of the portrait studio. She'd spent a lot of days trying to disappear and never being able to. She talked too much.

Chloe considered that. Was there a way to talk to Terrence? She didn't see how she could convince Terrence to take accountability for his actions. She didn't remember him ever admitting to any wrongdoing previously. She didn't see it happening now.

On the other hand, Terrence liked to brag. His arrogance had been his undoing before. Was it possible to use that now?

In her back pocket, her cell rang, and Chloe jumped in surprise. Fumbling for the phone, she looked at the screen in trepidation. The caller ID read CITY OF SEATTLE.

Reluctantly, Chloe answered.

"Hello?"

"Hello," said a woman's voice with a crisp, official tone. "Is this Chloe Jordan?"

"Yes," said Chloe.

"I'm Detective Caine with the Seattle Police Department. I would like to talk to you about Forest Valkyrie."

# 30

## *Forest*

# CLARITY

Forest looked up from the letter to Ash. Olly had slid down to the floor and was hanging on Forest's leg while sucking on one of his stuffie's paws.

"Are you OK?" Ash was worried. Ordinarily, Forest would try to mask whatever he was feeling so that his brother wouldn't worry, but at the moment, he was too shell-shocked to manage other people's emotions. "Forest?"

Forest had no idea what he looked like, but he knew what he felt. He felt like the bottom had dropped out of his heart. Chloe had seen right through him. Of course, she had. She could *learn* to be all right with disappointing him? No. Unacceptable. But that was what he had done. He had put her second and told her that she was the problem. But instead of hating him or being angry, Chole wanted to protect him. She was the victim. She was the one her family had tried to grind into a mold of Christian perfection. She was the one they had abused. How could he, for one second, think that Chloe was the problem? How could he be so damn petty?

"Want Chloe," muttered Olly around his stuffie.

Of course Olly wanted Chloe. Chloe gave him unconditional love. Something she'd never had from anyone, including Forest, and she gave it freely.

"Forest, you're freaking me out," said Ash.

"The Sound Transit job and the homeless camp..."

"Yeah, I saw the news. That's why you're working late. Chloe said. But they'll figure out it wasn't your fault."

"But it *is* my fault."

"What?"

"I was holding the job until Sound Transit cleared the site. I didn't realize I was squeezing the subcontractor. Or I did, but I didn't care. Also, I think I might have broken his nose."

"You punched your subcontractor?"

"He was going to hit Chloe. I just bounced him off the hood of the car." Forest tried to remember what he'd actually done. "And I probably did punch him a bit."

"Uh…" Ash was rapid blinking. "OK, question one: why was the contractor going to hit Chloe?"

"He's her brother, and he's an asshole. I don't think it's related to the encampment. I don't know… Maybe it is. Doesn't matter. Point is, he's the subcontractor. They were under contract for the Sound Transit job, but it was stalled until the city did something. My PM said money had been tight for them, and they wanted other work. But he's been unreliable. We didn't want to use them."

"So, you think he cleared the homeless encampment to kickstart the job?"

"Yes," said Forest looking at the letter again.

"Shit," said Ash. "You need to call your lawyers. You need to get a crisis management team together. The second anyone connects the dots between Chloe and those guys, you're going to have a problem."

"A problem…" What was Ash talking about?

"Yes, they'll say you told Chloe to tell her brother to clear it out. Or something equally stupid. We've got to get out in front of this."

Ash was being sensible.

I WILL DEAL WITH MY FAMILY AND DO MY BEST TO PROTECT YOU. Forest had been right—Chloe's family was a threat.

"Oh, who cares?"

Ash's eyes bulged.

But Forest hadn't grasped what kind of threat.

"I mean, seriously, who the fuck cares what people think? Besides, once I tell people I beat him up, they're more likely to say Terrence cleared out the camp to get back at me."

"Yes, but that would mean confessing to assault," objected Ash.

"Whatever," said Forest. "It's not like they haven't been flashing my arrest record around on the news already."

"Yes, that's my point!" exclaimed Ash, waving his arms.

"So I beat up the douchebag who was assaulting my girlfriend, so what?"

He'd been trying to protect his life. Why hadn't he grasped that Chloe *was* his life? He was still trying to keep things separate—keep little walls and boundaries between them.

"I really don't think you're taking the right view on this," said Ash. "Optics matter. Your company is going to take a hit."

"Yeah, probably. The bigger problem is that I need to find Chloe before she does something crazy. Who picked her up?"

"What?"

"Was it an Uber? A friend? Who picked her up?"

"I think it was a friend," said Ash, looking confused. "A woman was driving."

Forest grabbed for the tablet on the kitchen counter, trying not to move the leg Olly was attached to.

"Forest, your company is in the middle of a crisis. Chloe probably thought you needed to distance yourself from her."

Olly spotted a Lego under the table and walked away, freeing up Forest. He took the step he needed to reach the tablet.

"Yeah, that's exactly what she thought, but she's a Buddhist nun who believes in self-sacrifice," said Forest. Olly came back with the Lego and held it up to Ash.

"Buddhist nun," repeated Ash. "Oh. Is that where she learned kung fu?"

"What?" asked Forest.

"Kung fu!" yelled Olly and kicked Ash in the shin.

"Ow!" yelled Ash, hopping up and down and grabbing his shin and the edge of the counter.

Forest looked down at Olly in surprise. Olly looked up in equal astonishment.

"Nice shot," said Forest.

"Thanks for the support," snapped Ash.

"You're three feet taller than he is. If my son can take you out, then I think that warrants a compliment."

"Your son could take out a brick wall. He's a bowling ball of destruction!" Ash tried to get his leg up on one of the chairs for the island. He pulled up his pant leg to inspect his shin. It made him look like a flamingo, and Olly laughed at Ash's antics. Forest realized he was probably not parenting at his best.

"We don't kick Uncle Ash, bud," said Forest as he opened the home security app.

"Chloe kicks," said Olly sourly. "Want Chloe." He sat down on the floor and stuck Bear's paw back in his mouth.

"I know, bud," said Forest. "Me too."

"Forest, you need to stop and think," said Ash. "You need to get a damn lawyer on this situation."

"Olly, kick Uncle Ash's other leg," said Forest.

Olly laughed around Bear's paw, and Ash glared at both of them.

"Olly, why don't you kick Daddy?" suggested Ash. "Daddy needs a swift kick in the rear."

Olly looked confused.

"You're not wrong," said Forest, opening the nanny cam recording. "But it should have happened about two days ago. Maybe it would have stopped me from being an idiot."

He fast-forwarded to when he guessed Chloe would have returned from the office. He slowed down to see Rowan's people come in. Chloe let them take Olly, and then she went out of frame. He pushed the speed back up as Chloe collected Olly and then took him upstairs for a nap. He winced as he saw her take his phone call, and then she sat down on the couch and began to cry. Forest hit fast forward before he could break down himself. She looked so hurt. He hit play on a random spot. Chloe was on the phone.

"Daisy?" Chloe sniffed back tears. "No, I'm OK, but is that offer to crash on your couch still good?"

"Chloe?" asked Olly from the floor, standing up and trying to look at the tablet on the counter. Chloe paused and listened to whatever Daisy had to say.

"No, I'm OK. I just... I guess I don't get to stay here. The universe is being a little extra bitchtastic today."

Forest snorted. He understood that feeling. It was not a good day.

"Can you come get me? Or I can take an Uber or something if that's easier."

Chloe listened again.

"Thanks, Daisy. I really appreciate this."

Chloe hung up and looked toward the stairs and Olly's room. From this angle, he could see her face. She looked heartbroken.

"Chloe went to see Daisy," said Forest, and Olly perked up, recognizing the name. "And now you have to stay here with Uncle Ash while I go get her." He ruffled Olly's hair. "Don't worry. I'll bring Chloe home soon."

## 31

*Forest*

# RUN, FOREST, RUN

Chloe had dutifully entered Daisy's address into the In Case of Emergency Google doc, so Forest followed the map's instructions through the city to a narrow lot with a Craftsman bungalow. Darkness had fully fallen. It was another week before the winter solstice, and the turn of the planet would make the days longer again. He sometimes wondered what the hell he'd been thinking to leave all the sun of the Middle East for the constant drizzle and six hours of daylight that constituted Northwest winters. Then he remembered that he liked being able to go outdoors without melting.

He approached the front door and rang the bell, knowing that the dark probably made him more intimidating than he meant to be. So he stepped back and waited. The door opened about four inches and stopped. He thought she still had the security chain on.

"Hi," said Forest, attempting to get a better look at the woman in the crack of the door. He wished he'd been more proactive about meeting Daisy. All of Chloe's photos had been of Olly and the adorable Norah. The woman behind the door had long black hair and looked like she was probably Norah's mom. "Are you Daisy? My name's Forest Valkyrie. Our kids—"

"You!" hissed Daisy, yanking open the door. "You are the least supportive boyfriend on the planet."

"Uh…"

"She got attacked by her brother, and your first thought was to tell her what a risk she was?"

"Well, my first thought was to hug her, but..." He looked at Daisy's angry expression. "But then, yeah, I did that."

"Her family is not her fault! She is the victim, you asshole!"

"Yeah, I know," said Forest, unhappily. "I always say the wrong thing. And I'm used to her being so strong. I just went into problem-solving mode. Look, is she here? I'd rather be apologizing to her."

"Well, I would be happy to have you do that, except she felt so guilty about exposing you to *risk*," the air quotes around *risk* were vicious, "that she has done something dumb."

Forest felt himself go cold. "What did she do?"

"I'm not sure exactly. I went to change Norah. We're still working on some of the potty-training stuff."

"Us too," said Forest, feeling relieved that he wasn't the only parent struggling with that.

"But when I came out, I heard her give someone her parent's address, and then a few minutes later, a car pulled up, and she ran out and said she would be back later but that she had to do this now."

"Do this? Do what? What's she doing?"

"Well, I don't know, but I know she wanted to get proof that her brother attacked that homeless encampment! And when I texted her, she said she was turning off her phone for a little while but that she was going to take care of everything."

"What? No, no, no! Her brother is a psycho! Her family are abusive religious nut jobs!"

"I know that!"

"Shit! What is she thinking?"

"She is thinking her brother burned down the encampment because he was mad at the two of you, and therefore, it's her fault."

"No! It's my fault! He's the subcontractor on that job, and I wouldn't move his contract to another project. He burned it down so the job could move forward. This is *not* her fault."

"You couldn't have shown up earlier to say that?!"

"I came here as soon as I read her letter!" Forest flailed his arms in frustration. "OK, OK, uh... give me her parent's address. I'll go get her and call the cops. How long ago did she leave?"

"About an hour. But she already called the cops. They said, thanks for the tip, but Chloe thought they wouldn't do anything about it."

"I have the detective's direct line," said Forest. "I can call her, but... Just give me the address. I'm going to go get her."

"One sec," said Daisy. She dashed inside and then returned with a piece of paper. Forest grabbed it, texted Rowan the information, and then emailed it to the detective on the case. Daisy shifted her weight nervously from foot to foot. "You know they have, like, five adult sons or something like that, right?"

"Yeah," said Forest. "Don't worry. I have brothers, too. I'll bring her back."

"Yeah, but..."

"But what?"

"It's not just her family," said Daisy, biting her lip. "She's doing this because she thinks... She wants to fix it for you. She really thinks you want her to be perfect."

Forest's shoulders slumped. "No," he said tiredly. "Never. I want *me* to be perfect. Ever since I was little... I just thought if I was good enough..."

"Forest," said Daisy, tearing up a little, "if Chloe were here, she'd tell you you're enough just as you are."

"You're a really good friend," said Forest. "Thanks for being there for Chloe."

"Any time. Now go get her."

"On it," he said, grinning and backing up.

Forest voice-to-texted a message the detective as he drove. He'd given the detective's message the subject line of Emergency, but he wasn't sure the detective would read it or do anything about it. He supposed he could call, but he didn't think he had time to convince the detective of what was happening.

Rowan rang through as Forest sped through a traffic light and probably picked up a ticket.

"What's this address?" asked Rowan.

"It's where Chloe is and where I'm going to be. I need you to find Teddy and José and whoever else you used to go get Vivian out of that house and meet me there."

"Uh... Why?" asked Rowan, although Forest could hear him moving.

"Because her brother is the one who burned down the homeless camp, and Chloe thinks it's her fault, so she thinks she's going to go solve the problem."

"Solve the problem, how?" demanded Rowan.

"I don't know, but her brother is an abusive, violent nut job. I need to get her out of there."

"Forest, calm down," said Rowan. "You need to take a breath and think—"

"I've been doing nothing but thinking, and it's gotten me no-where. I need to go get Chloe. But she's got a bunch of brothers and who knows who else already there. I need some fucking backup."

"I am on my way," said Rowan, sounding like he was gritting his teeth. "But you need to slow down."

"No," snapped Forest. "I already know that they have zero problems hurting her. I will not wait while she is in danger."

## 32
## *Chloe*

# THE WHOLE PROBLEM

It took Chloe several long minutes to walk down the block to her parent's house. They lived in a much-modified rambler that had expanded forward and back to accommodate extra rooms and children. It looked like a second-story addition to the garage had also been completed while she'd been away.

Chloe shivered in her sweatshirt and wished she'd worn a heavier jacket. She wanted this done and over with. She looked behind her. Nothing moved on the street. A boxy, white Seattle Public Utilities van was parked a little way along the block, but no one was nearby. Somewhere, a dog barked. There were several white work trucks with Jordan and Sons on the side parked in the driveway. She could also see Terrence's sporty two-door parked off to one side.

Taking a deep breath, Chloe centered herself, then trudged determinedly up the walk. She knocked on the door and then stepped back. After a moment, the door opened, and her mother blinked at her in surprise.

"Chloe?"

"I need to speak to Terrence," said Chloe, happy that her voice was steady and clear.

"We're just clearing dinner away."

"Great," said Chloe. Her mother's arm pulled the door slightly wider, an almost invitation to come in. "I'll be waiting out front."

"Out front?" Her mother's voice was troubled.

"I will not come into your house," said Chloe. Then she turned and walked back along the path to the front yard. It hadn't rained in the last few days, but that didn't matter. The ground was still wet. Chloe didn't want to loiter like this was a stand-off at the OK corral. So she knelt down and meditated, slowing her breathing and centering herself in intention. She could feel the knees of her pants getting wet, but that was irrelevant.

"Chloe?" demanded Terrence, and Chloe exhaled and opened her eyes. Terrence's nose was swollen, and he had a cut over his eyebrow. The damage looked worse with a few days to swell up. Behind him, the family was filling in on the porch. She could see her father and mother on the top step, but only Terrence had come onto the lawn. Her father's hair was nearly white, but his beard still had a reddish-gold tinge.

"Terrence," said Chloe.

"Have you come to apologize?" he demanded sarcastically.

"No. I have come to ask you to go to the police and turn yourself in."

"Your *boyfriend,*" he sneered the word, "is the one who hit *me.* If I go to the police, it will be to file a complaint against him. But I guess Valkyrie's got enough troubles right now." Smugness radiated out of him.

"You can do that if you want," said Chloe. "That is your choice. I'm sure the police will want to know why you threw me against the car and threatened to hit me, but that's not what this is about. I am here to ask you to confess to your crime."

"What crime?" he yelled, leaning over her, spittle flying. "I didn't do anything wrong!"

Chloe remained kneeling but sat back on her heels, curling her toes into the ground. She could move quickly from that position but still looked vulnerable and calm.

"Terrence, I know you attacked that encampment," she said. "This is your opportunity to tell the truth."

"Shut up!" screamed Terrence, his arms waving wildly.

"Chloe," said her mother tentatively from the porch. "You're mistaken. You've made a mistake. Tell your brother you're sorry."

That seemed to calm Terrence down, and he stood on the lawn in front of her, breathing heavily through his nose. "That's right. Tell me you're sorry."

"No," said Chloe. "I am not mistaken. Terrence went to the homeless encampment last night and set it on fire. He was angry because Forest stopped him from hitting me. I don't know which of our brothers he took with him, but I know it was him."

"You don't know that. You *can't* know that," barked Terrence. But behind him, she saw Caleb and Will exchange white-faced glances.

"That encampment has been holding up the light rail project for months," said their father heavily. "They're all druggies. They're lucky nothing's caught fire before now. Terrence can't be blamed for that."

"Yes, he can. Because he made Molotov cocktails out of beer bottles and gasoline—just like he used to do when we'd go camping. Then he threw them into the camp from his truck. A truck that most likely had the Jordan and Sons logo on it."

"No, it didn't!" yelled Terrence.

"Oh, is it one of the magnet signs? You took it off first?" Chloe hadn't seen a logo on the truck in the video, so putting the statement out there was a gamble, but she saw it was correct. Terrence swallowed hard and almost glanced over his shoulder at the family.

"Did you cover up the license plate?" asked Chloe, pressing her advantage.

Terrence shifted uncomfortably, and behind him, the family was silent.

"Answer the question," growled their father. "They have parking enforcement cameras down there. Did you cover the license plate?"

"I… Yeah, I did. I just put some electrical tape over it."

"Oh, Terrence," said their mother, sounding disappointed.

"Those squatters have been blocking the project for months. We need the money," snapped Terrence. "And Valkyrie wasn't doing anything. They just kept putting out press releases about human dignity. Like he gives a shit."

"Those people are homeless and hurting," said Chloe.

"They are addicts. They just come to Seattle for the benefits. You know they get bussed in and dropped off."

"That is a conspiracy theory," said Chloe. "That is not reality. Statistics show that the majority of the unhoused population lived in the same county for at least two years before becoming homeless. *Those people,*" she made air quotes around the phrase that turned humans into alien others, "are quite literally our neighbors."

"They don't belong here! They should never have been here in the first place! Nobody gives as shit about them."

"You shall open wide your hand to your brother, to the needy and to the poor, in your land," said Chloe.

"Don't give me your Buddhist bullshit," snapped Terrence.

"That's Deuteronomy chapter fifteen," said Chloe.

"I don't see anyone helping me," said Terrence. "We're needy. We're working our asses off, and no one does shit. I guess you need to have a drug problem to get a free pass."

"Is that why you burned down the only home that they had? Because you think they were getting a free pass?"

Terrence took a long stride forward and loomed over her. "I burned it down because they were in my way. I did it because someone should have done it months ago."

"You did it because you were mad," said Chloe, looking into her brother's face, trying to find the younger person she remembered. Trying to recall a time when he hadn't been angry.

He leaned down, his eyes boring into hers.

"I did it because it was fun," he hissed.

Chloe felt a deep line of sorrow shoot through her heart like a lightning strike. "I'm so sorry," she said. "You must hurt so much."

Terrence blinked, and then, with a howl of rage, he grabbed for her throat.

## 33

## *Forest*

# MOP UP

Forest slammed on the brakes and was out of the car, leaving the motor running. He sprinted toward Chloe. Terrence was looming over her, grabbing at her. Forest knew he was never going to reach her in time.

His chest was burning, but time seemed to slow, and as he watched, Chloe rose up on her knees, seized Terrence, pivoted, and threw him in a long, graceful arc. Terrence hit the ground in a surprised heap. Forest could see the spray of water spring up from the grass as Terrence struck the ground. Then, time seemed to speed up again as two of Chloe's brothers surged forward. Chloe was up in an instant and kicked one in the gut. Forest had nothing quite so graceful in his arsenal, but a hard right cross sent one of them staggering back.

Forest swung at whoever came next and caught a glimpse of Chloe making a whirling move that ended with someone flying after Terrence. He didn't have time to think about it because someone was trying to grab him from behind. Forest elbowed backward, grabbed whoever it was by the hair, and pulled them down and around. Then, kneed whoever it was in the face.

There was a moment of silence as the men in front of them pulled back and appeared to be trying to regroup. Forest stood shoulder to shoulder with Chloe, staring down her brothers. He didn't know what would happen next, but he sure as hell hoped

Rowan showed up soon.

Terrence staggered to his feet, shaking his head. Chloe had flipped him like a damn pancake. Forest couldn't process that.

The men in front of him looked both confused and scared.

"Boys!" yelled the woman on the porch. Forest assumed it was Chloe's mom. She was clinging to the porch support and looked scared. "What are you doing? That is your sister!"

"This is none of your business!" the older man yelled, waving his arm at Forest. Forest assumed he was Chloe's father.

"Chloe is my business. Maybe I was unclear the last time Terrence came to visit, but stay the fuck away from my family." Forest took an angry step forward. Chloe's arm shot out and slapped across his chest.

"Terrence will have to take responsibility for his actions," said Chloe. "Beyond that, there is no need to fight."

Forest could hear more cars arriving and hoped it was Rowan, but didn't dare look around.

"I'm not going anywhere," yelled Terrence. "You don't get to come back here and ruin everything!" Terrence reached behind him and pulled out a handgun, but the air was filled with yelling before it was pointed anywhere.

"Hands in the air! Nobody move!"

Terrence slowly put his hands and the gun in the air. Forest froze as cops swarmed across the yard, but beside him, he felt Chloe breathe out a sigh of relief. Forest didn't know what would happen next, but considering his past history with cops, he didn't dare waste his shot. He grabbed Chloe and wrapped his arms around her.

"I love you. I'm sorry. You are perfect exactly how you are."

Chloe put her hands on both sides of his face and kissed him and Forest knew that no matter what happened next, everything would be all right.

"And now we have that on tape," said a dry voice.

Forest looked around and spotted Detective Caine. She was

wearing the same trench coat and thick braids that he didn't have a name for.

"Detective?" asked Forest.

"Was that clear enough?" asked Chloe.

"Clear as a bell," said the detective.

"What's going on?" asked Forest.

"I'm wearing a wire," said Chloe, lifting her shirt to reveal a black wire taped to her stomach. "The detective thought I could get him to confess."

"We would have been here a little sooner, but I was on the phone with your brother trying to figure out what the hell you thought you were doing." Detective Caine gestured to Forest.

"I was coming to get Chloe! I thought she had gone to talk to her family by herself!"

"That wouldn't be sensible," said Chloe, shaking her head, as she peeled off the equipment and handed it to the Detective. "I needed proof, and when Detective Caine called, I realized it was the best way to achieve harmony within our society. I believe in justice and working within the framework of the law."

"Unlike some families," said the Detective.

"Hey, I don't think you should comment on her family," said Forest defensively.

"I was talking about the Valkyries," said the Detective. She put her hand up to her earpiece. "And speaking of which, your brother is here."

"Shit," said Forest.

"Uh-huh. If I could have the two of you come this way." The Detective gestured for them to move away from the shouting Jordan family and the police.

Forest grabbed Chloe's hand, holding on tight as they walked. The Detective lead them through the maze of parked police vehicles. There was still a lot of yelling going on behind them. The Detective stopped them outside of a plain Seattle Utilities work van.

"Stay here," said the Detective and walked away.

Forest looked around, seeing all the neighbors looking out windows and standing on porches. The street lights were on, but they were overpowered by the flashing red and blue from the police cruisers.

"Did you do some sort of kung fu fancy flip thing back there and throw your brother on his head?"

"No, that was Judo. I learned that on the set of *American Samurai Ghost Terror*. The rest was kung fu, though."

"But… I thought that was just movie stuff."

"What do you think Olly and I do in the mornings?" she asked, her forehead wrinkling.

"Yoga?" he asked hesitantly. He checked her face. Her yoga poses had always seemed a little odd, now that he thought about it. "Not yoga? Kung fu?"

She nodded.

"Well, that does explain why he yelled *kung fu* and kicked Ash in the shin."

"What? When?

"Earlier tonight. Ash hopped up and down like a flamingo. It was hilarious."

"His first kick, and I wasn't there!" Her eyes were rapidly filling with tears.

"Oh, no, don't cry! He'll kick lots of other things, I'm sure."

"He shouldn't be kicking Uncle Ash at all," said Chloe, but she was still crying. "We talked about only using our skills when we're in trouble."

"I don't think he expected to make contact," said Forest truthfully. "He looked really surprised." Forest patted his pockets, found a dry baby wipe, and swabbed at her tears.

"But still," said Chloe, sniffing.

"What's going on? Why is Chloe crying?" demanded Rowan, coming around the corner of the Utilities van, which Forest realized was probably also a police vehicle.

"She's sad because she missed Olly kicking Ash in the shin,"

"His first kick!" said Chloe, taking the baby wipe.

"Oh, well..." Rowan looked to Forest as if Forest knew what to say. Forest grimaced and shrugged. He didn't know either. "We'll just tell him to kick Ash again when we get home," suggested Rowan.

"Right!" said Forest, relieved at this reasonable plan.

"He's not supposed to be kicking people! But I wanted to be there if he did."

"Completely understandable," said Rowan. Forest recognized his brother's patented soothing tone and heard himself in it for the first time. He used the same voice on Olly. "But you're OK? Forest said your family was violent."

"Oh, yes," said Chloe, with a sniff. "But Forest really punched the crap out of Will. And I threw Terrence on the ground again, and the police showed up when he pulled out a gun. So... everything's fine." She smiled, but her hands twisted the baby wipe around in a tight spiral.

"Fine," repeated Rowan, but his eyes flicked to Forest.

"There was a bit of a..." Forest hesitated, looking for the right words. "Thing."

"Uh-huh," said Rowan. "A thing like the time I got that call from the consulate in Marrakesh?"

"They started it! And anyway, Chloe was working with the police to get Terrence on tape," said Forest. "I didn't know that when I called you. They might be a little mad at me now."

Rowan chuckled and Forest realized that his brother had already known about the police.

"That's OK," said Rowan with a shrug. "Detective Caine already didn't like me."

"What?" demanded Chloe, looking offended. "Why not?"

"She doesn't like it when we solve problems independently."

"You weren't solving problems. You were running your own

military op in a residential neighborhood." Detective Caine returned, followed by a woman in a suit. The suit woman wore her sandy salt and pepper hair was pulled into a tight bun, and she looked grim. She looked like the kind of person who got called in to fire other people.

"And saving my girlfriend from a murderer," said Rowan with a shrug. "Not apologizing. Besides, I called this time."

"Only because you thought we would be faster!" Detective Caine looked outraged.

"And I was right. You were already here. I knew you'd be on top of things, but that's got to be some kind of record."

Detective Caine glared at Rowan, who only smiled in response.

Mr. Valkyrie," Detective Caine turned to face Forest directly, "Ms. Jordan's evidence clears you in conjunction with the burning of the homeless encampment. I have spoken to ADA Weber," she gestured to the woman in the pantsuit, "you and Ms. Jordan are free to go for the time being, but we will need both of you to make statements and a later time."

Ms. Weber stepped forward and handed them both business cards. "Don't leave town."

"But you should feel free to leave at any time," said Detective Caine, raising her eyebrows at Rowan.

"Now that I have seen that Forest and Chloe are unharmed, I'm happy too," said Rowan. "You're going home?" he asked Forest.

"Yeah, we need to stop at Daisy's to grab Chloe's stuff, but then we'll go get Ash off of Olly duty."

"I'll meet you there," said Rowan. "Vivian was going to go over and wait with Ash and Olly."

"Oh, OK," said Forest, feeling surprised at the show of solidarity.

"See you in a few," Rowan gave a wave and headed back the way he'd come.

"Your car is over there," said Detective Caine, pointing down the block. "We had to move it for safety."

"I did send you an email," said Forest apologetically.

"Yes, I got it. Please leave now. We will be putting Ms. Jordan's relatives in cars soon, and we feel your presence will only exacerbate the situation."

"Right," said Forest. He grabbed Chloe's hand again, pulling her away, but it wasn't until they were in the car that Chloe spoke again.

"Forest, what are we doing?"

"We're getting your stuff from Daisy's and going home?" It seemed like the right answer, but he wasn't sure if he was answering the right question.

"Forest, I broke up with you," said Chloe. Her eyebrows drew together, and she was still clutching the baby wipe.

"Well, yeah, because I was stupid, and you thought your family stuff was a problem."

"It's still going to be a problem."

"And I'm probably still going to be stupid," said Forest. "We'll work on it."

"Forest, I don't think you're getting it. This is still going to be a PR nightmare for your company."

"No, I get it. I just don't care. I want you. You're worth more than the company. Olly and I are better with you in our lives, and I don't really give two shits in a bucket what anyone else has to say about it."

"What about Olly's grandparents and the custody lawsuit?" asked Chloe nervously.

"There is still Cambodia. Look, I've had a lot of clarity in the last few hours, and what I know is that there is Olly, there is you, and there are my brothers. And everything else is just noise. We will get through it. I mean, I will probably freak out multiple times, but I know…" He looked at her in the glow of the dash lights. "I believe in us. Maybe that sounds crazy. But don't you think that maybe we could be an us?"

Chloe's eyes started to fill with tears, and Forest pulled over.

"Don't cry! Please! What did I say now?"

"We can be an us!" she said, fighting back tears. "I want to be an us. You and me and Olly! But sometimes I feel like it's you and Olly, and I'm not invited."

"I'm inviting. I'm saying. I'm declaring. I've been trying to keep everything separate because I wanted to protect myself. I said it was about Olly, but let's be real, it's about me. I get scared, and I panic, and I try to protect myself. I'm sorry. I want you. I want us." Forest felt like he was babbling, but he couldn't stop talking.

"I love you."

"Great. So next time, can you talk to me before you wander off to take on bad guys?"

"I just said I love you."

"Right. Sorry. I love you too."

He reached across the center console and wrapped his arms around her. Her arms went around him in return, and Forest let out a breath of relief that seemed to start in his toes and echo all the way through him.

"OK, this is better," he murmured.

Chloe let out her own sigh. "Yeah, it really is."

There was silence in the car, and Forest could feel himself unwinding like a watch.

"But seriously," he whispered, unable to stop himself, "please don't wander off again without talking to me. I don't think my heart can take it."

"I promise," she whispered back.

## 34
### *Chloe*

# HAPPY ENDING

Chloe sat on the couch with Olly on her lap. He was sucking on his fingers and barely even wiggling as they watched the Magic School Bus. He'd been extra cuddly since she'd returned, but so had Forest. Chloe couldn't say she was unhappy about it. Olly pulled his fingers out of his mouth with an unstoppering noise.

"Miss Frizzle come to our house for Christmas," he said.

"Yes," said Chloe, realizing he meant Vivian.

"Iguana?" It sounded more like ihwanna, but Chloe knew what he meant.

"No, Aunt Vivian doesn't have an iguana."

Olly looked disappointed about the lack of lizards in his future. She ruffled his red-gold curls, and he flopped back against her chest as if sitting up was too much effort. Chloe hugged him tight and considered the idea that Olly might be hers forever and ever if her karma held out. It was a magical thought.

Forest came in from outside, stomping off his boots. He had been going over the yard with the survey team to lay out the play area and pottery shed. Chloe couldn't believe he was trying to make all of her dreams come true with construction equipment, but she was starting to think that was how he showed his love. If the backhoe was anything to judge by, he loved her a lot.

"Mmm! Something smells delicious!" he called from the kitchen.

"I'm making beef stock for pho tomorrow. It will need to cook for another four or five hours."

"What? It smells like that, but I don't even get to eat it today?" He sounded outraged.

"No," Chloe called back. *"Bánh mì thịt* tonight."

"Those are the tasty sub things, right?"

"Yes," said Chloe, amused at his sandwich description.

"Sweet," he said, grabbing a drink from the fridge. He rummaged around in the kitchen for a few more moments and then came into the family room.

"They say I'll have plans by the end of the week," he announced, flopping down. Then he grinned at them. "You two look all cozy."

"Wan-an-ihwanna," said Olly without taking his fingers out of his mouth.

"Uh…" Forest looked at Chloe for an explanation.

"I believe he's asking for an iguana," said Chloe.

"Oh, that's going to be a hard nope, bud," said Forest without hesitation. "I don't need tiny dragons wandering around the place. We've got enough disasters going on without help from the reptile set."

"Dragon?" asked Olly, looking interested.

"No. Absolutely no dragons in the house," said Forest.

Olly made a disgusted noise, which made Chloe laugh. They finished off the Magic School Bus and made dinner together, helping Olly select his sandwich ingredients and discussing their respective meetings with the district attorney.

"It's weird," said Forest. "They keep acting like I'm getting away with something, and my lawyer keeps reminding them that I haven't done anything. I feel like Rowan must have just pissed them off so, so badly."

Chloe shrugged. "There is that vibe. Hopefully, Ash never gets in trouble. I hate to think how they'd treat him."

Forest snorted in amusement.

"Not likely. Ash was always the angel baby in the family. The only trouble he ever got into was the trouble we drug him into." He paused. "Why? How are they treating you?" His voice took on a hard tone that suggested he would have feelings about the answer.

"Oh, I keep getting condescending explanations of what words mean. Vivian says I will need to buy fancy clothes to make them stop. She says power dressing is a thing. I might actually take her up on her offer to go shopping. It's really annoying."

Forest made a face. "I'm sorry. That's pretty crap treatment when you're the one that made their entire case happen." Forest fiddled with his sandwich, then he glanced nervously up at her. "How are you doing with this? It's your family. Are you… Are you OK?"

"I feel terrible for my parents. Well, my mom, anyway. And I feel bad for my brothers' families. But what Terrence did was unacceptable. I can't look the other way. I'm not happy he'll probably go to jail, but how could I keep silent?"

"Your dad is taking over the company again," Forest said hesitantly. "I've had some calls. People are asking… well, they want to know what will happen if they keep using Jordan and Sons."

"What do you mean?"

"They want to know if Valkyrie will still work with them if they work with Jordan and Sons."

"Oh," said Chloe. She hadn't thought about the broader social and business implications of the incident. "They want to know if you're blackballing my family."

"Yeah, basically."

"What did you tell them?" asked Chloe, frowning. She knew the correct answer, but she wasn't sure she ethically had the authority to tell Forest what to do with his business.

"I wanted to say yes," said Forest. "Whenever you talk about your childhood, I get so mad about how they treated you. But then I Googled what Buddhists think about revenge and said no."

Chloe burst out laughing. "You just Googled?"

"Just like Jim is not my Black person Google, you are not my

Buddhist Google. I can do my own research. Also, I didn't want to put you on the spot. I wanted you to have time to think about it, but I needed an answer, so I Googled. Reddit is surprisingly thorough on the topic, by the way. But I can change my answer if that's what you want."

Chloe leaned across the table and kissed him. "Don't. Revenge taints your soul. This way is better."

"Yeah, I figured you would say that," he said, but he didn't look excited about a vengeance-free, karmically positive existence.

After dinner, there was tidying up and Olly book reading, and Chloe found herself standing outside Olly's bedroom listening to Forest read a book about washing your dragon. She went down the hall to their bedroom. All of her things were now in Forest's closet.

She was staring at the framed picture of infant Olly and Vera on the dresser when Forest came in.

"Oh. Uh. I can move that somewhere," he said awkwardly.

"Why?" asked Chloe.

"Well, Vera…"

"She's so pretty, and she looks like Olly in this one." Chloe patted the frame. "I'm glad you keep pictures of her. Olly doesn't understand it yet, but remembering her is important."

"Still," said Forest, picking up the frame and moving it across the room to the desk where there were a handful of other photos. "We'll get one of you and Olly, and I'll put it on the dresser."

"Is that what one does with dressers?"

"It's where you keep the underwear. That makes it the sexy spot to keep photos. So you keep the important person on the dresser."

Chloe laughed. "I didn't realize that was the rule."

"Possibly more of a guideline," he said, laughing himself.

Chloe stopped laughing as she realized what he was saying. She was his important person. He'd said it in so many ways in the last few days, and this was perhaps the smallest, but it was the one that meant the most to her. It wasn't a one-time event. It was the far more difficult, deeply ingrained little habit of life that he was willing to adjust for her.

Abruptly, she leaned in and kissed him.

"You are my important person, too," she said. "I don't own any photos, but I will get one and put it on a dresser."

Forest chuckled. "How about we just get one of all of us and put it on the same dresser?"

"That is more practical," she said as he tugged her closer and gave her neck tiny little kisses.

"Mmm-hm," he agreed. "You like practical."

"You know," she said, sliding her hands under his t-shirt, "I did *read* a book on yoga one time. I'm pretty sure I remember some of the poses. We could try them out."

That made him laugh again, but he peeled out of his shirt, leaving his chest free to be covered in kisses.

"Is there one where you wrap your legs around me like a pretzel?" he asked, still chuckling.

"We could try that," agreed Chloe.

"I am starting to think you are just making things up as you go along," he said, a grin stretching across his face.

"Hey," said Chloe, pausing in her removal of his pants, "I'll have you know that I do lots of research so I can improvise freely. Creativity takes practice."

"I…" Forest paused, trying to work through that one, which allowed Chloe to remove his belt in one long, sinuous snap. He let out his breath with a little woof. Chloe grinned and wrapped the belt around herself, turning around to give him a little shimmy with the belt across her ass.

There was another heavy breath, and then the belt was yanked out of her hands.

"Yeah, well…" She turned around, waiting for the end of the thought, but reasonably certain she'd already put an end to his thinking.

"Research this," Forest growled and pulled her shirt up. Chloe giggled and lifted her arms, but he paused when her shirt covered her eyes and tangled around her arms to kiss her.

With only her lips to guide her, Chloe sank into his kiss. Her heart began to pound as he put one hand on the small of her back and kept the other tight around her shirt. His chest against hers felt warm, and his lips were fire as they tasted hers.

His hand pushed the waistband, and her pants fell with a heavy thump to the floor.

"Forest," she moaned, tugging at the shirt around her arms. His laugh in return was wickedly smug, but he relented and pulled the shirt off. He tossed the shirt over his shoulder, his eyes dancing.

"You are not the only one who can be creative, you know," he said, kissing her again and backing her toward the bed. She would have responded that she hoped everyone could be creative in their own time and space, but her mouth was occupied with his. Then, her feet flew upward as he pushed them onto the bed, and she gasped in surprise. He dipped down to lick the entire length of her torso, which made her squirm in delight. When his face was buried between her thighs, Chloe sank her fingers into his dark hair and arched back for him.

"I love creativity!" she sighed. The pressure of Forest's tongue and fingers was everything, and Chloe centered herself on the pleasure of Forest, breathing deeply as he brought her right up to the brink and then pushed her over with just his tongue.

She lay there panting while he looked down at her.

"You look so happy," he said, grinning.

"So happy," said Chloe, reaching up for him.

"Better get used to it, crazy girl," he said, kissing her gently. She wrapped her legs around his waist and pulled him into her.

Could she get used to it? Could she ever get used to joy?

They moved together in the push and pull of love, and Chloe found her center again. Forest really could get her there every time.

Chloe sprawled across Forest's chest. Happy in the after-glow of sex.

"I do like your yoga poses," said Forest, and Chloe giggled.

"If we keep doing this, I might actually have to learn some yoga," she said.

"We are going to keep doing this," said Forest.

"I'll take a class," said Chloe, biting lightly at his chest.

As Chloe snuggled into Forest's arms, it occurred to her that maybe Forest was right. Perhaps this was going to be her life.

"I love you," she said, looking along Forest's painted chest to his face.

"I love you too," he said sleepily without opening his eyes.

Maybe Chloe would have the family she had always wanted. She and Forest would make it themselves.

"This is going to be such an adventure," she whispered.

"Best life ever," Forest whispered back.

# EPILOGUE
## *Christmas*

Forest closed out the Zoom call with Vera's parents. Months of lawyer's fees had evaporated with a negotiated settlement of monthly Zoom calls and the promises of summer visits. Forest had wanted to hate them, but Vera's mom had been crying practically the entire time. As Chloe had pointed out, grief made people do strange things. Olly hadn't been too impressed with his grandparents. Although Forest and Chloe had carefully saved their Christmas presents for Olly to open over Zoom, the moment the Legos came out of the box was the moment Olly lost interest. But overall, Forest had thought the call had gone well.

Olly had streaked out of the room, taking his Legos to be with the other Legos, and Chloe had gone to nibble at the leftovers. At least, that's what he hoped she was doing.

Chloe hadn't eaten very much at breakfast and the previous night had said she was feeling a little nauseous. If that continued, he would tell her to go to a doctor and not just drink whatever weird tea she came up with.

Forest stood up and stretched and realized there was a mountain of wrapping paper strewn across the floor. He began to pick up the paper as he considered how much his son's family circle had expanded in the last few months. Chloe went by, cheerfully humming a Christmas carol and nibbling a pickle. Forest couldn't help laughing at her—she was too cute for words.

It wasn't just Olly's family that had expanded. His had too. He guiltily wondered if he could convince Chloe that expanding even further was the best idea ever. He didn't want to rush her, but he couldn't help thinking that Olly would love a brother.

His own brothers had shown up in force for Christmas with more presents and food than had been asked for or expected. And Ash had looked happy that Forest had procured presents for their mom, but said she hadn't wanted to come. Forest knew he would have to do something about that but wasn't ready to face it yet. But at least Ash had seemed to accept that. Although, now that he thought about it, Ash hadn't seemed totally normal. Lately, he felt like he didn't really know what was going on with Ash. Forest felt like their disagreement over their Mom was driving a wedge between them, but he wasn't sure how to solve it.

"Do you think Ash ran out of here kind of fast?" asked Forest, looking up from picking up the explosion of Christmas paper.

"A little," agreed Chloe, licking her fingers as she finished her pickle. "Maybe he wanted to spend time with Harper."

"Who's Harper?"

"The girl he's seeing?"

"He's seeing someone? Since when?" Forest felt guilty. He'd been so busy with his own stuff. He should have checked in with Ash more.

"Well, Olly and I saw them before Christmas, and he accidentally texted me instead of her the other day and it was uh... warmer than I would say was appropriate for a random friend. He retracted and apologized and said it was for Harper. Over a month, probably? I don't know. I figured you knew."

"Huh. Why wouldn't Ash tell us he had a girlfriend? I swear he doesn't tell us anything that's going on with him!"

"Maybe he didn't want to be teased," suggested Chloe.

"I wouldn't! I mean, more than he teases us. Well, I'll pin him down at New Year's. OK, but speaking of my brothers, did you hear Vivian say *when we have kids?*"

Chloe laughed. "Yes, I did! It sounded very much like they have a plan in place."

"Those two," said Forest, shaking his head. "When do they not have a plan? I wish they were moving faster, though. I want Olly to have..." He trailed off, realizing he'd been about to say that he wanted Olly to have a sibling. "Anyway."

He combined all the piles of paper into one giant garbage bag and took it out to the garage. Christmas had been just as much fun as Thanksgiving and some how at least as much food. He grabbed Chloe's gift from the back of his car, where it had been sitting for three weeks, and brought it in.

Chloe was standing awkwardly in the kitchen when he got back. "Did you mean that about Olly?"

"Mean what?" asked Forest, already mid-way through handing over her last gift.

"What's this?" asked Chloe, examining the bag Forest handed her.

"It's the Christmas present I didn't think needed to be opened in front of my brothers," said Forest. "What did I mean?"

"The mind races at the possibilities," said Chloe, untying the ribbon holding the handles together. "Although, really, you already got me too many things."

"I got you things you can do and a new skirt that was hand-felted by a local artisan from recycled materials."

Chloe stopped and clasped the bag to her chest. "And I love it so much! It has pockets!"

"That was why I picked it, but one skirt and tickets to stuff are not things. So I didn't buy you a lot."

"They were wrapped around things."

"Christmas ornaments which we will re-use and cherish."

Amir's Christmas person had been a miracle worker who had knocked the gift-wrapping out of the park by attaching the tickets to charming wooden ornaments. Forest disliked outsourcing gifts, but he knew he never would have come up with anything half as good.

He also felt like he should have spent thousands more on Chloe, but instead had donated to her monastery and a homeless shelter in her name which had made her cry.

"That is true. But still… I don't need more things."

"You have specifically requested these. Just open the bag."

Chloe looked intrigued as she removed the tissue paper to see what was inside. She pulled out the soft package and tore off the next level of tissue paper he'd wrapped around it. Finally, the three-pack of Jockey For Her revealed itself, and Chloe laughed.

"Sorry," said Forest, "but the smallest I could find was a pack of three, so now you will have a spare."

"Thank you. I love them," said Chloe.

"You were asking me something about Olly?"

"Uh…" She took a deep breath and looked nervous. "You want Olly to have a cousin? Or maybe a sibling?"

"Well, I love my brothers. I just want Olly…" Forest cleared his throat. "We're a lot younger than Rowan. I think it would be better if Olly had someone closer in age."

"How about four years apart?" Chloe reached into her pocket and took out what looked like a COVID test in a plastic sandwich bag.

"What?"

"Well, if this is… I want this. He'll be four by the time… We haven't been very careful."

Forest squinted at the stick through the plastic bag. It had a pink plus on the display.

"I'm pregnant," Chloe blurted out. Her eyes looked big and a little bit scared, and Forest knew he should say something reassuring, but instead, he laughed.

"Is that panic laugh or yay laughter?" she asked cautiously.

"Both," he said, pulling her into him and crushing her with a kiss.

"Oh," said Chloe, smiling as they separated.

"This is going to be so much fun," he said, still grinning. "You're the best mom, and I can't wait to see you all round like a beach ball."

Forest wrapped his arms around Chloe and hugged her so hard he lifted her off the ground, and she giggled.

"I suppose we'll have to do the wedding fast," he said regretfully, setting her down.

"What wedding?" asked Chloe, tilting her head to look up at him.

"Ours." The confusion on her face made him doubt his next words. "We love each other and want to be together?"

"Oh, yes," she said, kissing him.

"And there's a baby on the way?"

"Well, the tests seem to indicate that. Although, currently, it just feels like puking is on the way."

"So we should get married?"

"Oh. No, I'm not getting married. That Never didn't change."

"But..."

"If you need a piece of paper to be with me, then you don't really want to be with me."

"I... but... baby and things?"

"Those have literally nothing to do with marriage."

Forest tried to realign his thinking. "OK, but... No. No, you're not allowed to wander off without telling me anymore. You promised."

"Yes, I promised."

"OK."

"I would definitely tell you first."

"Gee, thanks? Why are you weird?"

"You like me that way."

"Yeah, that's true," he admitted.

"And I think you love me," she added, drawing one fingertip along the back of his neck.

"Oh, that is very definitely true," he said, leaning down to kiss her.

"Ugh," exclaimed Olly, coming out of the playroom. "Daddy, stop hogging the Chloe."

"Never," said Forest.

## THE END

*Find out if Ash and Harper can
catch their own elevator ride to happiness
or if they'll get stuck at the...*

# LOVED IT?

# WANT A FREE BOOK?

For a free e-book visit:
www.**bethanymaines**.com

Blue Jones just stole Jake Garner's dog. And his heart. But technically the French Bulldog, Jacques, belongs to Jake's ex-girlfriend. And soon Jake is being pressured to return the dog and Blue is being targeted by mysterious attackers. Can Jake find Blue and Jacques before her stalkers do? For Blue, Christmas has never been quite so dangerous. For Jake, Christmas has never been quite so Blue.

# WANT MORE ROMANCE FROM BETHANY MAINES?

## TRY THE DEVERAUX LEGACY SERIES

The Deveraux Family: wealthy, glamorous, powerful… and in a lot of trouble. Senator Eleanor Deveraux lost her children in a plane crash, but she has a second chance to get her family right with her four grandchildren – Evan, Jackson, Aiden and Dominique. But second chances are hard to seize when politics, mercenaries, and the dark legacy of the Deveraux family keep getting in the way.

## TAKE A SNEAK PEEK AT BOOK 1

# THE SECOND SHOT

SATURDAY

# Maxwell Ames

*I have better uses for my mouth.*

The words were etched in his brain.

Maxwell Ames looked across the room at Dominique Deveraux and felt himself physically flinch at a memory-driven whip of embarrassment.

An eighteen-year-old Dominique had arrived at college with an ice queen reputation and a pair of legs that had fueled half the hot dreams on campus. But it hadn't been the legs that had gotten to Max—it had been her lips. Max had taken one look at Dominique and decided he wanted, no, *needed* to know what those lips felt like on his body. And he'd declared, drunkenly, to an entire frat party that he would melt the ice queen. He hadn't doubted for a minute that he could do it. He was a senior. He was a nationally ranked college wrestler—his body showed his effort—and he rarely had to do more than lift a finger to get panties to hit his floor. Perhaps it had been the liquor that had made him stupid, but whatever the reason, he'd simply walked over and told her what he wanted her to do to him. He recognized his mistake the second he heard the words come out of his mouth. Her horrified expression only confirmed how badly he'd misjudged. Then she'd gone from shocked to furious, but instead of slapping him, she'd pulled herself up to her full height, looked him in the eye, and declared loud enough for the rest of the room to hear: *I have better uses for my mouth.* And then he'd stood there and let her pour the entire contents of her red solo cup down his front.

And now, six years later, his father had dragged Max into the

Galbraith Tennis and Social Club and directly into revisiting one of his top ten stupidest moments.

"Dad," said Max, turning to look at his father.

"She donates two-k a year," said his father, staring across the party hall at a woman in beige everything. "She's worth like eighty million. Would it kill her to scrounge a little more change out of the couch cushions for needy kids?"

"Dad," said Max again.

"Yeah, what?" asked Grant Ames, finally making eye contact.

"You didn't say this was a Deveraux party."

"Uh, yeah?" said Grant, looking away again—probably scanning the crowd for more targets. "Oh, that's right. You went to school with them, didn't you? Dominique and Aiden? They're probably around somewhere if you want to dig them up. Eleanor usually commands appearances from the family at these little shindigs."

Eleanor Deveraux was running for congress. Again. Or still. Whichever. These *little shindigs* were fundraising events masquerading as cocktail parties. Max didn't know why she bothered. Her nearest competitor was a bitter Republican that sounded crazy even to his constituents. But his father, always on the hustle, spared no thought about why the party existed—he simply enjoyed that it did. And of course, it hadn't occurred to Grant to mention to Max who was hosting.

After the frat party incident, Max hadn't even had the courage to apologize to Dominique. His only consolation was that during all their other encounters she had treated everyone in the room with an equal amount of cool disdain—he hadn't been singled out. Generally, she hadn't even acknowledged him, let alone what had happened.

"You said we wouldn't be here long," said Max, looking back at Dominique. Her golden blonde hair was longer than the last time he'd seen her, laying in soft waves against her pale skin. Those lips that had made him lose his judgement were painted a wine red that emphasized their size. Her conservative pencil skirt and long-sleeve, high-necked blouse should have taken her allure down a notch, but as far as he could see, she was even more gorgeous than she had been in college.

Max had been with plenty of beautiful women—hell, his last girlfriend had been a model-slash-actress. Dominique shouldn't have been able to make the impact she did. But here it was, six years later, and Dominique still hit him like a Mack truck to the libido even when the only skin he could see was her knees.

"We won't be long, I promise," said Grant, scoping the room, oblivious to the direction of Max's gaze. "I need to make the rounds. Say hi to a few people and then we'll be off for burgers."

It was a lie. Max didn't know why he'd thought his first visit to his father's in over a year might warrant special treatment—particularly, since his entire childhood held evidence to the contrary. He wondered if there was a point in adulthood when a parent's failings stopped mattering so much.

Dominique nodded along as the guy next to her talked. He was a lean, good looking twenty-something with black hair and a designer suit. Max watched in surprise as Dominique burst out laughing at whatever he'd said—Dominique had never been very demonstrative in public. Her laugh made the guy grin, but, still talking, he leaned over and snagged something off her plate. Dominique smacked at his hand, but the man leaned further away, dragging the morsel with him, and popped it into his mouth. She flicked at his ear, miming patently faked annoyance. In equally mock penance, her companion lowered his head and held out his plate and Dominique made a show of selecting something in recompense. The only person he could remember bringing out that sparkle of playfulness in her had been her brother, Aiden. It seemed that the ice queen had been melted after all.

Still chewing his stolen goods, Dominique's companion looked up and scanned the room, homing in on the location of the other Deveraux family members. Max followed the man's gaze to the matriarch, Dominque's stately and poised grandmother, Eleanor, holding court by the bar at the far end of the long, narrow room. Then he shifted to Dominique's red-headed investment manager cousin, Evan, amongst a bevy of Wall Street bros in the middle of the room. And last, Dominique's brother, the equally blonde Aiden, hovering by the buffet table in front of a wide expanse of floor-to-ceiling windows.

All of the Deveraux children had lived with their grandmother after a plane crash had left them orphans sometime during their early teens. Max remembered thinking how nice that had sounded when his father had missed every single one of his college meets and was late for graduation. He supposed it hadn't really been pleasant for the Deveraux cousins, but at least they'd had each other and Eleanor.

Max realized, too late, that the scan was continuing on to the new arrivals in the room, which, in this case, were Max and his father. Max found himself awkwardly making eye contact with the guy and knew that he'd been busted staring at Dominique. He broke eye contact and turned to follow his father.

Max pretended to be absorbed in his father's conversation with a white-collared, black-shirted Jesuit priest. After a few minutes of discussing the endowments and scholarship funds, Max's eyes glazed over and he looked around the room, desperate for anything to take his mind off his desire to blurt out a question about pedophiles. How did anyone take priests seriously anymore? He found himself fidgeting with one of the tiny decorative pumpkins placed on the bar-height tables and biting his tongue.

With Halloween and the election around the corner, the party was decorated in a patriotic harvest theme. The red leaves and orange gourds seemed attractive, but Max thought the hay bales by the buffet table seemed a bit too folksy for the Deveraux, not to mention the tennis club locale. He suspected that the entire reason for their existence was to support the stars-and-stripes-bandana-wearing scarecrow. After all, a politician couldn't fundraise without at least a nod to the flag.

He snuck another glance at Dominique and realized that her boyfriend was scanning again. Same pattern—Deverauxes first, then new arrivals, then the rest of the room. There was something professional in the appraising stare, and Max felt the weight of it resting thoughtfully on him. Max checked his watch and angled so he could watch Dominique and her guy. She chatted in an easy, unaffected way, but at a minute fifteen, her boyfriend made another scan. Then again a minute later. It was definitely a more than a casual glance. Max tried to get a better look at the guy. What was he? Boyfriend, bodyguard, security? The suit was expensive, but he was drinking water as he watched the crowd.

Dominique reached out and put her hand on his arm, tugging impatiently, demanding attention. The guy laughed and complied, turning toward her with an affectionate smile. He was definitely not the hired help. For some reason, that burned. In the intervening six years, Max had put Dominique out of his head. Mostly. Sort of. Max would never have admitted it out loud, ever, under any circumstances, including a court of law, but Dominique had always been one of his go-to fantasies. He was perfectly sure that she hadn't thought about him once in that time. So why did he feel jealous of this guy?

Max turned back to his father and tried to focus on the conversation. Dominique was none of his business. What did he care if she dated someone with an over-active sense of security? None. Of. His. Business.

Grant moved on and Max followed him dutifully, the same way he had when he was twelve. He was a prop to his father's socializing. He met a dozen people and forgot their names instantly. Finally, he turned away from a blocky woman in a Chanel jacket and found his father about to introduce him to Dominique and her date.

"Max, I don't know if you've met Jackson, but you went to school with Dominique. Max is staying with me for a few weeks while—Hey, Frank! Frank! Be right back. I've been trying to get five minutes with that guy all month." Grant buzzed off and left Max staring uncomfortably at Dominique and her date.

"So, Max," said Jackson, his expression derisive, "do you need Dominique to get you another drink? We could send the catering staff out for some beer and solo cups."

Max glanced at Dominique, who was visibly restraining a laugh.

"No," said Max, trying not to feel like an ass—any hope that she'd forgotten him or the incident slipping away. "I think once was enough." Did she really have to tell everyone?

Dominique actually did giggle this time and her boyfriend looked amused by her laughter, but his attention was pulled away.

"Nika, what is Aiden doing?" asked Jackson, looking past Max.

"Um," she squinted toward the door, "exactly what you told him not to do?"

Jackson sighed. "OK, I'll be right back." He ducked around Dominique, his jacket swinging open. For a second, Max clearly saw the strap on a shoulder holster and outline of a gun. Max looked back at Dominque, but she seemed not to notice. She was watching her brother attempting to sneak out of the room and biting into her bottom lip with a frown. She transferred her gaze back to Max and smiled, but it was the same old cold smile.

"I'm glad you can laugh about that uh... incident," he said, deciding to man up and do what he should have done six years ago. He glanced down at the floor and realized that she was only conservative from the ankle up. Her heels were stacked, strapped, and had a black satin bow at each ankle that begged to be untied. "I really apologize for that," he said, tearing his eyes off her feet.

She looked startled and suspicious.

"I was a total asshole," he added.

"Um." She frowned, then smiled—a real smile this time. "Well, apology accepted."

It was his turn to feel surprised. He hadn't expected her to simply believe that he was sorry. "And I wouldn't say total. I'd go ninety-eight percent."

"Ninety-eight percent?"

"Well, I'll give you a one percent discount for being young, dumb and in college."

"Yes," he agreed fervently.

"And another one percent for standing there for the entire cup of beer."

"I knew I'd earned it," he said. She glanced over his shoulder, still following the action across the room.

"Your boyfriend's a little intense," he said.

"My boyfriend? You mean Jacks?"

He wanted to comment on the intimate shortening of their names. Jacks seemed weird, but he liked Nika. On the other hand, it really was none of his damn business.

"Does he always carry a gun?" he asked instead.

"Oh, you know…" she said, trailing off and not answering the question. Max decided that meant the answer was yes. "Grandma has gotten some… Well, they're death threats, really, in the last few weeks. She's chairing that Senate Committee Hearing on Absolex. And nothing brings out the crazies like Big Pharma."

"I don't understand," he said. "I thought that was about government fraud?"

"Absolex falsified research and then sold their drug Zanilex to the VA as a solution to treat complex PTSD. Suicide rates sky-rocketed. Turns out that, in fact, it makes the symptoms of PTSD worse, particularly the paranoia and depression. Or at least that's what Grandma intends to prove. She's going to haul the CEO out on the carpet next week. But ever since the hearings started, she's been getting hate mail."

Max looked around the party. "Where is the Secret Service?"

"None of the threats have been active. It's all kind of vague. And she's not a party leader or anything. So, no Secret Service."

Max frowned. If he had been Eleanor, he would have been

putting his foot down and demanding an investigation. He also wouldn't be hosting a party and looking as relaxed as she did.

"Besides," continued Dominique, "we have Jackson. Although, even he couldn't get her to cancel this stupid party. She claimed that we all just didn't want to go."

He raised an eyebrow and she looked guilty.

"That may be partially true. Anyway, Jacks said if she was going to insist on having the party, we should at least be smart about it. He gave us all rules and hired additional security. Of course, Aiden is not following the rules. I would accuse him of being willful, but it's more likely that he's just not taking the threats seriously."

Max nodded. His memory of Dominique's older brother was a sunny personality to whom nothing serious was allowed to adhere and who never seemed to get mad about anything.

"I expect Jacks will tell him about a secret stash of bourbon under the bar and rope him back in."

"Sounds like Jackson knows what he's doing then," said Max, turning to look at the two men who were now making their way back toward them. Aiden stopped to adjust the bandana on the scarecrow with a disapproving shake of his head.

"He does," agreed Dominique, looking up at him with a flash of a smile, "but Jackson isn't—"

Whatever she had been about to say was drowned out by the sound of a car engine and then a thunderous crash as a car exploded through the windows, slammed through the buffet table, plowed across the room, and buried its nose in the far wall.

## FIND OUT WHAT HAPPENS NEXT IN…

# THE SECOND SHOT

# ABOUT THE AUTHOR

 Bethany Maines is the award-winning author of action adventure and fantasy tales that focus on women who know when to apply lipstick and when to apply a foot to someone's hind end. When she's not traveling to exotic lands, or kicking some serious butt with her black belt in karate, she can be found chasing after her daughter, or glued to the computer working on her next novel.

# ALSO BY BETHANY MAINES

**CARRIE MAE MYSTERIES**
Bulletproof Mascara
Compact With The Devil
High-Caliber Concealer
Glossed Cause

**SAN JUAN ISLANDS MYSTERIES**
An Unseen Current
Against the Undertow
An Unfamiliar Sea
An Unfinished Storm

**SHARK SANTOYO CRIME SERIES**
Shark's Instinct
Shark's Bite
Shark's Hunt
Shark's Fin
Peregrine's Flight
Shark's Blood

**THE DEVERAUX LEGACY**
The Second Shot
*A PNWA Literary ContesttAward Winner*
The Cinderella Secret
The Hardest Hit
The Fallen Man

**THE SUPERNATURALS**
Wild Waters
A Little Red (3 Colors #1)
A Deeper Blue (3 Colors #2)
A Brighter Yellow (3 Colors #3)
Maverick
Hudson (Rejects #1)
Killian (Rejects #2)
Alekos (Rejects #3)

**GALACTIC DREAMS**
When Stars Take Flight Vol. 1
The Seventh Swan Vol. 2
*A Book Excellence Award Winner*
The Beast of Arsu Vol. 3